Three Days In Hell

By Emilio Iasiello

Beacon Publishing Group
ISBN (Paperback): 978-1-961504-27-1

Three Days In Hell
© 2026 Emilio Iasiello

Cover Layout by Lori Pace
Edited by Ashley Buchanan

All rights reserved, including the right to reproduce this book or portions thereof in any form whatsoever. For more information, contact our rights department at bpgrights@beaconpublishinggroup.com.

No part of this publication may be reproduced or transmitted in any form or by any means electronic or mechanical, including photocopy, recording, or any information storage and retrieval system now known or to be invented, without permission in writing from the publisher, except by a reviewer who wishes to quote brief passages in connection with a review written for inclusion in a magazine, newspaper, website, or broadcast. The web addresses referenced in this book were live and correct at the time of the book's publication but may be subject to change. All rights reserved worldwide.

Beacon Publishing Group, New York, NY 10001
www.beaconpublishinggroup.com

Manufactured in the United States of America

Dedication

For my family who keeps me inspired to write

"Do not fear those who kill the body but cannot kill the soul. Rather fear him who can destroy both soul and body in hell."
- Matthew 10:28

Table of Contents

Chapter One 1
Chapter Two 27
Chapter Three 39
Chapter Four 58
Chapter Five 108
Chapter Six 137
Chapter Seven 182
Chapter Eight 211
Chapter Nine 243
Chapter Ten 259
Chapter Eleven 270
Epilogue 288

Chapter One

The trailer park squatted on a patch of baked earth, crusted over like week-old roadkill under the desert sun. The road that led there wasn't a road so much as a suggestion, some gravel-strewn afterthought that peeled off a state route winding through the forgotten ribs of nowhere. Thirty miles outside of Helman – God's blind spot on the map – I was running a hustle dressed up in holy robes, trying to sell salvation in installments. A tiered path to the Pearly Gates, monthly rates applied. All for a "non-profit" outfit that feared God about as much as a con man feared confession.

My '88 Caprice rolled in like a wounded animal, dragging its belly across rocks sharp enough to shave a man's face. The old beater wheezed up to the park's center, a gravel crucible encircled by seven mobile homes, each one clinging to dignity like a drunk clings to his last bottle. It looked like the aftermath of a showdown: the wagons circled, nerves frayed, guns metaphorically cocked.

I stepped out into a wasteland dressed up as domestic life. Screens grimed over with years of indifference, rusted tin wind chimes made from empty beer cans, and folding chairs that promised front-row seats to decay. Trash spilled like loose guts across the hardpan. It wasn't so much a neighborhood as it was a slow-motion obituary.

I grabbed my fake leather satchel, the brown kind that tries to look classy but screams bargain bin – and picked my way through a minefield of dog shit. My destination: the nearest shack with something that resembled steps. Three of them, fashioned from warped wood and pride, leading to a porch resting on cinderblocks. Fancy by local standards. Rich folks, probably.

I knocked. Three times, sharp and official. A screen door rattled open and out came a man who looked like he lost a bar fight with a lawnmower. Mid-forties, skin like sandpaper, and the kind of eyes that could curdle milk. He opened his mouth, and a voice crawled out, dry and full of broken glass.

"What the hell do you want?"

Then came the cough – long, wet, and carved from the lungs of a man who's been kissing unfiltered Camels since puberty. He didn't cover his mouth. Why would he? Courtesy died a long time ago out here.

I wiped the spray from my face, let a plastic smile bloom. It was straight out of the training manual: Calm. Friendly. Deceptive.

"Hot one today," I said, pretending I wasn't already regretting every life decision that led me to this doorstep.

He squinted. "State your business."

Straight to the point. I respected that in a man. "Name's Bobby Santos, and I'm – "

"Should that mean something to me?"

Before I could answer, a voice growled from inside. A woman's voice this time, scratchy and mean like a record played backward.

"Tell him we're not interested, Jimmy!"

"Well, Jimmy," I said, tossing that tidbit into the pitch, "you're in luck. I'm not here to sell you a damn thing. I'm here to give you something. How's that for a change of pace?"

His eyes narrowed. Distrust crackled off him like static. "That so? What're you givin' away?"

I reached into the satchel like a magician pulling a rabbit – only this rabbit was pure pleather, gold-embossed, and stuffed full of gospel. The cross on the cover caught the sun like a dagger.

He saw it, sneered. "Go to hell." And moved to shut the door.

"Now hold on," I said, bracing the frame with my palm. "I'm not here to preach or pass a plate. Just here to offer you a book. Free. No sermon, no strings."

He spat. The wad hit the porch with a splat, just shy of my shoe.

"You show up uninvited, you're askin' for trouble."

"No trouble from me. Just a man, offering a Bible. What you do with it's your call. Read it, burn it, roll it and smoke it – I don't give a damn. I walk away clean either way."

His eyes stayed fixed on mine; they were red-rimmed and twitchy. Not just tobacco behind that glaze.

"What's in it for you?"

I shrugged, like a man explaining why he breathes. "The more I give, the lighter the warehouse gets. The lighter the warehouse, the better chance I make rent. That's the game."

He mulled it over. Poverty has a way of leveling the field; everyone understands when they need a buck or two.

"So, lemme get this right. You make money by giving away free books?"

"That's the grift, sure," I said with a smirk. "But it ain't as glamorous as it sounds. A lot of pavement, a lot of doors, a lot of spit. I give enough away, maybe I get to eat well next week."

He shook his head, still chewing on it. "You think I'm some dumbass?"

"No, sir. My brother's the funny one. My sister has the brains."

He snorted. "What's that leave you with?"

I grinned. "Personality."

I held out the Bible again. "I'll just set it here and be on my way."

Then I saw it – the smile that wasn't a smile. A flash of teeth that looked like they'd been chewing coal. That's when the gun came up, a revolver so old it probably had stories to tell.

"Go fuck yourself," he said, and slammed the door hard enough to rattle my fillings.

I checked my watch. Nine-thirty in the morning. The sun was already sweating bullets, and I was out one Bible and one shot at redemption.

Curtains twitched. Faces peeked. Hard faces, harder lives. People made brittle by circumstance. They stared at me like I'd broken into their church during confession, like I'd stolen the last slice of something they couldn't afford.

This place was a bust. I knew it before I ever stepped out of the car. A long shot, and I'd rolled snake eyes.

It didn't matter. Helman was waiting.

And Helman didn't sound like a place you walked out of smiling.

But it was all I had left. My final act, the last mark on a busted ledger. Either I made it work there, or I didn't make it at all.

And there was no resurrection for guys like me.

***

The truck-stop diner stood like a dying neon flame against a backdrop of dust and nothing, the last sorry oasis before seventy miles of asphalt hell. It catered to road-weary truckers, stray travelers, and lost souls trying to outrun something, usually themselves. A couple semis dozed on the far end of the lot, their engines ticking in the heat, and a guy with a wild beard was gassing up a Jeep that looked like it had been through a war and only half survived.

Hand-scrawled signs in the windows hawked *"World's Best Coffee"* and a lemon meringue pie that supposedly melted on your tongue. They sounded like promises hawked by a false idol, and part of me itched to ask a waitress how long they'd been selling the same damn dream.

The bell above the door gave a tired jangle when I stepped inside. It was the kind of joint where the only thing thicker than the grease on the griddle was the air of resignation. Maybe fifty seats total, and damn near all of them empty. The kind of emptiness that screamed *necessity*, not *popularity*.

Two truckers hunched at the counter, talking low and slow over their coffee, ass cracks peeking out from jeans that were doing the Lord's work holding on. Across the room, two more guys, local drifters or maybe day laborers, dug into their plates like the food might grow legs and bolt.

One had pancakes stacked like a gambler's debt; the other was working on a burger so dressed up it looked embarrassed to be in this place.

The waitress glanced up and gave me the same look you'd give roadkill you weren't sure was fresh or not. She jerked her head toward the open booths like she didn't care where I sat, just as long as I didn't bleed on the floor.

I took the booth in the back corner. Old habit since I was a kid and learned Wild Bill Hickok got his brains blown out because he didn't sit with his back to the wall. You only have to learn a lesson like that once, even if it's secondhand.

She shuffled over and dropped a menu like it offended her to carry it. Didn't say much, just jabbed her chin at the mug already on the table.

"Black," I said.

She returned in a blink, slinging the carafe like it owed her money and pouring what I hoped was fresh brew. The steam rising from the cup gave me some hope. The smell killed it.

"You want the specials?" she asked, chewing gum like it was the last piece on Earth.

"Are they worth the pitch?"

She didn't miss a beat. "Not unless your last meal was in 'Nam. If it ain't frozen, it's fried. And don't trust anything with mayo, unless you want to spend the next two days praying to the porcelain gods."

"Two eggs over easy. White toast."

"Eggs are safe. Bread's stale. You want a biscuit instead?"

I raised an eyebrow.

She shook her head. "Didn't think so."

Three Days In Hell

She disappeared behind the swinging door like a ghost in orthopedic shoes. I nursed the coffee, letting the bitterness scald my tongue just enough to remind me I was still alive. The place smelled like hot grease and lost time. The walls had been white once, but years of fryer fumes had yellowed them into a jaundiced haze. Booth cushions were torn open like slit throats, and the counter stools wobbled like drunkards.

If Helman was anything like this diner, I was walking into a graveyard wearing cologne.

I was halfway through a plate of rubbery eggs and dry toast that could've doubled as roof shingles when the bell above the door rang again. It wasn't the sound that got my attention. It was the shift in the room. Conversations stalled, forks froze mid-air. A man walked in with the kind of presence you don't ignore.

The sheriff.

You can spot the difference between a statie and a county badge from a mile away. State cops dressed like they were trying to impress a governor with creased uniforms, polished boots, and a posture that said they knew they could ruin your week with a citation pad. But sheriffs? Sheriffs were a different breed. They moved like they owned the dirt under their feet. Like the county line was the edge of the universe, and they were the sun around which all the sorry planets orbited.

This one was no exception with a paunch beneath the tan shirt, mirrored shades indoors, and the kind of walk that said he hadn't run in a decade. He scanned the room like he was looking for trouble or maybe hoping to catch it off guard.

I didn't flinch. Just sipped the last of my lukewarm coffee and let the sheriff make the first move. I was just passing through, after all. But a place like Helman? It had a way of turning a traveler into a suspect without so much as a warning shot.

Sheriffs were elected, which meant they could be bought, usually for less than you'd expect. I never met one who didn't have a little something going on the side, a quiet hustle that kept the taxman in the dark and paid for the occasional fishing trip or mistress. Civil servant pay barely beat out Sunday collection plates, and at least preachers had the benefit of guilt on their side.

The man who walked in wasn't a statie. Not even close.

He was in his forties, heavyset and thick through the chest like a butcher who liked his own product too much. He didn't move slowly, exactly, just with the kind of swagger that said he didn't have to rush. He walked in like he owned the deed to the place, which in a way, he probably did. Small-town power was always louder than its reach.

He had the face of a man who'd laugh while kicking a wheelchair out from under someone.

The waitress gave him a practiced smile as he approached the counter. They exchanged a few words, casual, maybe even friendly, but the kind of friendly that came with teeth. Then he leaned his back against the counter like a sun king surveying his dominion and scanned the room.

His voice was gravel in a whiskey bottle and it rose over the soft murmur of the diner. Bold. Abrasive. Meant to be heard and never mistaken.

His eyes fell on the two truckers. He stared long and hard, the way a man does when he's trying to decide if he recognizes someone from a mugshot or a memory. Whatever gears turned in that thick skull, it wasn't out of curiosity. People who thought that long in silence weren't planning birthdays.

Eventually, his attention landed on the pair in the booth by the window. His look changed to recognition and then interest. He strode over, all confidence and zero concern for interrupting a meal.

I played it casual, keeping my glances loose and my ears open. You learned a lot more when you didn't look like you were trying.

"Teddy-boy, how are they hanging?" Dupree said, his voice full of false warmth. The shift in their body language was instant. Tension cinched them tight. They didn't like him, not one bit. But they feared him more.

He wasn't just some lummox in a badge. He was that old archetype: the hometown football hero who peaked senior year and never got over it. The only difference now was the weight and the badge. And the bitterness.

"Morning, Sheriff Dupree," Teddy answered. His voice was polite, but his posture screamed discomfort. He was a wiry man, older than he looked from behind, hair thinning and streaked with gray. Life had clearly kicked him around, but not enough to give him a backbone, not in front of Dupree.

He set his fork down like it weighed too much.

Dupree just stood there, saying nothing. Letting silence do the work. The longer he didn't speak, the more Teddy folded in on himself. Then came the hand, big, meaty, and casual on Teddy's shoulder. Teddy flinched like he'd been goosed with a cattle prod. Dupree chuckled.

"Relax now, Teddy, you're wound tighter than a long-tailed cat in a rocking chair factory."

Teddy locked his eyes on some distant, invisible horizon.

Dupree turned to the man across from him, Bud, judging by the look on his face when the sheriff said his name. Bud had the slack-jawed terror of a man caught sneaking back into the henhouse.

"Bud, where you been hiding yourself? How's Mae? She good?"

Bud tried to fake a smile, but his fear hollowed it out.

"She's fine, Sheriff. Doing real well. Thanks for asking."

"That's good to hear." Dupree's voice was syrupy now, slick and condescending. "I stopped by the depot the other day. Henry said he hadn't seen you. I said, 'Now that's strange. Bud doesn't just go disappearing.' But here you are. Looking all cozy. Full bellies and good company."

Bud couldn't look Dupree in the eye. He glanced around the room like someone might come save him. No one would. Dupree reached out and turned Bud's chin toward him with two thick fingers.

"You want to tell me where you ran off to?"

Bud looked at Teddy, hoping for backup, but Teddy was off in some other place, his soul already halfway out the door.

"Nowhere special," Bud said. "Just out of town for a few days."

Dupree didn't press. Not yet. He dipped a finger into Bud's plate, fished out a couple fries, and popped them in his mouth. He licked his fingers with deliberate slowness.

"Nice to get out once in a while," he said. "Reminds you there's more to the world than this little patch of dirt. Richer places. Greener pastures. You get what I'm saying?"

"I don't know about that," Bud mumbled.

"Oh, come on, now. You trying to tell me Helman's got more to offer than upstate? Bud, if that's what you're saying, I've got beachfront property out on the mesa with your name on it."

"No, I didn't say that."

"I know you didn't," Dupree said. "Because if you did, you'd be lying. And we both know, aside from lawbreakers, liars are the lowest form of person in my book. Deceit is ugly, don't you think?"

"I do, Sheriff."

"I thought you might. So now that we're on the same page, you want to tell me where you went?"

Bud tried to swallow, but it stuck halfway down. He opened his mouth, but only a garbled sound came out. A cough rattled in his throat. Dupree slid over a glass of water. Bud drank like a man just rescued from the desert, finishing it in two panicked gulps.

"Try that again," Dupree said.

"I was at Carlson," Bud finally managed.

"Carlson! Now there's a place. Bigger. Richer. Wouldn't you say?"

"Yeah... it's a richer place."

Dupree nodded slowly, savoring the admission. "I'm glad you didn't lie to me, Bud. Because I know things. I'm the law here. That's my job. To know what's happening in Helman and everything that even touches it. And I know you were gone for three days. I know you brought back a little *inventory* folks have been whispering about. Tell me I'm wrong."

Bud stayed quiet.

"That's what I thought." Dupree leaned in, his voice dropping, oily and low. "And I know what that inventory sells for. I know what you made off it. And now, I know what I'm owed."

"It's not like that, Sheriff," Bud stammered.

Dupree picked up the fork from Bud's plate and pointed it at his eye.

"That's exactly what it is. And now I'm going to tell you how this goes. Or so help me God, I'll jam this fork into your eyes and feed them to you one at a time. How's that sound? We got a deal, or do you want to eat your eyeballs instead of that fine juicy burger?"

I'd never seen a man piss himself, but judging how Bud looked all frozen, clammy, and barely breathing, I figured I had now.

Dupree dropped the fork on the plate with a clatter. He plucked another fry and stuffed it in his mouth, licking the salt from his fingers before rapping his knuckles on the table.

"Uh-huh. I'll expect my slice of that pie in twenty-four hours. Y'all enjoy the rest of your meal."

He turned, then paused. "Oh, and Bud? Tell Mae I asked about her. Looking forward to her cornbread at the Festival."

Dupree spun on his heel, and that's when I made my mistake.

I looked too long.

He caught me watching. Our eyes locked. I broke it quick, but it was too late. I'd crossed into his orbit.

He ambled over, his belly and the polished grip of his sidearm coming level with my eyes. Instead of a badge or a flag, his collar held a gleaming high school class pin, the kind worn only by men who still remembered touchdowns and pep rallies.

He didn't speak right away. Just loomed, waiting for me to look up. When I did, he greeted me with a smile that didn't touch his eyes.

"Hello there, friend," he said. His tone had all the friendliness of a cocked hammer. "I don't think I've seen your face around here before."

"I just came in off the road for some food," I said, shifting under his gaze.

"Work or pleasure?"

"Excuse me?"

"You're traveling," he repeated, slower this time. "Is it for work, or is it for some other purpose?"

"Work. Headed to Helman."

That got his attention. He placed a deliberate hand on the table.

"Fancy that. I happen to be the sheriff in Helman. Mind if I ask your business there? You being a new face and all. Unless, of course, it's a secret."

"It's no secret, Sheriff."

He nodded once. "Go on, then."

"I'm giving away Bibles."

His brow furrowed, confused. "Bibles? Why would you want to do a thing like that?"

I get that question a lot.

"I have to ask it," he said. "Comes with the job."

I reached into my pocket and pulled out a business card. White stock. Plain logo. Just enough ink to be taken seriously.

Dupree regarded the card, working his jaw like he was chewing a thought. Then he slipped it into his shirt pocket.

"That's a peculiar profession, wouldn't you say? Giving away Bibles? Hell, folks can swipe one from any motel they stay in. And they don't."

"I don't make the business decisions," I said. "I just follow orders."

"And that pays?"

"It can."

"How much?"

The gleam in his eye was suspicion looking for a foothold, so I just gave a faint smile, no teeth.

"See," he continued, "I'm asking because it sounds a hell of a lot like one of those cults. That what this is? You running some scheme? Trying to soft-sell the locals into something?"

"No, sir." I reached into my satchel and pulled out a Bible. "This one here's an honest-to-God St. James. No edits, no footnotes, no funny stuff. Just the Good Word, same as it's always been."

He flipped through it, eyes scanning as if expecting a hidden map or secret code. The tiny font must've irritated him because he tossed it back to me like it bit.

"Well, what do you know," he said, sounding disappointed there wasn't more to sink his teeth into. "Just when you think you've seen it all. So, tell me, Mr. Bible man, you like selling these for a living?"

"I'm not selling them," I clarified. "I'm giving them away. But to answer your question? No, not really."

He nodded, as if that made sense. "And how many you figure on handing out in Helman?"

"As many as I can. I work on quota. Got a trunk full."

"No shit. And you really make money doing that?" he asked again.

"Not nearly enough," I said, picking at a thread on my lapel.

He nodded again, chewing on that for a moment. His suspicion dimmed, replaced by a flat sort of boredom.

"All right then. You hand out your Bibles. But I don't want to hear about any funny business – no shaved heads or confusing the kids about what's what. I'm the law in Helman, and if you so much as fart in the street, I'll smell it. And when I do, I'll know more than you want me to. Catch my drift?"

"With both hands."

He gave me a sour look, then turned away. Called out a goodbye to the waitress and strolled out the door like he'd just blessed the room. I stared at my half-eaten eggs, my appetite gone.

The waitress didn't approach until his cruiser pulled away.

"My, my, my," she said, eyes still on the window. "What on earth did you do in a past life to get his attention?"

"I didn't do anything. I was just here."

"In Helman, sometimes that's all it takes."

"He wanted to know my business," I said, sipping cold coffee. "He always that friendly?"

"You mean *nosy*? Yeah. Every face is a dollar sign to him. An unexpected windfall. Did you tell him?"

"Yeah. He's the sheriff."

She raised a brow. "If he can turn a profit off you, that badge becomes a tool for business, not justice. Let me put it this way. Nobody makes five dollars in his dung heap without one going straight into his pocket."

"Ah," I said, starting to see the picture. "So, he's *the* man."

"Dupree? In Helman?" she laughed once. "Hell no. He *wants* to be, but he ain't. There's someone else, someone who gets *three* of those dollars I mentioned."

She looked at me expectantly, waiting for the obvious follow-up.

I didn't bite. I'd been in enough places to know: if you don't *need* to know the top dog's name, don't ask. Especially when all that really matters is the size of his teeth.

She glanced down at my plate. "Didn't finish your food."

"I'm guessing that's not a first."

"Not by a long shot. Want something else?"

I pushed the plate aside. "How's the lemon meringue?"

She gave me a look like I'd asked to borrow her dentures.

"You seem like a bright fellow."

"I know basic math and how to spell 'Wednesday.'"

"Then let me ask you, see any lemon trees around here?"

"No."

"I think you found your answer." She smirked and slid the check toward me. "Have a nice day."

***

Instead of transitioning into a more urban environment, the road into Helman unfolded like a slow-moving panorama, rugged, semi-arid flatlands stretching wide beneath an enormous sky, with distant mountain ranges jagged on the horizon like the back of a sleeping beast. The land was pocked with gullies and wind-carved crevices, the kind of terrain you imagine the moon might have had, if it were painted in rust and red swirls.

Three Days In Hell

A few scattered ranchers let their cattle range across patches of earth where irrigation gave just enough life for tufts of stubborn, chewable grass. If it weren't so damned hot, this might have been the kind of place someone could stand losing themselves in. The space had a way of demanding introspection. It was quiet. Endless. And the skies here were some of the bluest I'd seen, rivaling even the ocean-bordering states.

Up ahead, I saw an old man atop a rusted John Deere, dragging something that kicked up a hazy wake of dust. The tractor, chipped and green, wheezed and coughed over the broken terrain like it was tired of the work but knew there was no one else to do it.

I slowed as I passed, curious.

The driver was shirtless beneath his overalls, his skin leathered into permanence by years of sun and wind. His arms worked the wheel with easy authority, muscle taut and wiry. On his head sat a battered, near-conical hat, its original shape long forgotten. His face looked carved from wood: a crooked nose, scraggly beard, cheeks that had been flayed by the elements and hardened by them in equal measure. He didn't look like he belonged to the land so much as he'd been born *from* it.

As I eased by, he glanced at me with eyes like knot holes in old barn wood – dark, unreadable, and not entirely welcoming. I might have waved, but I was too busy trying to process what he was hauling behind him.

A horse.

Dead.

A massive one.

Even in death, it was impressive, easily the largest horse I'd ever seen. It wasn't sleek or built for racing, and it didn't have the fire of a wild mustang. This one had been a worker, thick-muscled, barrel-chested, a plow-puller. Maybe a lifeline for that broken patch of land in the distance, the one he was heading toward, shimmering like a dream through the heat waves.

The horse's mane dragged in the dirt behind it like a fallen banner. Its great body heaved slightly with the bumps in the earth, and in some strange, mournful way, it looked like it still breathed. Even death couldn't rob it of its strength.

I'd never seen something so beautiful and so sad all at once. A loss like that, out here where every living thing counts, must have cut deep. Enough to set back a season. Maybe two.

The man turned away, eyes returning to the horizon as he coaxed the tractor forward. Dust curled in his wake, and behind him, the carcass followed, silent, loyal even now.

***

According to the office backgrounder, Helman had had its day.

Once.

And from the way things looked, that day was a long, long time ago.

Like any town scraped from sunbaked clay and dirt, Helman struggled for existence. But like a stubborn agave, its roots eventually took hold. A few visionaries caught a flicker of possibility and saw more than just dust and distance; they saw potential. All it took were a couple of good breaks to lift this stubborn little outpost into something resembling a town with a future.

The first break came with the arrival of a family who believed in the land, believed it could yield more than heartache. The second came when silver ore was struck deep underground, giving Helman its first real taste of prosperity. And then came the whispers of oil, rumored to lie hidden beneath the basin's cracked skin. That promise rang like a hymn through the valley. Locals swore they could hear angels singing that Helman was the next promised land.

Talk of black gold reached the state capital and soon came blueprints for a new highway to cut through town. There was even talk of railway freight, passengers, and the works. Helman, once a dusty, cattle stop, started buttoning its collar and standing a little taller. Construction crews poured in. Businesses staked their claims. Banks handed out loans like candy. Helman was no longer just surviving; it was becoming.

For a time, it felt like a true, God-ordained miracle.

But the fire-bush turned out to be a sparkler in the rain.

The oil? A fiction. Just a slick scam to pry funding loose from gullible officials. The silver? Overestimated and quickly depleted. The construction? Abandoned, the union crews gone as soon as the checks bounced.

Empty frames of buildings stood like bleached ribcages, littering the town like the corpses of better days. Businesses packed up and pulled out. The smart money went somewhere else, somewhere that delivered.

Helman didn't fall.

It evaporated.

The true believers stuck around, thinking the tide would turn again. The others, the wise ones, read the tea leaves and left before the rot set in.

The state pulled its highway funds. The railroad found another route. The promises went elsewhere. Helman stood still, watching its golden future loaded onto flatbeds and railcars heading to towns that didn't flinch when opportunity came knocking.

Now, there was no reason to come to Helman, unless you were into ghost towns. Most who passed through didn't bother to stop. Truckers and wanderers barreled down the sun-bleached main street, on their way to the river gorges, the distant mountain trails, or the deserts between. California waited at the end of the road. Helman was just a mile marker you forgot as soon as it was in your rearview.

Like a child caught in lava mid-scream, Helman stood frozen in time, cursed to endure without progress. It had enough to survive, but survival here was its own kind of slow death. The daily grind bled spirit. Even the strongest buckle.

And for the dreamers? It was worse.

Dreams in Helman were treacherous. They shimmered just long enough to be believed, then dissolved as soon as you reached for them.

No, Helman wasn't struck by tragedy. It was infected. A slow, crawling cancer that hollowed it out from within, until only a brittle shell remained.

Its heart still beat, barely, at the intersection of Paradise and Hope, streets named with cruel irony. Any business that still clung to life was found there. Depending on how you looked at it, they were either lucky or cursed. Lasting costs something. Money. People. Soul. And in a town this scorched by economy and heat, that price was nearly unbearable.

Helman sprawled like the aftermath of a star that exploded and never reformed. A few other roads splintered off, some paved, others shattered and sunken, leading to the town mechanic, the junkyard, the sad little bowling alley. But there weren't many.

Three Days In Hell

The schools were gone.

Families homeschooled or gave up entirely, trading education for day labor to help pay the bills.

The people? They lived like ghosts. Some huddled above dying businesses. Others squatted in crumbling red clay homes that ringed the town like a prayer circle made of regret.

A development of "new" homes sat off on a bluff, half-built, half-dreamed. Their skeletons lurched in the dry wind, frozen promises of what might've been.

My stomach sank at any thought of making Helman a quick trip.

Aside from a pair of old men parked on chairs outside a storefront, the streets were empty and silent in a way that made me wonder if the town had already died and just hadn't figured it out yet.

Finding Motel Indigo wasn't hard. It was the only one left perched at the edge of the main drag, a couple of bends away from the interstate that funneled people into, and more often out of, Helman. The office sat wedged between two low-slung wings of rooms, one of which was clearly closed for good. I wasn't surprised. Nothing I'd seen suggested enough demand to justify opening ten more rooms just to have them sit vacant like forgotten coffins.

The man behind the desk looked about ten years older than me and wore his bitterness like body armor. His unshaven face was topped with a gray-bristled mustache that all but swallowed his upper lip, either a conscious choice or just neglect in action. His short salt-and-pepper hair spiked up like desert scrub. The nametag on his stained shirt read "Woody," which fit him: splintered, stiff, and unwelcoming.

For someone in the hospitality business, Woody seemed allergic to hospitality.

The lobby smelled of dust and stale air. Two neglected gumball machines squatted by the door beside a mustard-colored sofa that hadn't seen a cleaning crew since Clinton was in office. The complimentary coffee in the carafe looked like it had curdled into something halfway sentient. A rack of faded tourist pamphlets drooped with age, their corners yellowed and curling like fallen leaves.

All signs pointed to the Indigo having seen better days, if it had ever seen good ones at all. I braced for what the carpets and sheets in the rooms might look like.

Woody let me stand at the counter a full minute before speaking.

"Got a reservation?" His voice sounded like it had been filtered through gravel.

"Do I need one?" I asked, letting the sarcasm ride.

"Don't be wise," he snapped. "I don't need any wiseasses in my place. You wanna be funny, take it outside."

Part of me wanted to turn around and leave. But the nearest real town was over an hour away, and I wasn't about to make that commute every day. I put on my best friendly face and softened my tone.

"I'm sorry," I said. "Been driving all day. I'd like a room, if you've got one. Please."

He studied me like I was a half-rotten melon, then grunted and slid a ledger toward me.

"Credit card. ID. Sign the book, if it's not too much trouble."

If he wondered what I was doing in Helman like the sheriff had, he didn't show it. His eyes had seen too many travelers roll through town. Unless someone's business touched his, it wasn't worth his attention.

He pulled a key from the wall behind him. Room One.

"You can't miss it," he said.

"Sure," I said. "It's right before number two."

The room was at the far end of the open wing. One window faced the parking lot. The other offered a sweeping view of the endless dry folds of land stitched between jagged mountain ranges. It might have been breathtaking, if the windows weren't streaked with grime thick enough to obscure the details.

I retrieved my suitcase and a brown paper bag from the back seat. Inside was a bottle of bourbon. A lesson learned early: always travel with alcohol. You never knew when the office was sending you into a dry county. When it came to drinking, religious types were unpredictable, either preaching abstinence or praising the miracle of water turned to wine. I'd seen drunk Catholics and teetotaler Protestants, all quoting the same book. The God squad was funny that way.

I grabbed a towel from the bathroom and spread it across the bed. This was the kind of room where you stayed off the comforter and slept in your clothes just in case you rolled over onto someone else's dried fluids.

I sat down and poured myself a heavy glass of second-tier Kentucky's finest. The carpet was sticky, stained with what looked like either cheap wine or half-digested regret. A table squatted nearby, too small to be useful. One of the chairs had two legs mummified in duct tape, barely fit to support a taco combo, let alone a human being.

The walls were decorated with cheap prints of desert cacti, the kind of watercolor crap a bored kid might churn out when left alone too long. The nightstand looked like it had been through a knife fight, etched over the years with names, initials, and crude symbols that made it feel less like furniture and more like an artifact from a jailhouse.

I opened the file I'd pulled from my suitcase and began flipping through pages. According to our records, Helman had about 365 full-time residents, one for each day of the year. I was supposed to unload seventy-five Bibles, collect seventy-five names, and send back seventy-five leads. *Seventy-five*.

I thought about my supervisor and shook my head. That idiot actually got one over on me, a rare move for a man who couldn't play checkers without help. He sent me here for one reason: to disappear. Getting seventy-five people to take a Bible was a stretch in *any* town, even one that wore its religion on its sleeve. But here? This place was like the backside of God's own mistake. Seventy-five was a pipe dream. But I was locked into the contract now. I'd be here however long it took, which meant I'd be out of the way, and conveniently forgotten.

I drank the bourbon too fast. For the second pour, I measured two fingers, just like Luanne used to. She always poured it that way with a hand around the base of the glass, liquor up to the top of her index finger. Luanne knew how to handle a bottle. She was a drinker, a smoker, a free spirit. And she was fun. Too much fun.

I liked Luanne more than I should have, and more than was good for me.

Women had always been my weakness, maybe even my curse. I convinced myself that I didn't need them, that I could love 'em and leave 'em. It felt like power. But Luanne cracked through that armor, dug deep, and pulled out something I didn't want to see.

She was the reason I ended up in this godforsaken place. And as much as I hated her for it, I couldn't stop thinking about what she was doing now. And worse, *who* she was doing it with.

Three Days In Hell

No doubt she had company. Luanne always had company. Nobody knew that better than I did. God gave her a body that made people, men and women, look twice. And she used it like a thief with a lockpick. Before me, there was Dexter. Before him, Sampas from accounting. Each one thought they were the player until they found out she'd played the game better and faster.

When it was my turn in the batter's box, I thought I had her figured out. I thought I'd get my fun and be the one to walk away when it was over.

Turned out, I was just the next name carved into the nightstand.

But here I was in Helman. I'd pushed my luck, and I knew it now. I did what I'd never done, what I *shouldn't* have done, and got in too deep. Now I was paying for it. Being fired would've been too merciful for cuckolding Hank. No, in his eyes, I had to pay properly.

I raised my glass and studied the bourbon. If I held it just right to the light, I could almost catch the color of Luanne's eyes, the depth, the warmth, just before she'd close them and lean in for a kiss.

Truth be told, my first instinct was to bolt. Bibles be damned. But Hank had made himself crystal clear: if I ran, he'd report me for stealing the company's inventory, inflating the numbers to make it sound like grand theft. With my record, the cops wouldn't think twice. I'd done too much time for less, and I had no appetite for a third strike.

Being trapped; that was the worst fate for a man like me. You learned real quick to avoid it at all costs. But I was already there. No money. No backup. No place to run. And even if I did run, I knew exactly where I'd end up: behind bars, this time for a long haul. Prison time.

I had to hand it to Hank. The bastard had done his homework. He knew I was an opportunist, someone who looked for angles, for advantages. Maybe Luanne told him. Maybe he figured it out on his own. It didn't matter. One way or another, he knew how to deal a sentence dressed up as a job.

He gave me just enough rope to hang myself, and I was the kind of fool to tie the knot myself.

That's what you get for sleeping with another man's wife, and not just the sex, but the fantasy that came with it. Thinking you could have the woman, the escape, the win. Thinking you could get away clean.

At least this cell had the kind of bars I liked to see through.

I drained the rest of my drink and lay back on the bed, staring at the flickering neon that spelled out *Motel Indigo* to a world that wasn't watching. No other flies buzzing toward that light. No cars. No hope of another twenty-dollar bill in Woody's register tonight. Just him, back in his room, watching television or staring at nothing.

I wondered if this was what dying felt like. Those moments when the spark flickered, then faded, then flickered again, each time the intervals growing longer until one day… there was no spark left.

Chapter Two

Yeah, his name was Hank Twohy, sure, but nobody ever called him that. Around us, he was "Shank," and not the prison kind, though the vibes were similar. He didn't stab people, not literally anyway. He just made sure the poor saps working under him got screwed on the regular. It was his thing. Man had a gift.

Shank was shaped like a beer keg and covered in hair like a cheap rug, but that didn't stop him from acting like he ran the joint. He had that special kind of confidence only nepotism can buy. He didn't earn his job. He got it because someone up the food chain had the same last name and couldn't be bothered to climb any higher. But the thing was, his family didn't have faith in him, but they didn't want him starving either. So, they stuck him in middle management and hoped the paperwork wouldn't kill him.

It didn't. Shank was just smart enough to keep the circus going. Managed six of us "customer engineers" – the company's cute name for Bible delivery boys with sales quotas. We weren't selling religion. We were selling *brand awareness*, or so they said. The Bibles were free, yeah, but everything else cost. Trinkets, keepsakes, little chunks of "holy" this and "blessed" that, all mass-produced in sweatshops a continent away.

The hustle was simple: hand out a Bible, grab a name, an address, a glimmer of trust. That was all we needed. You'd think giving away something for free would be easy, but people these days? Suspicious. Can't blame them. Too many snakes in the grass. I got more doors in my face than a repo man during Christmas.

Still, we always found a few gullible enough to play along. That's when phase two kicked in. A new crew would sweep in, guys who looked like census workers but acted more like loan sharks. They scouted the place, sniffed out the soft spots, and passed the intel up the chain. And then the real action happened.

The closers. Now those guys? Artists. Suits sharp enough to slice bread, voices like warm syrup. They knew how to drain a wallet without ever pulling a gun. Life savings, pensions, insurance payouts, even antiques, it didn't matter. If it had value, it was on the table. One guy even walked off with a family's classic car collection. Honest to God. Said it was for "the Lord's work." Apparently, Jesus liked ChevyBel Airs and Dodge Coronets.

And because they brought in the big bucks, they got the VIP treatment. Separate offices, bigger checks, actual respect. Us grunts? We weren't even allowed to breathe in their direction. Shank made sure of that. He didn't want their cologne mixing with our sweat.

Now, a guy in my shoes might've been tempted to fudge the paperwork. Pad the numbers. Make up a Mrs. Margaret Holyman at 123 Bible Lane. But the company? They had safeguards. Every Bible had a serial number. Every serial needed a legit name. No name, no pay. Fake a name and just like that, you're a criminal. Not just fired. *Prosecuted*. Dragged through court like some two-bit thief.

They even had this "three strikes" rule. Two mistakes? Okay, you get a pass. Bad weather, dead leads, whatever. But a third? You were toast. They'd fine you, fire you, and toss your ass to the cops. And trust me, the company had friends in uniform. Shank's uncle or cousin or whoever wrote big, fat checks to the state police every year. Buy a little goodwill, buy a little muscle. Real cozy setup.

So, yeah, we played along. Didn't mean we liked it. But it was a roof, a paycheck, and better than selling timeshares in Florida. Barely. Every day we walked the line, Bible in one hand, quota on our back, praying the next door wouldn't get slammed too hard.

Funny thing is, I never believed in what we were selling. But I believed in the hustle.

It wasn't exactly a steppingstone to greener pastures, but then again, nothing in my life ever was. I had a real knack for landing jobs that didn't pay. My mother used to call it a talent, said it with a smirk, like she was halfway impressed and fully disappointed. She never had much hope for me. She claimed I lacked ambition, couldn't read the signs even when they were lit in neon. She wasn't wrong.

Now, my younger brother, that was a different story. She'd stacked a whole damn deck of dreams on him, and for a while, it looked like maybe she'd bet on the right horse. Everything he touched turned to gold, at least through her eyes. He hated it. Being the favorite meant living under a microscope, and he wasn't built for that kind of pressure. Then came the MS. Last year of high school, the bastard hit him hard, and within a decade, he was glued to a chair and fading fast.

Once he couldn't be the hero anymore, she wrote him off like a bad investment. Wouldn't even look at him. Too painful, she claimed, but really, she just couldn't bear watching her best shot at glory rust away in front of her. He became another liability in a life already full of them. Whatever she thought he'd do for her? That died right along with his mobility.

Funny thing, while she was busy ignoring him, he and I got close. I guessed misery's got a way of leveling the field. She'd spent years trying to turn us into rivals, but once we were both on the same end of the shit-stick, we figured we might as well help each other clean it off. I started taking him out, giving him some air, some scenery that didn't reek of failure and old guilt. Got to know him, finally. Then he went and put a bullet in his brain.

Anyway, my mom always figured I was built for two things: manual labor or prison. I'd already done a stint in the second, which made me eligible for the first. And while working for a bunch of holy rollers wasn't exactly my style, the gig paid just enough to keep the wolves at the door instead of inside the living room. They gave me a tie and a busted suit and expected me to pass for respectable. Joke's on them; I've pulled bigger scams with less.

The job was a dumpster fire, and Shank was the human equivalent of a migraine. But his wife, Luanne? She made the whole thing bearable. Just enough curve and color to keep the eyes happy, and in an office packed with secondhand testosterone and first-rate loneliness, that went a long way.

I never figured out how Shank landed her, but I suspected it was his family's money. He didn't have any looks and even less charm. He put her behind the desk as our secretary, which was like hiring a showgirl to balance your books. She hated numbers, couldn't answer phones without rolling her eyes, and typed like she was using a chisel and stone. But she wore red lipstick and tighter dresses than the HR manual allowed, and that was good enough for the suits upstairs.

Me? I didn't have a girl. Never really did. I never saw the point in keeping one around when you could borrow someone else's for less effort. Real relationships took time, energy, cash, all things I either didn't have or didn't want to part with. But other men's girls? They were easier. More fun. Most of them were halfway out the door already, just looking for a nudge. They wanted their cake and their cupcake, and I was fine being the frosting on the side.

I'd barely been out of the joint two weeks when I saw the ad for the job. Still shaking off the stink of steel bars and state food. My plan was simple: work a few months, stash some cash, and get the hell out. Head west. California, maybe. Some place with surf, sun, and no one who knew my name. Hell, an island in the South Pacific sounded even better. No parole officers, no debt collectors, no ghosts.

But plans were like promises in this world; they didn't mean much. Like my mother always said, I fed my vices more than I ever fed my ambition. And by payday, my wallet looked like a crime scene. And broke? Broke didn't get you laid. Not the way I liked to be anyway. Only women who stuck around when you were running on fumes were the ones who charged by the hour or used you like a clearance rack sex toy before tossing you back in the bin.

Luanne? She was a cocktail of both.

She wasn't dumb, not by a long shot. She played the airhead card, but she was always watching. Calculating. Trying to figure out who in the room might be the next rung on her ladder. She reminded me of a kid standing outside a bakery window, waiting to see which pastry looked the sweetest. She didn't need to do much. Just drift around the office like smoke, flashing a smile, twirling a strand of hair, dropping hints with that lazy Southern drawl like a fishing line to see who'd bite.

And we bit. God, did we bite.

After work, we'd sit around nursing cheap whiskey and wounded egos, swapping stories about what we'd do with Luanne if we ever got the green light. None of us ever did. But that wasn't the point. She gave just enough to keep the fire burning and the fantasy alive. That was her real talent, keeping hope on a leash just long enough to make us chase.

Flirting was just another hustle, a game of angles and bait, like picking pockets with words. Half lie, half theater, and all wrapped up in a shiny little package with a bow on top. Hell, in some ways, it wasn't all that different from what I did. She sold sex the way I sold bad investments and broken dreams, always with a smile, a wink, and enough smoke to hide the mirrors.

You talked sweet, let them think they're in control, then you steered them where you wanted to go in the first place. Flirting was just sex sales. You dangled the goods, asked questions that received answers without ever giving up your own. Words did the touching. A glance? That was a challenge. A hair flip? The bait. And if she fixed your tie with both hands, friend, that was not flirtation; that was clearance for takeoff.

The only real difference was, I was in the business of separating suckers from their wallets, not their pants. But the mechanics? Practically the same.

Looking back, Shank was a fool for keeping Luanne behind a desk. She'd have made a hell of a customer engineer, probably could've run the place if he wasn't so scared of getting outshined by his own damn wife. That kind of ego? Fragile. He thought putting her in a skirt behind a typewriter would keep her close and keep her loyal. But you didn't lock a wolf in the henhouse without expecting feathers to fly. And with an office full of lonely men and a woman like Luanne? He basically set the table and invited the wolves into his house for dinner.

Eventually, I'd had enough of being the guy with nothing but bar tabs and cold sheets. I decided I wanted her. Not for keeps, just for the ride. So, I paid attention. I watched how the other boys tried to win her over. Dexter was all flash, and Sampas? Sampas thought being persistent would do the trick. Eight days in, she tossed him like expired milk. That's when I made my move.

I started small. The kind of things women notice before you ever say a word. You let them see you watching the room, but not them. You do the little favors. You become useful without being obvious. Luanne clocked it fast. She could smell a fellow hustler a mile off, and she liked it. I wasn't just playing the game; I *understood* the game. And for six glorious weeks, I was the new pastry in her display case.

We kept it clean at first. No stolen glances. Just "Yes, Mrs. Twohy" and "No, Mrs. Twohy" and the occasional paper jam rescue like I was a damn office hero. Anybody sniffing around for gossip came up empty. We were professionals, on the surface. Beneath it? Animals, starving and smart enough not to shit where we ate, at least not in the beginning.

Outside the office, we stayed invisible. No motels, no receipts. We met like strays, on foot, in alleyways, empty parking lots, abandoned stairwells. Places where the only audience was peeling paint and broken glass. No one followed us, no one caught us. Not until we stopped caring.

Because when the boss left town, all bets were off. Strategy meetings were our mating calls. We'd screw like sinners in her car, in my rat-trap apartment, hell, even in Shank's own recliner. There's nothing quite like lighting up a cigarette with someone else's lighter while drinking their whiskey, wearing nothing but sweat and smug satisfaction after you screwed their wife blind.

But the thing about animals? They get sloppy. Especially when they're in heat. And Luanne and I were always goddamn feral.

There was a high you got when you knew you were doing wrong and didn't care. It wasn't just the sex; it was the crime. The thrill of cheating the game. Of owning what was never yours. And when your morals are on life support, the rush is even sweeter.

So, when Shank found out, I wasn't shocked. Truth is, I think he'd known for a while. He just didn't have the spine to do anything about it. But he got his proof. Photos. Maybe a hotel clerk got sloppy, maybe a neighbor got nosy. It didn't matter. What matters was he confronted Luanne first and gave her the classic ultimatum: the fun was over, come home, or get cut off.

She didn't blink. She chose the money. I might've had better moves in the bedroom, but I couldn't compete with a trust fund. Luanne knew how to play the long ball. She'd ride the wave just long enough to feel alive, then paddle back to shore where the safety net was waiting.

Me? I got something different.

Shank told me to meet him at the Triple Clovers, a bar that smelled like regret and cheap cigars, with a clientele that thought that being labeled a felon was a compliment. I figured he'd want to blow off steam. Yell, fire me, maybe land a punch or two for honor's sake. I was ready to take it on the chin. Fair's fair, I thought.

But the second I walked in, I knew it wasn't that kind of meeting.

He didn't say a damn word, just gave a nod. Not to me, mind you. To the two gorillas flanking the jukebox. They were on me like a tax audit, dragging me into the middle of the room before I could even blink. Then came the fists. Kidney shots, gut punches, kicks when I was down. It wasn't a fight; it was a statement. And Shank? He just sat there, sipping his Tom Collins, smiling like he'd paid for front-row seats.

I was thankful they left the bones intact. No broken fingers, no busted knees. Just enough hurt to make a point. The big one even had a Jesus tattoo on one arm and praying hands on the other, like that balanced the scales.

Eventually, Shank waved them off and invited me to his booth like we were old pals. He slid me a napkin and a glass of bourbon like it was a peace offering instead of a post-beating courtesy. I dabbed my nose, tasted blood, and waited.

Then he laid it out.

He said I had a shot at redemption. Said if I played ball, kept quiet, followed orders, he'd ship me off to a satellite office in another state and let me keep earning.

Hell of a sermon, considering the cross tattoo and all.

And me? I took the deal.

Because guys like me? We don't get second chances. We take the first offer that doesn't come with a pine box.

He assured me I'd just have to do what I always did. Hand out as many Bibles as I could. The thing was, it was a tough territory, the toughest he'd ever seen, but he knew I was up for the challenge. But he made it clear in no uncertain terms that if I tried to run, he'd reach out to his friends on the force and tell them that I had embezzled funds from an upstanding Christian employer who tried to help a former con acclimate himself into regular society. His bottom line: push the Bibles or push a button on a press that spat out license plates. It was my choice.

At that point, I took the bourbon in hand and swallowed it in two gulps. It was bitter and cheap and stung like a swarm of hornets down my throat.

Two questions popped into my head. "What if I didn't want to go?" I asked. "What if I wanted to just quit my job?"

Shank set his finished drink on the table. His thick lips twisted into a smile as if he had been hoping I'd ask him that very thing.

"You wouldn't leave here alive."

***

I paid my rent for the next month and spent the next couple of days getting my affairs in order. When you didn't have much of a life, you found out that the organization process didn't require a lot of time. My apartment could be rented tomorrow with minimal effort on the part of the landlord to get what few things I had into storage or on the street corner.

Word had made its way around the office. Shank made sure of that.

I was *persona non grata*. Everyone conveniently found other places to be when I showed up those last few days before my trip. It felt exactly like the time I was expelled from my first high school, and my class didn't know what to do when I gathered my stuff before being escorted out of the room. Luanne didn't even acknowledge my presence. She busied herself with the copier or the fax machine, humming to herself like nothing had happened, like we hadn't spent the past month and a half rubbing skin and swapping spit. She had forgotten the banter we had and the little smirks we had shared when someone said something funny that reminded us of the last time that we were together.

But what totally hurt, what really burrowed under my skin, was how her eyes dismissed me like I was rattling a can for spare change. One moment, she couldn't get enough of my attention, the next, her eyes dismissed me without a second thought.

See, the problem was, somewhere between sneaking sex and spending those little moments together, I had fallen for Luanne. I hated to admit it, but that was God's honest truth. For the first time in my life, a woman got to me. And it was a strange feeling. An uncomfortable feeling. But one that held me in a way I'd never been held before. That's when I realized I wanted Luanne. Instead of me stringing her along, the hook got switched, and she drew me into her instead of the other way around.

But that pain was nothing compared to the realization that I was the one who wanted more, and I couldn't have it. Don't get me wrong. I knew about her other affairs. We all did. But they were just one-offs, quick flings to fill her dance card as she looked for a more substantive alternative to meet her needs. I was that alternative, or so I thought. My problem was that she had come to mean something to me, and in giving up that, I gave up everything of any value, and she knew it. She had tested my limits, and I came up short.

The day before I was to head out to Helman, Luanne was already working with Spencer, a new kid Shank hired right out of the Bible Thumper College an hour up the road. The kid was good-looking in a fresh-faced sort of way, and two minutes didn't pass before Luanne started her hair twirling in Spencer's presence. On my way out the door, she was sitting on Spencer's desk at the back of the bullpen, giggling at something that the college boy had told her. She had her skirt hiked just high enough to show the top of her nylon and the garter snap that kept it in place. She didn't even glance in my direction as I passed by carrying the box of my desk supplies. I was going to make an off-colored remark but checked it when I smelled something familiar.

It was thick and sweet-smelling, and reminded me of a freshly baked chocolate cupcake when it's pulled from the oven and set on top of the counter to cool off before topping it off with icing. She had found her new pastry all right and couldn't wait to dip two fingers into the frosting to taste it.

Chapter Three
Friday

Friday morning announced itself with the sun blaring in through the thin gauze hanging listlessly in front of the windows as an excuse for drapes. The night before, I had aired out my slacks and jacket and meticulously laid out my clothes for the next day on the other bed. I came prepared with the only two suits I owned, so I had to be judicious about how I wore them and how I cared for them. I doubted if Helman was the type of place that had a bustling dry cleaner with turn-around service. The prior evening, I noticed a room with a coin-operated washer and dryer sold small boxes of detergent and made a mental note to pick up some quarters before returning tonight.

After a shower and shave with a slap of cologne, I was ready to suit up adjust the tie Luanne gave me, but it was too nice for a town like this. Too clean, too hopeful. It felt like a splash of color on a corpse.

Exiting my room, the hot breath of Helman panted in my face like a fat dog in August. The kind of air that sticks to your skin and makes your clothes feel like wet burlap and it was early morning. I spotted the maid two doors down, busily organizing her cleaning equipment on her cart. She was a heavyset Hispanic woman with heavy, sagging cheeks and eyes that surrendered any idea of hope long ago.

She didn't hear me approach, preoccupied with humming some sad song whose rhythm and depth were indicative of an origin south of the border.

"Hey, there," I called out to her. "Excuse me. Ma'am?"

I reached out to tap her arm. The touch startled her, and her face showed both fear and confusion. She removed her earbuds and waited for me to talk. She didn't seem accustomed to talking to guests, and it showed. I tried to put her at ease with a soft smile.

"You got any good places to eat around here?"

When I repeated the question, her blank expression told me she didn't understand a word I had said, which made me wonder why she even bothered with the earbuds. She kept staring at me as if the longer she looked, the more apt I'd be to start speaking her native tongue.

I blew out a mouthful of hot air. My Spanish was woefully inadequate for one-on-one engagement, and getting a word out of her was like pulling teeth. Plan B was engaging in charades.

"Eat? Food?" I said, pantomiming forking food into my mouth.

She gave me another subtle tilt of her head, only this time her face brightened when it clicked, and she nodded enthusiastically, lifting a meaty arm and mimicking my gesture so fervently that her triceps disappeared under a roll of undulating flab.

"*Ah, sí, sí*. Eat, eat."

She then pointed a fat finger at some unseen destination in the direction of downtown Helman. She didn't say a name and just nodded over and over like a bobblehead doll. It wasn't much help, but then again, I couldn't imagine there were more than a couple of places to strap on a feedbag if I was lucky.

"Can I get more towels?"

She cocked her head to the side again, but I didn't have it in me. I figured I'd ask ol' Woody for some when I got back.

I smiled broadly. "Have a good day."

I headed to my car and got in and started it up. I turned on the radio and was greeted with the news telling me that today was going to be a real scorcher, with temperatures to hit the mid-nineties by ten o'clock. It was a little after eight already, and it felt like the devil himself was cupping my balls and holding a blowtorch to the bottom of them.

***

El Gallo y La Luna occupied a corner two blocks away from the main intersection. The name of the restaurant could still be seen scrawled along the chipped concrete wall near its entrance. Though the colors had long since faded, hints of green, red, and orange were still visible, though their brilliance was only a suggestion of their former selves. It must have been something in its time, the bold, bright paint catching anyone's eye walking down the street. Not any longer, not that it mattered much. Residents knew well enough where it was, and that's who the owners relied on to pay to keep the lights on and the frying oil hot.

I'd been to greasy spoons in other cities, but *El Gallo y La Luna* made them look like spacious, regal accommodations. Eight tables with two chairs each offered patrons a place to eat. A set of swinging doors led to an equally tiny kitchen where three cooks worked a shared flattop station and oven. Two locals with sun-burnt faces eyed me suspiciously as I walked in and sat at one of the tables. They immediately paused their forks when they saw a face they didn't recognize enter. Because there was no reasonable explanation for my patronage, I was an oddity to be stared at and questioned. In a town that didn't have many other interests, newcomers were something fascinating to watch with curiosity.

The laminated menu bore the filth and crust of years of spilled salsa and refried beans. Thankfully, there was English underneath the Spanish scrawl, and I perused the various fried offerings, gauging which would do less harm to my GI tract. The waitress was a young Hispanic woman who looked to be the next generation of a family-run business. She was predestined to run until she had kids to groom and indenture when their time came around. Like the two men at the table, she was genuinely surprised by my presence, an unfamiliar face in a very familiar town. Polite and to the point, she took my order and quickly retreated to the kitchen. I did my best not to acknowledge the three faces of the cooks crowded around the pass-through to eye the new guy.

The coffee was cold, the food oily, and it made me wonder why anyone would come here to eat unless they had forgotten how to cook for themselves. The two men at the other table kept looking in my direction as I pushed my fork around the plate, looking for something edible to spear in the mess of intermingled mush. They were rugged men with rugged faces, and I guessed that even when the economy was flourishing in Helman, these were not the types accustomed to wearing slacks and a pair of wingtips. They tilled the soil, whether making things grow or scraping out the material value, whether it was oil or silver, from within its depths. I wondered what they did now, the land being what it was and Helman looking like an area where things went to die.

"You don't like?" the waitress asked in accented English when she checked up on me. Her expression was genuine, her voice tinged with legitimate surprise, and I could tell that the meal had been cooked by family and not just an employee.

"My eyes were bigger than my stomach," I said, offering an apologetic smile. I did not want my first impression to offend whatever father, mother, sibling, or cousin made this gross concoction in the back of the house.

She was sharp enough to know my response was a fib but accepted it because I was a new customer and, by extension, an unexpected profit. Her nametag read "Catalina," and she had long jet-black hair that she kept in a tight ponytail. When she raised the carafe of coffee in a gesture to ask if I wanted more, I reluctantly nodded in assent to her pour.

"You a local?" I asked, and then added after looking at her nametag, *Catalina*. "You live here?"

"*Sí*, all my life."

"Is it always this quiet?"

She offered an apologetic smile. "It's a small town, *señor*."

"Tell me about it," I said cheerily. "Where I grew up, you could swing a dead cat and hit every business downtown."

Catalina's expression told me she missed my meaning. I quickly abandoned humor and decided to use the direct route to get the information I needed. I glanced out the front window. The streets were practically deserted. There was an old Ford pickup truck and a dirt-covered Chevy in a mostly empty row of parking spaces.

"Where is everyone? Where does everyone go? I figured such a good café as this would be full of customers."

She blushed another embarrassing smile. "This is Friday," she said. "More come later for lunch, but there are not a lot of people in Helman, *señor*."

"No kidding," I said. Then trying a new tact, "I'm new in town. I want to see people. Where do I go?"

It took a few seconds for her to understand my question, and when she did, she shrugged, nodding her head in concession. She removed a rag from her apron pouch and scrubbed at something on the table. One of the cooks in the back who had been listening to our conversation growled something in Spanish to Catalina, and her mood quickly changed. "I go back to work, *señor*."

"One more question, please." She hesitated long enough for me to ask it before she scampered away. "Do you have a church around here?"

She paused mid-departure. "Yes, of course," Catalina responded.

"Where?"

Her head cocked. "You want to see the church?"

I smiled, trying to put her at east for any misgivings she was having sharing that piece of information with me."

She pointed as she gave me directions. "There is Hope Street. Go all the way to the end of town. You see a big white house at end. Helman House. The church right next to the house."

"Helman? Like the town?"

Catalina smiled the way you would when a child solved a simple math problem correctly. "It wasn't always so," she said. "The people change it many years ago. The town was very small. Farms. Farmers. Not many buildings. Then Helman family came. Much business. Mining. Jobs.

Everything – boom!" She released a long sigh, her smile dissipating with the air in her lungs. "But then, no more boom."

"But they stayed. The Helmans, I mean."

She nodded again. "Their name. Their town. Now only one left."

One of the cooks called out to her and said something in Spanish. Catalina smiled at me and set the check on the table. She started back toward the kitchen.

"Catalina," I said. "What was the town's name before?"

"*Soledad*," she said. "It means, how you say?"

"Desolation." That word I knew.

She offered a weak smile before disappearing behind the swinging doors. This wasn't the first town run by a wealthy name, and it certainly wouldn't be the last. But it did seem odd that the family stuck around after the writing was on the wall. Rich people stayed rich by keeping on doing the things that made them rich in the first place, which made me think that maybe Helman wasn't as dried up as it appeared to be. Just because the town wasn't making money didn't mean that Helman wasn't.

I took a final gulp of that horrible coffee and turned in time to watch the table with the two men throw all subtlety out the window, checking out Catalina bend over to retrieve a tray of silverware from the bottom shelf. One made eye contact with me, and I glared at him until he abruptly looked away. I found leching to be one of the most disgusting acts a man could do, and that said a lot coming from someone who had an affair with another man's wife. Immoral or not, that was consensual. What they had done was nothing short of visual assault.

I removed a bill from my pocket and then thought better of it and replaced it with a smaller denomination. I felt things looking up already. The town had a church. And churches had followers. And poor churches in depressed towns needed Bibles more than anyone. And I had a whole stack of them in my trunk, ready to spread around. If things started to fall my way like I knew that they could, Helman would be a quick stop after all.

I grinned as I headed out the door. Ol' Shank thought he was going to screw me over with this gig, but it looked like it was going to bite him in the ass.

***

Standing in front of the church, I understood why Catalina answered the way she had. The town had one alright, and judging from the size of the structure at one time, it had catered to the souls of a large, God-fearing congregation. Unfortunately, the construction was dilapidated, but judging from what was still left standing, it had been glorious in its day, the pride of a spiritual community, and a beacon of all things religious and all the things that come with those trappings.

But what I saw was a shell of that magnitude, a structure in a state of morbid and unyielding decay. The stone and concrete still stood in place, but its façade bore the chipped marks of weathering and faded spray paint tracing, capturing profane images and slurs. Windows that had featured stained glass were long gone; all completely shattered with just jagged fragments jutting out of the individual frames. The front door had been removed from the hinges and lay on its side, leaning up against the crumbling building. The front parking lot macadam had been infiltrated by weeds that erupted from the ground only to die in the elements. Random litter had collected over the days, months, and years, blown in by competing winds only to catch hold of a defunct parking marker or random cactus, to be forever trapped in a frozen moment in time. There was no sign of resurrection or revival here; the church had perished regardless of the promises spelled out in the Bible.

In the rear, a small graveyard survived, though there was little indication that any living soul in town maintained the memory of those buried. The headstones were old, the etchings long since eroded and illegible. The ground must have been softer back then, as it was now too hard caked now to imagine the point of a spade breaking the hard surface.

Much of the ceiling had collapsed, exposing great strips of blue sky above. Dirt and debris had accumulated in the corners where flash-flooding swept in dirt and turned it into sludge. Near the altar, I found branches and brush around the base of a broken altar where animals had made their temporary dens at one time or another. The few rows of wooden pews that were still standing had been vandalized, with profanities and lewd drawings scrawled over them, probably the work of *Gatos Locos,* the name of that gang spraypainted in gold and black on the walls. The podium that held the tabernacle had been stolen long ago, along with anything that might hold any material value. The church was more of a mausoleum than a place of worship. There was no priest, and there was no congregation. I was back to square one.

I stepped outside and took in the town. The silence at the top of the hill was thick. Not peaceful. Just… empty. The kind of silence you only find in places that used to matter. I tried to imagine how it looked in its heyday, with crowds bustling through the streets and the clamoring of merchants conducting business. A mining town would have entertainment for those hardworking souls who disappeared into the earth to spend their money when they emerged from the tunnels and collected their paychecks. There'd be bars that pulsed with loud music and gambling halls erupting in cheers after the lucky toss of the dice or the pull of a slot machine's arm. And for those whose vices tended more toward the carnal, there were prostitutes and whorehouses that could relieve a miner of his hard-earned cash in a different way. Nights must have been filled with the cacophony of debauchery reminiscent of any Sodom or Gomorrah. And like any place battling Satan's propensity for good times, the poor church stood like a lone candle flame flickering mercilessly in the howling storm that was the seven deadly sins.

The Helman House stood above it all.

The church might have succumbed to events, but the Helman House not only survived, but flourished. It beamed vibrantly in the morning hours, looming large above the town in a prominent place next to the church, the way only politics and religion could in small municipalities. There was a heartbeat to the place; you could feel it, if you stared long enough. It wasn't just the way the wind pushed the fountain's spray into a fine mist or how the marble glinted like polished bone. No, this house was alive in the same way snakes were alive: cold-blooded, silent, and always watching.

The residence's pristine front and power-washed walls made the white exterior gleam in the sunlight and stand out from the rest of the structures it overlooked. I didn't have to see the rest of the town to know this was by far the largest and most impressive residence, complete with a white stone fence marking its perimeter. However, unlike the nearby buildings lumbering beneath its elevation, the Helman House was neither crafted in stucco nor adobe, nor did it show the aesthetics of the Southwest influence.

A house for a king was a castle, a clear differentiator from the shacks of the surrounding gentry. The Helman House was such a distinction, a Spanish-themed hacienda constructed from the marble harvested on the Mediterranean coast, such as in the Almeria and areas of Murcia and Alicante. It projected power and wealth, designed expressly for the people's admiration or envy, a totem to be aspired for but never actually achieved by anyone below a certain economic and social threshold. At least, not by Helman's citizens. Mining work was for people living in canvas tents and shanties, whose wives contributed to the camps and were integral to the survival of the family.

Something struck me oddly about the Helman place. Compared to its surroundings, it looked remarkably well-kept, up-to-date, and clean – an odd combination given the condition of the rest of the town. Parked in the driveway was a newer model convertible sedan, and near that, a small marble fountain where a carved fish spat water in a high arc. I understood the concept of family wealth, but usually, there came a period when the money ran dry, and all that you had was the fading trappings of the way things once were. When their coffers ran dry, old money still had houses that looked impressive at a distance, but like any Money painting, its deterioration became more noticeable the closer you got to them. They needed more than fresh paint jobs and a little spit to make dull things shine again. Their roofs had gone neglected over the years; window frames needed to be replaced; cracks in the foundations needed to be repaired. Their interiors weren't much better either. Fancy furniture yellowed over time and across generations. Drapes were usually outdated, and the windowsills seemed in perpetual need of thorough dusting. Termite damage could be found in areas where the wood was hollow, and if you looked at the high vaulted ceilings, you'd see the unmistakable rings where water stains betrayed a small but steady leak from one of the pipes.

    Not this house. No, this place was kept with the type of care that only comes from care and diligent attention to detail. Unlike the denizens clutching to the poverty level, someone was obviously not relying on good fiscal investment and trust funds to get by the tough times. It was clear that he was still making money while others were not. The question was how. There didn't seem to be any commercial enterprise dictating this type of opulence or disposable wealth. And yet, this person had it.

    I headed back to where I parked my car and saw some kid in his late twenties tinkering with some tool to jimmy my trunk open. He was lanky and lean like a hungry coyote. He didn't have much finesse in getting into locked things as he took little care in obfuscating his struggles as he aggressively fiddled with the lock before finally wrenching the trunk-lid free.

    "Hey! What the hell do you think you're doing?" I yelled.

    The kid looked at me. The anger in my voice startled him because he froze long enough for me to cut the distance between us before he bolted. He took off down Decatur Street before darting to his left onto a dirt access road. I pursued him hard, though my cheap dress shoes didn't help much on the uneven, unpaved ground. The faux leather pinched in places, and I felt the contour and point of every rock I stepped on in the process. It didn't take a track coach to figure out I didn't have a snowball's chance in hell to catch him. The kid was jackrabbit-fast and had the advantage of knowing the nooks and crannies of the terrain. I pulled up in surrender when I saw him hurdle a couple of trashcans blocking his entrance into an alley.

Fuck it, I thought and headed back to the car, fishing out an old crushed and empty pack of cigarettes from the inside pocket of my jacket. I tossed it on the ground.

No sooner had I retraced my steps than who did I see digging through my trunk for a second time? The damn kid. He had a brass set on him, alright. And brains enough to lead me on a wild goose chase, only to double back and see if he could find something worth stealing.

This time, he looked up at me with a grin on his face. His eyes held no fear of being caught this time because his efforts yielded an unsatisfactory result – I had nothing worth stealing. He held up one of the pleather-bound texts of collected scriptures.

"Bibles? You chased me down for a bunch of Bibles? I thought you had something worth taking."

"That's not my property, but I'm responsible for it," I told him. His demeanor was more agitated than nervous, expecting a score and coming up shit-assed empty. For a kid who tried to rob me blind, he seemed assured that I wasn't going to break his hands for trying to steal from my car.

"Son-of-a-bitch," he said, fanning through the pages that flashed with gold gilding. "These are honest-to-God 'let there be light' Bibles. You some kind of preacher or something?"

"No, but I was sent here by one. Owns a big ministry. And he doesn't like his things taken from him." I pulled the book out of his hands and let my fingers run over the cover. "See that craftsmanship? The gold embossed inlay? That's top-quality stuff right there," I said, reminding myself that Christ loved the miscreants, and remembering the company didn't have any policy about giving the Good Book to thieves.

The kid continued his eyeballing. "And there's no coke inside? Pages aren't cut out and hiding some pills or something?"

"You watch too many movies, kid." I tossed the book in with the others and slammed the trunk shut.

The thief shook his head, dug into the front pocket of his faded jeans, and pulled out a soft pack of cigarettes. He flipped out a crooked butt and stuck it in his mouth and lit it with a quick snap of a rusted Zippo.

"Hell, the way you came at me, I figured you had something of real value. I could have killed you."

"With what? Your sharp personality?"

"I could have been packing heat for all you knew."

It was my turn to grin. I had run across men with guns in my day, and this guy was not of that caliber. I held out my hand, and he handed me the pack. I took a cigarette for myself, accepted the lighter, and handed both back after I lit it.

"Real value, eh? Like what?"

He shrugged. "I don't know. Like a laptop or smartphone. Big ticket items."

"But not diamonds," I said.

"No offense, mister, but you aren't exactly the spitting image of a person walking around with a pocketful of raw uncut."

"But packing coke, I'm that guy," I said sarcastically.

His face brightened, which made him seem younger, making me recalculate his age in my mind.

"You wouldn't be the first that tried to slip under the radar," he said. "Don't get me wrong. I didn't figure you for volume distribution. Just maybe something along the personal consumption line. You know, something that a man could pawn that might be worth something. Got to make a buck where you can."

"Kid, you got some imagination," I said. "How old are you, anyway?"

"Why? You looking for a date?"

"Knock it off," I said. "What's the matter with you? You got a wisecrack for everything?"

"Strange face waltzes into town wearing a cheap suit – no offense – and pushing Bibles is either a front, a grifter, or a pedo."

"That's not much of a choice," I said.

He shrugged. "You wanted to know, I told you. But I got to ask. What's with the Bibles, man?"

I let the question hang a minute. We stood there smoking our cancer sticks, both wondering what this chance encounter would amount to.

"For a cheap thief, you sure ask a lot of questions," I said. "You writing a book?"

He grinned at me. "I'm curious."

"Well, leave that chapter out."

He laughed and held out his hand. "Bins," he said.

"What, 'Bins'?"

"Bins. My name."

"That's your name?"

"Nickname."

"What was the other option?"

"Bartholomew Ignatius Nicodemus Servopolous."

I took his hand and shook. "You parents hate you that much?"

"Like I owed them money," he said. "But what are you going to do?"

"Well, Bins, I'm Bobby Santos."

"Santos," he said. "Like in saint?"

"I haven't been one since the doctor slapped my ass when I was born."

Bins laughed and dragged off his smoke. I surmised the bleak town from this elevated vantage point. The streets were still like dry riverbeds. There was little to no foot traffic and minimal vehicle activity. It appeared like the residents had boarded themselves into their houses, afraid to come into the light. One thing was becoming increasingly clear: if I was going to unload these Bibles, I needed a plan.

"How would you like to make some money instead of stealing it?" I asked Bins.

"Doing what?"

I shot him a look. "You broke into my car, and you're afraid if I may ask you to do something illegal?"

He smiled and shrugged. "It's called irony."

"I need information," I said.

"What's the pay?"

"Depends on the quality." I dug into my trousers pocket, removed a twenty-dollar bill, and handed it to the kid. "Let's start with what happened to the church?"

He snatched the bill and tucked it into his jeans pocket. He paused briefly, appearing to go through a mental rolodex. When he found what he was looking for, he opened his mouth. "It burned down."

"I see that. I want to know how."

"I'm not sure, exactly," he said. "I wasn't around then. But from what I've heard, it happened about the same time this town started to head down the shitter. It was a pretty steady decline from what I've been told. When the mines shut down, there were fewer offerings in the Sunday basket, if you catch my meaning. More bars opened, and more crime happened. Then, people stopped going to church altogether. Things just got worse from there, I suppose."

"So, all of a sudden, people stopped believing?"

"What do you mean?"

"A church has a following. Even a bad economic stretch doesn't mean people stop thinking there's a God. Some even believe that's when people turn to religion most. I'm assuming they're still here. If they don't go here, where do they go?"

"Beats the shit out of me. The last priest sent to get the church on its feet disappeared a few months ago. Probably saw this shithole for what it was and took off."

"Where'd he go?"

"Look, mister, I don't know why no one goes to church anymore. But would it matter if they did? Look at that shithole. I think it needs more than a few thousand dollars to fix up, and in case your eyes don't work, look around. No one has that kind of scratch."

I nodded to the lavish Helman House next door. "He does."

Bins smiled again. "Where are you from, buddy? There are the haves and the have-nots. And those among the former didn't get to where they are by helping the latter."

He wasn't wrong. I removed a handkerchief and blotted my brow, and no sooner had I wiped the sweat off before it beaded up again. The heat had to be well into the nineties by now.

"You ever think about putting that coyote energy to better use?" I asked.

His grin faded, curiosity blooming behind his sunburnt face.

"Depends," he said. "Better for who?"

"I need to know the lay of the land here," I said. "Can you help me with that?

"As long as you can keep on producing Andrew Jacksons, I'll find you a house and a girl and whatever else you want."

"I just need you to point to places that may have more than three people to whom I can give away my Bibles."

"The town's not that big population-wise, but it stretches farther than you'd expect. You can save yourself some dough and just poke around on your own."

"The charm hasn't rubbed off on me. Besides, it's been my experience that small towns like this don't like it when strangers just start showing up and knocking on doors. A more planned approach usually works out best. Churches have always been good for that, but since you don't have one…"

"Plan B," Bins said, finishing my sentence with a smile. "Tell you what. You fork over more of Jackson's brothers, we'll see if we can't get you prime real estate at the Chili Festival."

"The chili what?"

Bins smiled and played coy. I exhaled loudly and passed over another twenty-dollar bill.

"Tomorrow's Helman's annual Chili Festival," he said with a hint of pride in his voice. "It's quite the big deal around here. People come from all over."

I couldn't tell if he was being serious or trying to pull one over on me. I hadn't seen more than a handful of people since I came into town and couldn't imagine from, since there wasn't any significant town in a hundred-mile radius?"

"A chili festival," I said skeptically. "Here."

"I know what you're thinking, but trust me, it packs them in. There are all sorts of competitions. Who can eat the most bowls of chili in ten minutes? Who can eat the hottest chili, shit like that? The big one is the heat challenge. How hot can you go? Winner takes home some fat coin. It draws crazy big crowds."

"Crowds. Here? I'll believe it when I see it."

Bins laughed. "Wait and see. For another twenty, I'll draw you a map of how things will lay out."

"Let's see how you earn the first two. Come on, get in the car."

"Where are we going?"

"You're going to tell me."

Chapter Four

Bins didn't bother dressing his words up in Sunday best. Helman was a small town on the books, but that was about the only thing pint-sized about it. It sprawled out like a dying man's last breath; wide, dry, and choking under a mean sun. Two roads stitched it together like the veins on a corpse. The buildings lining the strip were mostly hollowed-out husks, their signage standing like tombstones memorializing the faded names of dime stores, dive bars, laundromats, and busted dreams.

The windows were shattered, jagged mouths grinning with broken teeth. Could've been the handiwork of kids with too much time and no direction, or booze-soaked adults lobbing rocks just to feel something.

The heat crept in even with the windows down, thick and stale like bad whiskey. Sweat ran down my forehead in waves, and I had to keep swiping at it before it blinded me. The air had weight, the kind that made you feel like the desert was leaning on your chest.

Bins rode shotgun, grinning like a mutt on its first ride through town. The wind whipped through his hair and he damn near stuck his head out the window, tongue practically wagging.

"How long you say you lived here?" I asked, eyes still on the sunburnt road.

He chuckled. "Aw, look at you, playing nice."

"You ever stop running your mouth?"

"Nah," he said. "It's part of the charm. Pop moved us here after he got outta the service. I was ten, maybe. He thought the mines would make him rich. They didn't."

"They know what you do for cash now?"

Bins gave a shrug like it didn't matter, and maybe it didn't. "They're both gone. Pop drank himself into an early grave. Ma sold sandwiches to the railroad crew. Last I heard, she was slinging tacos from a truck two states over, selling burritos to guys without green cards."

"So, why stick around? Guy like you ought to be pulling bigger scores in a city with some pulse."

He looked out at the dying landscape and said, "No place like home."

"If this was Dorothy's home, she'd have stayed in Oz."

"Who's Dorothy?"

"Forget it. Tell me something useful. This town's on its last legs and it knows it, like an old prizefighter bleeding out on the ropes."

Bins snorted. "Helman's hell, man," he said, and grinned like he just cracked the code to the universe. "Get it? Helman, hell- man."

"Yeah. Real cute," I muttered.

"Cute as a Monday morning kitten."

He lit a cigarette, took a drag like it was his last, and leaned back. "Town's been dying slow for decades. It doesn't croak, doesn't thrive. Just limps along. It's got one of everything, and not much else. A diner, a bar, a flick house, and a grocery store that sells canned hope by the aisle."

"No church."

He nodded. "God gave up before the rest of us did."

I leaned on the wheel, scanning the town for angles, anything that looked like a play worth making. But every way I turned the problem, the answer stayed the same: there was no clean score here. Just dust, heat, and the long, slow grind of nowhere.

"Look," I continued, "I'm here to unload my inventory, and then I'm gone. The catch is that I have to attach real names, addresses, and phone numbers if they have them, for it to count. Otherwise, I'm shit out of luck. I think this chili thing or whatever is going on tomorrow might be the place to do it."

"You're going to have to get the big man's blessing first," Bins said.

"The big man?"

"Helman."

I picked up what he was putting down. "Helman. Like the town? Like the house?"

Bins pointed at his nose to show that I had hit the nail on the head.

I pulled the car off on the road's shoulder and started to steer the wheel to turn the car around. Bins grabbed my arm and squeezed tightly.

"What do you think you're doing, Cochise? You don't go to the house uninvited. It doesn't work like that."

"How does it work exactly?"

"There's a protocol to be followed. A parlay. He likes what he hears; you'll get an invite, all right."

"And where do I find him to make this parlay?"

"He goes to the Iguana. He's there most nights. I'll put you in the same room as him. After that, it's up to you."

"You know Helman?"

"I know everybody, Bobby. Sometimes that's an advantage. Sometimes not."

"So, why don't you rob him? I mean, if he's as rich as you're saying, it seems to me he wouldn't miss a few pieces of silverware or whatever it is rich people have that's plentiful and disposable."

Bins' normally jovial attitude took a turn. The smile and wrinkles quickly disappeared. He lit up a new cigarette.

"I'll tell you what, Bobby. There are two types of stupid. One's a guy sticking his hand in an operating garbage disposal to pull out a diamond ring. The second's a guy being ordered to do the same thing, only there's no diamond ring on the other end. The first is risk versus reward. The second one is just the result of bad thinking. Do I need to tell you which one robbing JB Helman falls under?"

It wasn't the most eloquent analogy, but I received the message loud and clear. But just in case I didn't, Bins added to his adage.

"See, I may live a less than satisfactory life, but I like living," he said quickly. "JB runs this town, which means he runs everything that's in this town, including the law, the undertaker, and the shovels that bury people in places out in that desert. And I'll tell you something else, Bobby Santos. There's a lot of holes in that desert. Filled holes, and I'm not joining them.

"Where do you want to go first?" Bins said, changing the tone of his voice along with the topic of discussion.

"Well, I suppose we should start on the edge and work our way into the center. I got to see everything. Know what's what and meet anybody worth knowing."

Bins looked down at the floor of the car and saw a couple of filled water bottles. "You got any more of these?"

"I don't know, a few in the back. Why?" I asked.

"If we're starting from the outside-in, we got to drive to the mines," he said, sliding down in his seat and getting comfortable. "That's what spurned Helman into existence and the reason why everything is as it is. They're about twenty minutes away."

With that, polite chit-chat came to an end. Bins puffed his cigarette thoughtfully, looking at the burnt-out scenery that stretched well into the distance. I didn't know what to make of my new friend, but as was often in these situations, I was reliant on his help if I stood any chance of getting out of there in any reasonable amount of time. How much he could be trusted was still up in the air, and something that I would have to keep a close eye on.

I turned on the radio and found a station. The DJ joked about the heat before putting on some classic twanger music. My white shirt was pitted with sweat. Temperatures had hit 98 degrees, and it wasn't even lunchtime yet.

***

Even in its graveyard state, the mining compound wore the ghosts of industry like an old war medal – tarnished, bent, but still shining in the right light. The chain-link fence had long since given up the pretense of security. Scavengers had torn it apart, the gate hanging sideways like a drunk clutching a lamppost. The security booth? Just a skeleton that was burnt out, gutted, and empty, like a coffin left open in the sun.

Three Days In Hell

The parking lot stretched wide and cracked, littered with the sun-bleached carcasses of machinery picked clean of anything worth hauling. Three squat buildings stood around it, boxy and quiet, monuments to a time when paychecks still rolled and lunch breaks meant something. Out back, a dirt trail cut through the hills like a scar, leading to the belly of the beast – the mines.

It was a hell of a view. Beautiful in that bleak, end-of-the-world kind of way. A monument not to what man built, but to how fast he tore it all down when the gold ran dry.

Bins climbed out of the car and took it all in like he was spitting on a grave. "What a shithole, eh?" he said. "My old man busted his back here. Sunrise to sundown. All he got for it was a bottle of cheap liquor and a bad liver."

I didn't say anything. I was too busy soaking it in. Bins was a local who had never seen much outside the county line. To him, ruins were just rust and rot. But I'd walked the ruins of Rome, and I'd seen history's ribcage up close. This place? It had the same bones. Just smaller, meaner. Like the American Dream had coughed up a lung and left it here to dry.

Suddenly, a dented white minibus chugged out from a side road and parked beside one of the buildings.

"What's that?" I asked. We hadn't passed a single car since leaving Helman's borders.

Bins flinched. Quick. Too quick. "Nothing," he muttered, eyes darting away. He tried to turn me too, like a magician redirecting attention before the trick went south.

But I saw it. And he saw me see it.

"I thought the mines were shut."

"They are. Let's go. There's more to see."

From the corner of my eye, I saw the bus door wheeze open. A grimy, hunched man stepped out looking like he crawled out of a ditch. Behind him, four girls followed, no older than twelve, eyes wide and locked in a shared fear. Last off was a familiar face in an unfamiliar place: the sheriff from the truck stop, Dupree. Clean uniform. Dirty conscience.

The grimy man grabbed one of the girls, shoved her through a side door.

"We gotta move," Bins said. This time, no jokes. No smile. Just a cold sweat and a loaded silence. He saw Dupree clock us from across the lot, eyes narrowing.

"Who are those girls?" I asked.

"Get in the car," Bins barked, practically shoving me behind the wheel.

I didn't argue. His look screamed danger and I wasn't about to question it. We pulled out without a word, the compound shrinking in the rearview mirror like a bad memory you don't quite forget.

Five miles later, Bins finally opened his mouth.

"What does it matter who they are? They're here now. Just... forget it."

"They didn't look too happy."

"What are you gonna do? Burn the place down? File a complaint?"

I glanced at him. "The sheriff's running girls now?"

"Everything moves over that border," Bins said flatly. Then he shot me a look. "How do you know Dupree?"

"Met him at the truck stop. Didn't like him then either."

He nodded, like that filled in a missing puzzle piece. "He runs the day-to-day, and for his efforts, Dupree gets a piece of it."

"Including kids?"

"Including anything that turns a buck."

I gripped the wheel tighter. "That's a special kind of evil."

"This is Helman," Bins said seriously. "Everything's evil."

We made it to the mine. It looked like the rest of the town – dead, silent, and waiting for the earth to finally swallow it whole. The tools were still where the workers had left them, like they expected to come back after lunch but never did. Tracks led from a busted depot straight into the yawning mouth of the mountain. The sign above it read *Helman Silver Mine*, black letters peeling off gold paint.

We didn't go in. There was no need to. Some places didn't hold answers. Just empty echoes. And the only thing those mines had left was a history of men who dug too deep and never came back up.

After the uneventful visit, Bins took me to a few other equally uninteresting places before heading back to town. Each was more depressing than the previous one. They were like scars or broken bones that hadn't healed properly. They were noticeable and ugly and a reminder of something bad that had happened there.

The sun hadn't let up, but somehow the town had stirred itself from its stupor. By the time we rolled back in, Main Street was wearing a canvas banner like a cheap party dress, fluttering in the hot wind: *WELCOME TO THE GREAT CHILI FESTIVAL*.

Somewhere between the morning silence and our return, life had been hammered together by the hour. The wooden skeletons of vendor stalls stood crooked but proud, their canvas awnings not quite managing to pretend they were shade. Proprietors had already set up makeshift kitchens with grills, smokers, propane burners, and cast-iron pots preparing to cook in heat that could sear a steak right off the sidewalk. Madness, I thought. A special breed of idiot to simmer chili under this kind of sky.

Down one of the side alleys, a rickety carnival outfit had erected a few sad rides for the kids. A lopsided Tilt-A-Whirl, maybe a knock-off Ferris wheel that creaked in the wind like a rusty hinge. But for a town that looked ready to kick the bucket, the Great Chili Festival was a jolt to the chest, a spark on the defibrillator.

We parked near the edge of town, not far from the motel, and walked the strip on foot. Bins was in his element, shaking hands, slapping backs, trading wisecracks and IOUs. He'd told me he was well known, and that wasn't a lie. People nodded at him like he was part of the furniture. Some smiled. Others scowled. But they all knew who he was. And by extension, they took one look at me and figured I had to be cut from the same stained cloth.

My suit didn't help. It marked me like a neon sign that read "outsider" in bold letters. I caught the looks; suspicion wrapped in polite nods. Their faces were maps of hard years: sun-cracked, wind-burned, life-scarred. They didn't cry anymore, but they hadn't forgotten how. Their eyes held a kind of permanent grief, like they'd buried too many dreams and just kept digging.

When they asked what brought me to Helman, I danced like it was the state fair and gave them a soft-shoe shuffle of vague answers and easy charm. You don't play a hand straight when no one trusts the deck. These folks didn't have time for strangers and even less for smooth talkers. If I was going to get any traction here, it wasn't going to be with the truth, and certainly not with Bins as my wingman. Petty thief, known liar, lovable nuisance... He wasn't exactly a badge of credibility.

Still, he said he'd set up an introduction with someone who mattered: JB Helman himself. Told me to meet him at the Iguana for drinks. I asked where it was, and he laughed like I'd just asked if the sky was up.

"You'll know it when the sun dips," he said. "Trust me."

Easy for him to say. I was dragging around a suit that clung like wet skin and probably smelled worse than it looked. There wasn't a dry cleaner within a hundred miles, and even if there was, it'd sooner throw my clothes out back and shoot them.

Back at the motel, something had shifted. The second wing, which had been a ghost town that morning, was now filled with a ragtag collection of pickups and battered sedans. It looked like the junkyard had come to life and decided to take a vacation. Rusty bumpers, cracked windshields, and dented fenders huddled together on the pavement like dogs waiting out a storm. Whatever brought them here, it wasn't comfort. It was desperation.

I wondered if Woody, the motel's gatekeeper, was relieved or just pissed. Hard to say. A full house meant business. But it also meant noise, trouble, and people asking for towels they wouldn't return.

A family rolled up while I was watching. Fat father, fatter mother, three loud kids stuffed into shorts and sugar-stained T-shirts. The old man had a key clenched between sausage fingers like it was the Holy Grail. They bumbled toward a room like livestock heading for the trough, squealing and bumping into each other with nervous glee. Out-of-towners, definitely. Corn-belt types with their pink skin, soft hands, and wide eyes ready to be wowed by funnel cake and chili too spicy for their delicate constitutions.

The thing about Helman was, if it had a pulse at all, it came from this festival. People showed up like flies to a carcass, drawn by some mythic promise of flavor and fun, ignoring the rot beneath. I couldn't blame them. Everyone needed a reason to smile, even if it was fake and disappeared by morning.

I showered off the sweat and dust but couldn't seem to rinse away the rest. The water wouldn't get cold enough. I dried off, hit myself with a little talc, and climbed onto the bed in clean boxers. It was barely four, and the heat still clung to the walls like regret.

My thoughts went back to the problem. Always the same one. I had a trunk full of Bibles; too many to sell, not enough to forget. Door-to-door wouldn't cut it. I'd be dead of heatstroke before I made a dent. No, this job needed one clean break, a single score, big and fast. Like robbing a church bingo night or flipping one hot hand at the blackjack table into a full escape.

I pulled out my notebook, hoping for divine inspiration. Pages full of past jobs, sketches of schemes from oil towns, bayou outposts, panhandle dives. Some half-wins, some losses. None of them helpful now.

Then I saw it. Scrawled in my own handwriting like a whisper from another life: a capital "L" and a phone number underneath it.

Luanne.

I wanted to hate her. God knew I had reason. But hate was a luxury, and I was fresh out of it. Luanne didn't twist my arm. No one put a gun to my head. I danced into the fire with my own two feet, and she just happened to be holding the match.

Three Days In Hell

She wasn't some naive sweetheart swept up in the storm. She could play the damsel, sure, but she knew her way around the other role too. She didn't just walk into rooms; she *tilted* them. The kind of woman who made you forget what your mother warned you about.

I remember one of our lunch-hour flings in my car in the back of a boarded-up Dairy Queen a few blocks from the office. The kind of place where ghosts might've lined up for cones once, now a cracked parking lot surrounded by nothing but bad decisions. We'd gone at it twice, sweat sticking our clothes to the vinyl like crime scene tape. Now we were post-coital and post-cigarette, windows down, heat baking the sin into our skin.

She was quiet. Staring at something past the world, past me, out where the road curved into the unknown. That look was half-smile, half-farewell. Played like a move in a game only she knew the rules to.

"What's wrong?" I asked. But Luanne in distress never quite rang true. She wore helplessness like an ill-fitting dress that was tight in the wrong places, and the seams ready to pop.

"Nothing," she said, drawing that word out like it was a lullaby. The kind you hum before slipping poison in someone's drink. "I'm real good, sugar."

"That the face of someone who's good?" I reached out, gave her a playful squeeze. She batted my hand away like a bored cat.

"There's nothing to say," she said. "Sometimes I get quiet, that's all. Just thinkin'."

"Yeah? About what?"

"What else? Life. Mine, mostly." She flicked her cigarette out the window. Watched it bounce once before dying in the dirt. "I just wonder sometimes... if where I am is where I'm supposed to be."

I looked at her sideways. "What the hell does that mean?"

"I'm still on the right side of thirty," she said. "Everything's still where it should be." She unbuttoned her blouse's top clasp, like punctuation to the thought. "But it won't stay that way forever."

"You're young. You're beautiful. You're –"

"You don't get it," she said. "At night, I lie there next to Hank, and I feel like I'm watching someone else's movie. Like I got cast in the wrong part. Maybe I missed the cue, maybe I skipped the audition, I don't know... but I'm sure as hell not where God intended me to be."

I shook my head. "You're chasing ghosts, baby."

She slid closer. Her perfume was sweat and ash and something else I could never name but always remembered. She kissed my neck with those lips that promised the end of the world and then whispered, *"I want more."*

"More?"

"More," she repeated, soft as sin. And a slow smile creased her mouth.

That was the moment. That's when the floor gave out. The second I stopped walking and started falling. Adam had his apple. I had Luanne. Same script, different garden.

I picked up the motel phone. Dialed half her number before I stopped myself. What was I expecting, salvation? Closure? She'd probably answer just to hear my voice and then hang up like she was snuffing a candle.

That ship had gone down with all hands. No survivors. Just a wreck you couldn't look away from and couldn't rebuild either.

I hung up and clicked on the TV. Some old sitcom flickered to life. Laugh track played like background noise to a funeral. I lay back on the bed, the ceiling fan chopping the silence into uneven pieces.

Helman didn't sleep, not really. It *waited*. Waited for its next secret to crawl out from under the porch and make you wish you'd never come. I didn't know what the night had in store for me, but I knew it wasn't rest.

In a place like this, you didn't make plans. You stayed light on your feet, kept your head clear, and your heart locked tight in your chest because whatever was coming around the bend?

It wasn't gonna knock.

***

The Iguana didn't look like much in daylight, just another sun-bleached box on a street full of forgotten promises. Could've been a school, a storage unit, maybe even a halfway house. It had the bland, municipal charm of a place nobody cared about until they needed to. If you weren't looking for it, it wasn't looking for you.

But come nightfall, it changed its skin.

A flickering sign buzzed to life in orange and blue neon script: *Iguana*. A trumpet wailed somewhere inside, jazz laced with tequila and regret. The front doors pulsed with noise and sweat. And out front, the girls were already circling, half-dressed, full-lipped, and eager to separate the out-of-towners from their hard-earned, booze-loosened cash.

They looked like trouble. They *were* trouble. Pretty faces painted over the same bruised canvas I'd seen getting off that bus outside the mines. I didn't need a second guess; they were cargo. New stock. And just because they were dolled up didn't mean they weren't prisoners. You can't perfume a chain and call it a bracelet.

I must've stared too long, because one of them clocked me, lips curling into a grin like a blade unsheathing. Their sales pitch came next, dirty poetry dressed in euphemism. Offers whispered like sins you confess only in the dark.

Bins caught me gawking and chuckled like it was all a joke. He nudged me forward toward the door, where a human mountain stood watch. The guy looked like someone carved him from an oil drum. He was thick, hard, and bolted to the ground. His face was expressionless, a blank slab with attentive eyes that watched like sniper scopes.

"Tyrus, my man!" Bins said, tossing out a hand like they were old pals. Tyrus didn't bite. Just gave us a look like he was mentally fitting us for coffins, then jerked his head toward the door.

"Friend of yours?" I asked sarcastically.

"He doesn't talk," Bins said. "Got his tongue cut out."

"No kidding? Who did that – Godzilla?"

"Everyone takes a beating from somebody," Bins said. "His smackdown just happened to be biblical."

Inside, the Iguana was its own animal, resembling a post-war saloon by way of back-alley casino. A collage of noise, neon, and people tried to lose themselves. The décor didn't follow any rulebook; it was border-town eclectic with just enough grime to feel dangerous.

The air was thick with sweat and booze. It was the kind of place that clung to you long after you left, like the smell of regret on your clothes. Gamblers sat hypnotized at machines that blinked and beeped like alien shrines. They didn't care if they won. Losing was just a tax for the hope of hitting it big.

The bar didn't need a sign. We found an open spot where an old bartender worked like a machine too tired to complain. His eyes were fogged with cataracts, but his hands moved with the efficiency of a man who'd served more drinks than funerals.

Bins ordered Tequila for both of us without asking. One shot down, the second refilled before the glass stopped rattling. I said nothing. It wasn't the worst idea I'd had today.

I scanned the room. Locals, tourists, drifters, junkies, pickpockets, all of them part of the same ecosystem. I read faces like a priest reads confessions. The twitch of a lip, a hand too still, a laugh a beat too late. These were my trade secrets. The kind that told you who had something to hide, who had something to sell, and who was looking to be saved by the wrong kind of angel.

I told Bins I was taking a lap and slipped away to see what the Iguana was *really* offering.

In one corner, under pink neon that screamed *XXX* like it was proud of it, the girls worked the crowd. Local flesh, local cash. Tired, rough-handed farm boys dumped paychecks to see more skin than they'd seen in months. The girls weren't much older, dancing like it was the only thing between them and another ride out of town.

Across the room, near the back, the gamblers held court. Loud. Greasy. Vicious. They barked and slapped cards on felt so worn it looked like a crime scene. These were the foremen, the middlemen. The ones who bled the workers dry and still cried being poor. They didn't notice the girls, they'd been around long enough to know what they could buy, and where to find better.

They weren't here for distractions. They were here to win. Or lose ugly.

I watched the room churn. Everything had a price in Helman. It just depended on how much you were willing to bleed.

And tonight, the Iguana was open for business.

Drifting to the right of the bar, I paused outside a side room pulsing with orange fluorescence. Above the doorway, a crooked sign blinked: *Press Your Luck*. The game was anything but.

Inside, a wiry man with rooster hair clutched three darts in one hand and aimed the fourth at a poor bastard standing against the far wall with an apple balanced precariously on his head. The rooster let his darts fly, none of them even grazing the fruit. One embedded in the drywall a good foot off target. It was a miracle they hadn't left the guy looking like a pincushion. When his five were spent, they traded places. Money changed hands. Spanish curses filled the air like smoke.

Next door, another circus.

Four men stood around a pool table, but no one had a cue. A rat-faced hustler flitted between them, whispering quick pitches before flashing open his jacket. A flash of chain. Cheap gold. Maybe fake. Probably stolen. Each man shook their head or waved him off until finally he saw me watching. The instant our eyes met, the mood shifted. Suspicion flooded the room. One of the men stepped forward and yanked the beaded curtain closed, cutting the scene off like a bad act in a worse play.

It wasn't hard to figure out the Iguana's business model: no rules, no ethics, just as long as the cash kept flowing. Everything was tolerated – hell, encouraged – if it greased the gears. Morality had no seat at the bar.

I turned back, found Bins already waiting with another drink in hand, amber and reckless.

"Find what you were looking for?" he asked, handing it over.

I sipped. It burned on the way down but didn't answer the question.

Bins took my silence for something else and chuckled. "So, you like our little slice of heaven?"

I nodded at the chaos around us. "I think I know why the church folded. Temple Mount wouldn't've lasted a week here."

Bins slapped me on the back, grinning. "This ain't a good place to save souls. You might want to head north, find yourself a pew and a choir."

"I'm not here to save souls," I said, eyeing the room, "just trying to unload some Bibles."

His grin widened. "Then maybe this *is* the right place. Sinners per square foot, you're looking at a record."

"A moveable feast," I muttered, watching one of the backroom girls tug a farmhand behind a curtain.

Bins lowered his voice. "Hey, you might be better off trying someplace else."

"It's here or nowhere," I said. "That's my hand and I got to play it out."

His tone changed; it was less smug, and more resigned. "Then I guess you're stuck like the rest of us."

The bar had found its rhythm. Bartenders worked like cogs in a relentless machine that poured, wiped, and poured again. Neon chili pepper lights blinked along the walls, giving the place a festive air if you ignored the desperation soaking into the floorboards. The whole place throbbed like a migraine.

Down the bar, a woman sat alone.

She wasn't like the others. Not local. Too polished. Too poised. Her hair was bottle blonde, but it was done right. Not barfly right – *professional* right. Her dress was sequined and low-cut, not vulgar, but deliberate. She nursed a drink in a small glass, her chin resting lightly in her hand.

When she caught me looking, she released a slow, sleepy, and dangerous smile.

"I'd ask if you were going to buy me a drink," she said, "but it seems I already have one."

"There's always the next round," I answered, a half-beat too quick.

She took the bait. Downed her drink with the kind of elegance that made you forget what you were watching. She flipped the glass upside down on the bar, caught the younger bartender's eye, and ordered another. This time, she pointed at me.

"He's paying."

She didn't wait for my response, playfully slapping her hand on the empty stool beside her. I took the cue, took my drink, and stuck up two fingers for the bartender so as to make sure the lady wouldn't be drinking alone.

"You here for the Festival?" I asked.

She released a short bark of a laugh as she produced a small clutch purse and removed a gold cigarette case and lighter in the process. "No, no, you were doing fine. You introduced yourself, and it got you a seat. Don't ruin it with boring talk that you really don't have an interest in pursuing." She took a cigarette out and placed it in between her perfectly lipsticked mouth. She turned her smoky eyes toward me and waited patiently. I picked up the lighter and lit her, then paused my free hand over her case. She nodded her assent, and I helped myself to one.

"Point taken," I said, exhaling a stream of blue smoke from my lips. "But in my defense, I don't find myself in places like this often."

She took a deep pull from her cigarette and released it slowly through her lips, watching the smoke curl listlessly around the glass in her raised hand. "Places like what exactly?"

"Charming scraps of forgotten Americana." I couldn't gauge her reaction, but when she snorted in return, I knew I had chosen my words correctly. She was sharper than most in this room.

"Scraps is about right," she said. "I don't know about the charming part. Unless you like the stench of a cesspool in the dead of summer. I haven't seen you before, so is this just a short stay at Helman, or are you relocating?"

"The former," I said, sipping my drink. "The Festival was a surprising coincidence. Lucky me."

"That's all this town has," she said, taking her own turn with the glass. "Every other day of the year, this place is a graveyard and junkyard all wrapped into one. But when the Festival arrives, well, all the creatures come up and out of their holes to suffocate in the heat and press their sweaty flesh together, eating unusually hot chili peppers until their digestive systems are tortured almost beyond repair."

"Maybe that's half the fun," I said, putting back the rest. I didn't set my glass down before the younger bartender refilled it. He was a good bartender, anticipating rather than reacting. I felt bad that he was regulated in this town. He'd make big money in a place like New York. He also shot me a curious look, and I wondered if he didn't think I was muscling in on someone he thought of as his girl. I let the stink-eye pass. I was a passer-through, after all.

"Maybe. But ask any of these *perezosos machismos*, and they will tell you that by eating the Devil's own tears, the heat cancels out. Your mouth still feels like a blacksmith's coal pile, but your body will at least think it's cool."

The overall noise of the bar ebbed and flowed. But despite it all, one voice seemed to cut through the noise. The timbre and tessitura were distinctly female, but there was a weight behind it, an emotive quality that combined the depth of a gospel singer with the growling desperation of Mexican folk music. When the woman started to sing, the room obediently became quiet. A Siren's call sounded, and because it had, everyone turned their attention to the small backstage that was immersed in darkness. The stage lights suddenly turned on the moment the singer finished the first stanza revealing a raven-haired woman in a flaming red dress in front of a slender microphone stand. The illumination brought out the surge of sexuality in her body. The swirl of silky fabric clung to her body's sweeping, unapologetic curves and pressed against her flat stomach in a seamless sheen. I didn't know what she was singing, but the words seemed to have sprouted from a place of personal pain and travesty.

She mesmerized the audience with her beguiling tone. All other actions stopped. There was no more gambling, no more drinking, no more side hustle with the farm workers. The singer was the sole attraction, and everyone paid her that respect. The woman didn't croon as much as she told us a story, swaying slowly back and forth, her dress contorting to the movements of her body. She needed freedom for her performance, and it paid off. The slow, soulful introduction steadily gave way to an upbeat tempo. The spirited guitar riffs sent a jolt into the room.

Three Days In Hell

The woman stepped down from the stage, gracing the audience with her presence. She was a true professional at her craft, giving a little bit of attention to the men at the small tables on the floor as part of her game of tease and denial. She captivated them with the slightest smile, dangling that promise in front of them, only to rip it away before they stood up from their chairs, trying to grasp it. Pecking order established, she'd brush her long hair away from her eyes, revealing two of the deepest, darkest soulful eyes that ever were before moving on.

"Who's that?" I asked the woman next to me. She let out a bored sigh. In a way, I could tell this wasn't the first time she had been upstaged by the singer and had to play second fiddle to someone above her class. The singer was dark, deep, and mysterious, a little bit scary in the way beautiful women could be when they had a tint of danger in their eyes.

"Amelia," the woman at the bar said when she knew that any chance that she might have had in tapping my wallet slipped through her fingers. She finished her drink and stood up. She knew that she had been replaced and that to remain would be nothing short of cheapening her own value. She didn't wait for me to protest or even say goodbye before she disappeared into the room like a puff of smoke dissolving into the air.

The song ended in a crescendo, and she nailed the note and made her voice last even after the guitars were silenced. The room immediately erupted in a well-deserved raucous applause, and she took the accolades with a reticent bow and smile. She owned the room, and because she did, it gave her the right to languor in the adoration of those in it. She meandered slowly toward the bar, periodically stopping to hear some praise from ogling, sweaty men who gave her compliments as well as a fair share of lewd comments.

I leaned into Bins without taking my eyes off the singer. "Who's Amelia?"

Bins sipped his drink without looking up, but the corner of his mouth twisted into a knowing smile, one that said more than he was willing to say outright. "That's a loaded question."

I glanced sideways. "I didn't ask if she was loaded. I asked who she was."

"She's the kind of woman who could make a priest ask for a private confessional," Bins said, still not looking at her.

He didn't have to look; I did enough for both of us. I watched Amelia glide across the floor, the crowd parting like a tide for her. Her eyes scanned the room, not seeking attention but acknowledging that she already had it. She was cool, detached, magnetic in the way a storm cloud is beautiful, ominous, and full of promise you'd be wise not to chase.

Amelia reached the bar, placed a single manicured finger on the counter, and the older bartender whose cataracts hadn't dulled his instincts had already poured a glass for her before she even sat down, setting a large bucket of ice next to it.

She didn't look at me. Not yet. But she knew I was watching. She had the kind of power that didn't ask for your attention; it *assumed* it. And when it had it, like she had mine now, it didn't let go.

I knew women like Amelia. Not many, but enough to know they didn't make missteps. If she had decided I was worth talking to, it wouldn't be an accident or even a flirtation; it would be pure strategy. That gave her an edge of treachery, an allure of danger. And not the cheap kind. This wasn't some half-drunk femme fatale playing dress-up in the backroom of a cantina. She carried herself like a birthright, and exuded a kind of superiority that didn't shout, but whispered, and made you lean in closer just to hear the words that would ruin you.

"A word of advice," Bins muttered, voice low. "You want to survive this town, hell, just get through the next twenty-four hours, you keep your eyes on your business and your hands to yourself."

"Too late for one," I said.

I downed what remained in my glass and set it back on the bar with a little too much force. I searched for cigarettes in my jacket pocket, removing my motel key, a stick of gum, and a half-used book of matches. I took a cigarette out of the pack and lit my smoke.

Amelia turned, slow as honey off a dull knife. Her eyes found mine and held there, cool and unreadable, neither welcoming nor warning. Just that quiet burn of curiosity. And calculation. She popped an ice cube in her mouth like a bon bon.

The kind of look that didn't ask a question. It *dared* you to answer one.

"I'm Bobby," I said. "Bobby Santos."

Her smile curled at the corners, slow and smoky. The kind of smile that had seen lies born, raised, and buried all before breakfast. She didn't bother responding to my introduction right away. Just let the silence hang like a noose between us.

"'Business,'" she said, tasting the word like it was something bitter stuck in her teeth. "No flirtation. No mystery. But gentlemanly. Polite. But a little too clean for a man whose eyes say he's seen things... and whose key is to a motel that doesn't belong to him."

Her gaze dropped – barely. A flicker toward the telltale corner of the stolen keycard poking out of my pocket. She wasn't guessing. She was *noticing*.

I smirked, shrugged like it didn't matter. "You always greet your guests with psychoanalysis and suspicion?"

"I like to know what I'm drinking with," she said, crunching an ice cube between her teeth like it was someone's last chance. "Especially if I might enjoy it. Or regret it."

"And which one am I?"

She popped another ice cube. "That depends," she said. "What kind of business are you in?"

I blew out smoke. "What makes you think I'm here for business?"

I glanced out across the Iguana at the bodies moving like shadows in heat, music pulsing like a fever. The kind of place where every corner had a secret and every secret had a price. The booth gave us the illusion of privacy. But illusion was the currency here. Truth was just something folks bartered for in whispers.

"I don't know you," she said simply.

"I used to be a salesman," I said finally. "Now I move Bibles."

That got a laugh out of her, a low, throaty, whisky-colored sound that ran over me like silk dragged across a gun barrel.

"Bibles," she said, shaking her head. "That's rich."

"People still get them. Hope's got a good resale value."

She traced a line in the condensation on her glass with one sharp fingernail. "Hope doesn't keep the lights on in Helman. Fear does. Desire. Debt."

"I noticed."

She looked at me again, and her smile vanished like a match snuffed between fingers. "You give off a distorted vibe... You're running from something. Maybe someone."

"Does it matter?" I asked. "I didn't bring trouble with me."

"No," she said. "But trouble finds men like you. Same way a moth finds a flame."

"What makes you say that?"

"You're here. In this town. This isn't the first stop in someone's travels. But it's often the last."

She leaned in close enough for the citrus sting of her breath to cut through the tequila and smoke between us.

"So, what are you really doing here, Bobby Santos?"

"I told you."

"And that includes visiting old mines?"

How did she know that? My reaction gave me away and this time, her smile came slower. Smaller. Real. I burned my finger on my cigarette and crushed it out on the ground. She offered me another.

I lit it and looked at her for a long moment. She wasn't a mark. Not someone you could grease with charm or blind with bullshit. She was a storm in silk, the kind of woman people warned you about too late.

So, I gave her what I hadn't given anyone in years. The only thing that would hold enough value to keep the conversation going.

The truth.

"I used to sell Bibles," I said. "Then I started selling lies. Now? Now I'm not sure if I'm buying them instead of selling."

This time, her smile came slower. Smaller. Real.

"I like that," she said.

"Which part?"

"All of it. Especially the part where you don't know which side of the transaction you're on."

"I need to talk to someone about getting a spot at the festival. I can push my product there."

"Then you need to talk to JB."

"I hear he's the man that controls things here."

She pulled back. The air felt colder without her in it.

"No one's really in control in Helman," she whispered. "Not even the ones who think they are."

And just like that, I saw it clear.

She didn't just *live* in Helman.

She *was* Helman.

The commotion that broke our stare wasn't two hearts bursting for each other. It came in the shape of Sheriff Dupree, dragging some poor bastard by the collar of his greasy shirt through the front doors of the Iguana. The guy's heels scraped the floor, hands limp, eyes wild. But no one gave a damn.

Nobody blinked. The degenerates at the tables barely looked up. A few drunks didn't even pause mid-swig. Just another night in Helman. Just another man being taught a lesson by the law.

Dupree didn't say a word. He hauled the man into one of the side rooms like a butcher dragging meat to the back. The door slammed behind them.

Then came the ruckus. Thuds. A crash. A muffled plea. The kind of sounds you didn't mistake for anything else unless you were desperate to believe in something kinder. And in Helman, no one was that desperate.

When Dupree came back out, his breath was even, but his knuckles glistened red under the yellow bar light. He wiped them on a rag that used to be white and now wasn't.

His eyes scanned the room like a wolf checking the perimeter of its den before they found mine.

I looked away.

He didn't.

His stare on me was like a nail being driven into wood, slow and deliberate. No expression, just a promise. The kind that says you've got a foot in a grave and someone's already checking your shoe size.

I reached for my drink but didn't lift it. Just held the glass and watched the way the tequila caught the light, like gold in a coffin.

Behind me, Amelia didn't speak. She didn't need to.

In Helman, some silences said more than a thousand words.

Dupree strode over to us. Bins subtly bowed away from the bar, avoiding the presence of the brutal law man. Dupree nodded deferentially to Amelia and helped himself to a drink that the bartender set in front of him.

"Aren't you just the bad penny, always turning up."

Amelia regarded me curiously. "We met at the diner outside of town," I said.

"Have a good time, did you?" Dupree said downing his drink and glaring at me through malevolent eyes. "Get a good eyeful out at the mines?"

"I was just getting the lay of the land," I said, trying to keep the edge out of my voice. "Curious, that's all. I wasn't poking around.

He leaned back in the booth with the lazy satisfaction of a man who knew he'd thrown a wrench into something he didn't quite understand but enjoyed watching break just the same.

"Curious men end up dead in Helman," Dupree said.

"Or worse," Amelia countered. "Useful."

Dupree turned abruptly to Amelia, swirling the remaining liquor in his glass. "You think he's useful?"

Her eyes didn't leave mine even when she answered the sheriff. "I'm still figuring that out."

"JB won't like it if he is and not accounted for."

Amelia didn't speak right away. She just looked. And it was the kind of look that stripped varnish off wood, not out of malice, but precision. The warmth she'd allowed herself before – the playful smiles, the soft teasing – had shut off like someone flipped a breaker.

"The sheriff's right, Bobby," she said, reaching for another ice cube. But this time she didn't eat it. She held it in her fingers, watching it melt as she spoke. "JB doesn't like ghosts. And you, well, you have the scent of one. You show up from nowhere, sniff around his town, make friends with a thief who's barely tolerated, and take an interest in places that no one with a working compass wants to be near."

Her voice didn't rise. It just *tightened*.

Are you playing an angle, Bobby?" she pressed.

"You know what the first rule of a good salesman is?" I asked.

Neither answered. Dupree looked bored. Amelia watched the ice cube slip smaller between her fingers.

"Never knock on a door unless you already know who's behind it," I said.

Dupree leaned forward. "And who's behind the door in Helman?"

"Someone going to give me a second chance."

That landed with a thud, and not the poetic kind. The kind that said someone stepped on a body in the dark. Amelia stared at me long enough that her disappointment hit harder than her suspicion. Then she stood.

"You should go."

"What?"

"Whatever brought you here, I don't think it's going to get you what you want." Her voice was calm, but final.

"How do you know what I want?"

She didn't get a chance to answer. For a second time that evening, the narcocorrido music and raucous banter abruptly stopped suddenly as if something had sucked it right out of the room.

Bodies moved out of the way. Not politely. Not fearfully. Instinctively.

And then I saw him.

They wheeled him in like a general, rolled over the threshold like a ghost with a payroll: Jude B. Helman. JB for short.

He had to be in his mid-sixties, maybe older. His body seemed frail, but there was no weakness in him. His hair was white, parted clean, and his shirt probably cost more than a car. His body was wiry, sharp at the elbows, taut at the forearms, and he moved like a man who didn't need to walk to own the ground he was on.

I didn't need an introduction. Hellman made introductions obsolete.

One of the waitstaff offered a drink. He ignored it. He was scanning the room. Not for the curious, or the drunks. He was looking for the important people. The *useful* people.

And he found them.

Amelia. Dupree. Not me.

I didn't even register in his eyes. Not yet.

But that was fine.

In Helman, it was always better to be underestimated before the first deal was struck.

"Things are looking advantageous tonight," Helman said, his voice low and papery, like it had been soaked in old bourbon and lit on fire a few times. He scanned the room with a look that measured profit more than pleasure. "Comforting to see the Iguana's still the place to be the night before the Festival."

"Of course, JB," Amelia purred, like velvet with a knife tucked inside.

"That's the way I like it," Helman said, eyeing the bottle in front of Dupree. The sheriff didn't need a nudge to be told what to do; he flagged down a waitress who brought over a fresh glass like it was holy sacrament. Dupree poured. Helman drank. No wince, no breath. Just a swallow and silence.

"We get our merchandise today?" Helman asked no one in particular, but the question had Dupree's name stitched on it.

"Delivered and processed at the mines," the sheriff said, straightening just a bit.

"And my something special?"

"As ordered."

Helman nodded. "Good, good. I see more bodies in town than last year. More souls for the offering to the chili lords, so to speak. With money and assholes to burn."

"They don't always go hand in hand," Amelia teased, that smoky smile playing on her lips. "Money and assholes, I mean."

"Damn close enough," Helman grunted, knocking back his drink again. He extended the glass, and Dupree filled it without hesitation. The routine was smooth, choreographed, and mechanical. A ritual older than regret.

"Are we all set to go tomorrow morning, Sheriff?"

"Most of the tents are up. Wiring is going on as we speak. Smokers are lit."

"Hot damn." Helman grinned like a man about to auction off a town and keep the deeds. "This is going to be the best Festival we've ever had. I feel it. Numbers are gonna be strong this year. Real strong."

"There's something I need to talk to you about," Amelia said, her voice now cooler, quieter. Business talk.

Helman finished his pour and gave a slight nod. Amelia stepped behind him and pushed the wheelchair toward a back room, Dupree falling in behind like a dog on a leash made of obligation and blood. The door shut with a hush that sounded like a secret being sealed.

As if summoned by opportunity, Bins popped out of the shadows and slid into the chair across from me like a cockroach that knew when the lights went out.

"Well? What did he say?"

"What did who say?"

"About the Bibles, man. That was Helman."

"Didn't have the chance to bring it up what with Sheriff Wahoo making it real clear he's got a trigger finger for strangers."

Bins nodded, lips pressed thin as he glanced across the room at the women parading men toward the velvet-curtained back. Transactions with no receipts.

"If you want to move that product, Helman's the man. He blesses that kind of prayer, but at a cost."

"Everybody wants a cut of someone else's pie," I said, watching a man stumble toward the bar, shirt half untucked and a grin too wide for the room. "I have to say, with the way people talk about him, I didn't expect him to be…"

"In a wheelchair?" Bins finished for me, no judgment in his voice, just facts.

"Yeah."

"Don't let the hardware fool you. He's twice as mean because of it. What he lacks in legs, he makes up in leverage. Hell, he scares me more now than when he could walk."

"So, that's recent?"

Bins shrugged. "It happened over the past few years. An accident down a flight of stairs or something."

I nodded. "You think I can meet him tonight? I don't want to miss tomorrow's foot traffic."

Bins smirked and lit a cigarette that looked like it had already died once.

"You're in Helman, Bobby Santos," he said. "The only time that matters here is his."

We sat for the next twenty minutes, drinking, waiting, watching the Iguana turn into something unholy. The place swelled with bodies, shoulder to shoulder, wall to wall, until the air felt thick with perfume, sweat, and the scent of lies barely concealed.

If Babylon had been dropped in the American Southwest, it would've looked like this. Neon-stained sins dressed up as entertainment. A tent revival for the damned.

A room for every vice. Gambling, hustlers, two-dollar whores, and side acts no man with a mother should admit to seeing.

And tomorrow?

The Festival.

If tonight was the preamble, the Festival was the gospel.

And I was still figuring out whether I was the preacher or the sacrifice.

My eyes wandered to the curtain near the back where Dupree had earlier messed up that guy.

That's when I saw one of the young girls who arrived that morning at the mines with Dupree.

The madam exited from the back room first, an older woman with a tank top gone gray and a gut pushing out of hot pink shorts that should've retired a decade ago. The girl followed her. She couldn't have been more than eleven. Her onyx-black hair hung in loose waves down her back, brushing the shoulders of a too-thin dress meant for someone trying to look invisible. Her shoes were scuffed, one untied, as if she'd been running or dragged. Wide, frightened eyes darted around the room, taking in the low lights, the leather furniture that smelled of old cigars and older secrets, the men who didn't smile.

She didn't speak. She barely breathed.

She stood there like a question mark at the end of a sentence no one wanted to finish.

In her silence, there was a terrible untouched and untainted purity that was wholly unprepared for what waited on the other side of that curtain.

She didn't know it yet, but she was standing at the threshold between two worlds.

And one of them was about to swallow her whole.

The madam turned her slowly, displaying her like a showroom dummy to two men who sat hunched and hungry, eyes gleaming under the low light.

Then a familiar rough voice cut through the din of drunken chatter: Dupree.

"No! No! You stupid whore, that's for the boss not these shitheels!"

The madam paled like she'd just seen a ghost crawl out of the floorboards. She opened her mouth to explain, but Dupree got there first. He must have left the pow wow with the boss, and when he saw Helman's prize about to be spoiled, the sheriff cracked her with the back of his hand and sent her sprawling against the wall.

The young girl shrank into herself, folding up like paper under a boot. The madam, still dazed, scrambled up and apologized in a slurry of Spanish. She yanked the girl away from the circle of eager eyes and vanished behind the curtain.

"What did I miss?" Amelia asked.

I turned to her. The meeting had ended and now she emerged looking more clever and dangerous than before, if that was possible.

"Nothing," I said.

"You hungry?"

"I could eat."

She gave Bins a dismissive smirk. "I'll take it from here." Then she turned to me with that smile. "This way," she said.

She didn't need to look back. Her walk invited pursuit, not permission.

I followed.

She led me down a hallway I hadn't noticed before. It was narrow and short, the kind of corridor buildings grow like tumors over time. It smelled of old plaster and lemon oil, like a funeral parlor that didn't bother pretending. The walls were hung with photos from Festivals past: men caked in sweat and dust, women with lashes like knives, children perched on floats that looked more like nightmares than parades.

At the end stood a thick wooden door. Amelia pulled a brass key from the chain around her neck and slipped it into the lock. The door opened with a sigh.

The room inside didn't match the rest of the Iguana's chaos. It was cooler, quieter, cleaner, built for whispers and decisions, not for dancing. A circular table dominated the space, surrounded by eight carved chairs that belonged in a mansion, not a border-town bar. The lacquered wood glowed honey-gold in the low light, the craftsmanship unmistakable. An unopened bottle waited at the center beside two glasses and a wide ice bucket sweating quietly in the dark.

No jukebox. No chatter. Just the ceiling fan cutting slow circles above us, and the faintest scent of sandalwood and citrus.

She motioned to a chair. I sat.

Amelia picked up a phone mounted on the wall and spoke softly in Spanish. Her voice wasn't rushed. Everything in here moved on its own time.

A minute later, a server arrived. She was another young girl, older than the one from earlier, but not by much. She carried a silver tray laden with sliced carnitas, fresh tortillas, lime wedges, and an assortment of regional delicacies. She set the food down without a word and vanished just as fast.

Amelia poured the tequila. Smooth. No flourish. No fanfare. Just clean movement like she'd done it a thousand times for a thousand different kinds of men.

She handed me a glass.

"Welcome to the real Helman," she said.

We drank.

The tequila went down smoother than a lie told too many times. No burn, just heat and smoke that curled in my gut like a lit match in a puddle of gasoline. It rolled through me the way good firewater should, searing away whatever doubts were still clinging to the corners of my mind.

The walls were dressed in faded oil paintings, heavy things that seemed to watch the room like sentries. Men in iron and braid, all long dead, their names erased by time, but their eyes still fixed on conquest. One looked like a conquistador, stiff in his tarnished armor, sword raised to a God who never answered. The last wore an officer's cap and rode a tank like it was a throne, his mouth curled in a sneer as his enemies disappeared under steel treads.

There were women too. Ghostly faces locked behind gilt frames, their beauty cold, clinical. Eyes like mirrors, offering nothing back. Queens without kingdoms, saints without salvation.

"You like art?" she asked, voice like smoke from a long cigarette, pouring another round.

"I like it the way I like jazz. I don't know much about it, but sometimes it hits just right," I said, taking the glass.

"It's all just taste. Subject and style don't matter. There's no truth in art. Just perspective."

"You an artist?"

She smiled one of those sly, slanted grins that made you forget how dangerous pretty could be. Then she filled her own glass, generous again.

"Not the kind who plays with brushes."

"You sing nice," I said.

"'Nice' is what people say when they're too polite to say what they mean."

"What should I have said?"

She supplied a smile for an answer, as if she was collecting my questions, saving them for later.

"Are these your relatives?" I asked, nodding toward the gallery of grim faces.

That got a laugh out of her. She set the bottle down and walked over to me, all grace and mystery. No answer, again. She just lifted her glass.

"So careful," I said.

"You drink with someone for the first time, you drink like strangers. Formal. After that, maybe you drink like friends. But first, the rules matter."

"To breaking the ice," I offered. "To friendship?"

She shook her head. "To possibility."

Then she slammed her glass into mine, hard enough that I thought it might shatter. It didn't. We both drank like we were trying to kill something inside.

She nodded to the table, and I followed, refilling our glasses this time. My hands weren't exactly steady.

"These people, whoever they are, don't belong to me," she said, eyes drifting to the paintings. "But I come in here and I study them. I watch the way they hold their mouths. The set of their jaws. The tilt of the head. They're frozen, but not dead. Not really."

"When I look at paintings, I try to figure out what's going on. That's all. I don't romanticize it."

"That's because you look, but you don't see. Try harder. For me. What do you see?"

I looked.

And something shifted. The longer I stared, the more the canvas stared back. These weren't mere portraits. They were warnings. Every brushstroke bled menace. These weren't men; they were monsters dressed as soldiers. Tyrants in oil and gold-leaf. I saw echoes of Stalin in the dead eyes. Mao in the tight lips. Hitler in the calm, cold cruelty of the stare.

"These are terrifying," I said finally. My voice cracked. My throat was dust.

"They should be," she said softly. "Power doesn't wear a smile. It grits its teeth. It takes. It bleeds the world dry before it gives back."

"What are you saying?"

She looked down at her glass, then back at me, like she was deciding whether to tell me a secret or a lie.

"I'm saying history doesn't make heroes. Just survivors. Power isn't gifted. It's seized. And it's always paid for, whether it's in blood, in silence, or in ruin."

Before I could get a word in, there was a knock at the door. Two young waitresses filed in with their eyes down, backs straight, and hands steady as surgeons. They moved like they'd rehearsed this a hundred times. Trays of food, polished silverware, linen napkins folded with military precision. No chit-chat. No smiles. Maximum respect.

They didn't look at Amelia. Not directly. They waited in silence, like statues with good posture, until she gave the nod. Then they vanished just as quick as they came, like they were afraid the room might swallow them whole if they lingered too long.

Three Days In Hell

"That's a lot of respect for a singer," I said, watching the door click shut behind them.

Amelia smiled, tight and knowing. She made me a plate without asking, stacking it neatly like a hostess and not a queen, but the vibe was closer to royalty than service. Then she made her own, spooning braised pork with the kind of care a sculptor might use shaping clay.

"I pay them," she said simply. "I like good service. They like good pay. Everybody wins."

"So, this is your joint," I said, taking the plate. "You run the place."

"And sing."

"And sing," I echoed, chewing on the pork. It was rich and sharp, almost aggressive on the tongue, a flavor that didn't ask for approval, just took it. "There's more to Helman than meets the eye."

"The town?" she asked, pouring more tequila. "Or the man?"

"I'm beginning to wonder if there's a difference."

That made her laugh, low and smooth like a blues chord plucked at midnight. She slid my glass closer and filled it again, the tequila sloshing quietly like a secret being passed.

"You're an interesting man, Bobby Santos."

"How so?"

"You watch things. People. You clock the room. You weigh what's said, and more importantly, what isn't."

"I'm observant," I said, stabbing at another mouthful. "You've got gambling. Fights. Girls. Liquor that doesn't taste like turpentine. And somehow, a town full of folks who look like they haven't seen a good payday since the Depression. That's a contradiction."

She shrugged like she'd heard it before. Took a cube of ice and ran it down her cheek, letting it melt slow against her skin. Her face was slick in the candlelight, catching shadows like a film reel catching frames.

"People want what they want," she said, softly. "Doesn't matter if they can afford it. Hunger doesn't care about your wallet. And this place? This place feeds needs. Simple as that."

The room got quiet again. The kind of quiet that feels like a loaded gun under a pillow. I chewed my food and watched her, thinking about what she said, and more about what she didn't.

There were stories in this place. Heavy ones. I just didn't know yet if Amelia was the author… or the final chapter.

"You say you were a salesman, and now you hand out Bibles," she said, cocking her head, her voice wrapped in velvet and suspicion. "You don't look like a missionary. Does that make you a religious man?"

"No," I said. "But I'm God-fearing. Sometimes."

"Sometimes?" she echoed, her lips curling around the word like it tasted foreign. "That doesn't sound like someone who believes at all. Tell me, how can one fear something they don't think exists? *Sometimes.*"

Her question hit like a sucker punch. I opened my mouth to answer, but nothing came out.

She hushed me with a raised hand as music drifted in from the speakers. A light, almost playful accordion led the charge followed by a man's voice, sandpaper-scratched and full of longing. She closed her eyes. Just like that, Amelia was gone somewhere else, someplace quieter, away from the weight of this town and the eyes of men like me.

For fifteen seconds, I just watched her. There was no fire, no front, just a woman alone with the song. It was the first time I saw her without her armor. She looked like someone no one could reach, not without getting burned.

"I just don't like some of the things I see," I said, quietly.

"Like little girls," she replied.

Her words cracked across my face like a backhand. My eyes flared, and I felt the heat rise, but just as fast, it was gone. Rage was useless here. She was testing me. We both knew it.

"I don't have a moral compass," I said, voice low, even. "But I still know which way points north."

She gave me a look that could've meant anything or everything. "You're angry. You saw something that didn't sit right. The girl. I saw your face. Most men here don't even blink."

"Neither did you."

She didn't flinch. "I blinked a long time ago. Learned it doesn't change a damn thing." She studied me now, not the way a woman studies a man, but like a wolf studies another predator. "Is that what you're really here for, Bobby? To change things? Bring Helman into the light?"

I knocked back the rest of my drink, let it burn down the back of my throat like bad memories. "The only thing I want to change is my luck. Ten years of bad hands and I figure I'm due for a better deal."

She exhaled through her nose, calm and steady, then set her glass down like it was a chess piece. "So you say. But you should know, there's no rescue fantasy here. No white hats. Just fences, dust, and men who hold power like a knife at your ribs. Helman doesn't get saved. You either survive it, or you become part of it."

A thick and heavy silence crept into the room like a fog. It was the kind that let you hear every sound from the other side of the wall: slots clanging, voices raised in laughter and despair, and time being bartered away one coin at a time. The music from earlier swelled again, this time louder. The accordion rolled over us like a tide. A *bajo sexto* throbbed beneath it, deep and menacing, while trumpets sliced through like gunfire dressed as celebration.

"You know this song?" she asked.

"I know the type. It's a *narcocorrido*."

She arched a brow, amused. "You say that like it's a bad thing."

"The music's good," I admitted. "But the subject matter... not exactly bedtime stories."

"That's a narrow read," she said, her tone sharpening. "You hear facts, things like names, deaths, headlines. I hear emotion. Regret. Fury. It's a love song, Bobby. Just like *Romeo and Juliet*."

"Only in this one, Juliet's holding the gun," I muttered.

She smiled. Not sweetly. There was violence in the way her lips exposed her teeth.

"And Romeo's already bleeding out in the backseat."

"So, are you God-fearing?" I asked.

"I fear nothing," she said, eyes narrowing just enough to cast shadow. "I think you'll find the Festival quite the attraction. You'll be surprised what Helman has to offer."

Her tone iced over, cool and distant. A door closing. I got the hint.

"Dinner over?"

"I think so," she replied. "Don't you?"

Three Days In Hell

I stood, folded my napkin like it mattered, and set it on the table. "Thank you for your hospitality," I said, trying not to sound like a schoolboy sent home early. I wondered where exactly the evening had gone sideways.

She looked at me with something between amusement and pity. "Don't act like a beaten boy. Dinner's over, but not our time together. Unless you've got somewhere else to be?"

I thought of my motel room with its dusty curtains, a bed with sheets that smelled like past sins, and a flickering bulb over a cracked mirror. "I'm a stranger in a strange land," I said.

She smiled and pulled out a cigarette. Lit it with a match she struck slowly, deliberately. She held the flame in front of her, watching it flicker like it was telling her secrets. Then she let it burn down, right to her fingertip. It hissed against her skin before snuffing itself out.

"Doesn't that hurt?" I asked.

She shrugged, smoke curling from her lips like a whispered confession. "There are things that burn worse."

"What burns worse than fire?"

Her eyes locked on mine. No flinch, no blink, just the kind of look you get from someone who's seen too much and learned to stare it down.

"Ice," she said.

Then she moved. Slow, fluid. She stepped closer until her chest brushed mine like a promise or a threat. She reached past me, grabbed my glass, and pressed it into my hand, guiding it toward my lips with a touch that lingered. Then she took her own, her fingers never quite leaving my skin.

She held my gaze the whole time. Unwavering. Like she was trying to read something buried behind my eyes.

"You want face time with JB?" she asked finally.

"I do."

"I'll speak with him tonight. If he wants to meet you, he will." Her voice was soft, but the words carried weight. "Just understand something: when you stand in front of him, you better know *exactly* what you're asking for. Because once you're on his radar... you never leave it."

She poured us another round. The tequila hit the glass like the click of a loaded chamber.

"Now," she whispered, voice dropping into something heavier, almost tender. "We drink as friends should."

The rest of the night came in fragments. Blurred edges, tilted angles, the kind of night that lives more in feeling than memory. The tequila kept flowing, and when that well ran dry, Amelia found new ways to keep the current going – rum, mezcal, even some smoky stuff I couldn't name. I don't know how long we stayed holed up in that private room, but eventually we drifted out, carried by the tide of music and voices into the Iguana's main floor.

We didn't get the chance to simply exist in each other's orbit. The regulars had expectations. They called for her like faithful disciples, and Amelia, never one to deny an audience, took the stage.

She slid into the spotlight like she was born there, her voice rising over the crowd like smoke from a slow fire. She sang with that same liquid heat. songs of smugglers and rebels, of men who moved powder and pills across blood-soaked borders. They weren't just ballads; they were odysseys. Anti-heroes fought and fell to the pulse of *Cucaracha* horns and the deep, thudding soul of a *guitarrón mexicano*.

Three Days In Hell

Despite the south-of-the-border flavor, there was something ancient in her delivery. Something *epic*. These weren't just traffickers; they were tragic warriors, mythologized and mourned. Her voice turned them into fallen titans, each swallowed by betrayal, impossible odds, or the cold, final hand of law enforcement.

From the crowd, I caught flickers of something darker. A few hardened locals stiffened with the opening lines of certain songs. Faces dropped. Eyes dimmed. There was pain in those reactions like they weren't just remembering the lyrics. They were remembering the men.

Somewhere along the way, I lost Bins. He disappeared into the crowd, probably in pursuit of a warm body or a cold wallet. It didn't matter. Amelia had already taken the reins. She led me by the arm through the maze of smoke and noise, introducing me around as her "new friend."

It was a magic phrase. One moment, the faces were wary, appraising me like I was fresh meat. The next, they smiled, nodded, clapped my back. Amelia's hand never left mine as she moved us from group to group, each name more surreal than the last: *Augusto, Nessus, Thiago, Filip, Helena, Francesca*. They came at me like a dream. Maybe a warning.

The booze flowed. The music throbbed. The dancing grew wild and chaotic, like a ritual spiraling out of control. The shadows swelled in the corners, swallowing details, faces, time.

I don't know when we left. I just remember the feel of the night air, thick and heavy, and Amelia's arm around me, guiding me out like I was drunk on something deeper than alcohol. She led me to an old crimson '49 Buick Roadmaster convertible. Or maybe it was crimson. The

Iguana's neon bled colors into everything, and the tequila had long since taken creative liberties with my perception.

I leaned against the cool metal as she opened the door, then half-lifted, half-poured me into the passenger seat.

The leather interior swallowed me whole. I let my head fall back and closed my eyes, the thrum of bass and memory still echoing in my ears. The door clicked shut beside me, and for a moment, the only thing I could hear was the sound of Amelia lighting another cigarette.

She seemed disturbingly lucid for someone who'd matched me drink for drink, maybe more. While my thoughts slipped like a busted clutch, Amelia moved with poise; she was fluid, sharp, utterly unaffected. The liquor didn't seem to touch her. It was like her bloodstream ran on something else entirely. Power, maybe. Or purpose.

She belonged behind the wheel of that heavy old Buick the same way she belonged on the stage – completely. When she fired up the big V8, the engine purred with restrained menace. The vibrations rumbled under me, and I groaned, rubbing my temples.

"My head's spinning," I muttered.

"I'll drive slowly," she said. No pity, just control.

We didn't talk much after that. I kept drifting; my eyes opening then shutting again, chasing a balance between nausea and lucidity. She turned on the radio, letting the music bridge the silence. Outside, the town thrummed with life. Firecrackers popped in the distance. Guitar strings were plucked. Trumpets bleated out half-tuned fanfares. Maracas rattled. Every corner sounded like it had its own band; Helman's own orchestra of revelry and rot.

The motel lot was overflowing. I wondered how old Woody was handling his newfound popularity. Guests milled about like ants around a sugar spill. A cluster of them gathered near a sputtering grill, where the thick, greasy perfume of chorizo soaked into the air. They didn't know each other, but they shared something in common: same location, same fever dream of a night. Festival cohesion. Like those coastal towns that bloom in the summer and sleep through the cold, these people had come to burn bright, fast, and loud.

I told her my room number. She helped me out of the car like a man twice my age, led me through the maze of metal and noise. When we reached my door, she took the keys from my hand and opened it like she already lived there.

"I'd ask you in, but –"

She ignored me, stepping inside and flipping the lights. I stood there for a second, embarrassed by the cheap, threadbare surroundings. After the decadent decay of the Iguana, my motel room looked like a cinder block confession booth. She didn't seem to care. She headed into the bathroom, emerged with a glass, and poured herself some of my bourbon like she was entitled to it. Maybe she was.

Her eyes were darker now. Heavier. The same look I'd seen in women who knew exactly what they wanted, and expected you to know it, too. No explanations. Just signals. If you missed them, you didn't deserve the prize.

"It's late," I offered, trying to toe the line between respect and resistance.

She stared at me. Didn't blink. The space between us tightened like a noose.

"There are a hundred men out there who'd kill to be where you are right now," she said.

Before I could reply, her lips found mine; they were soft but assertive, sweet but searing. Her body pressed into mine with heat and sculpted precision. I tasted her lipstick, her hunger, the hint of danger she carried like perfume. Her tongue teased mine before retreating, leaving me dazed and wanting. She smiled when she saw what she'd done.

"That was nice," I breathed. "But honestly... I'm not exactly firing on all cylinders."

That didn't faze her. She hiked up her dress and produced a small, clear packet with a pink powder, emptied it into her bourbon, stirred it with a finger, and handed it to me.

"Drink this."

I looked at it. "What is it?"

"It'll help with your... issues."

"What is it?" I asked again, slower.

She leaned in, eyes locked on mine, unblinking. "Drink, and you'll find out."

I took it like a dare and downed it in one gulp. It tasted like medicine that had expired sometime last decade, and it hit my stomach like a brick. But seconds later, I could feel it working. The fog started to lift. My coordination returned. The spinning slowed to a manageable tilt.

I exhaled. "Better. What the hell was that? B-12?"

"It's a local remedy," she said, brushing off the question. "Every culture has its cures for indulgence."

She placed her hand on my chest.

"I can feel your heartbeat."

"That's not the only thing still alive," I said, grinning.

She didn't smile back. She unbuttoned my shirt slowly, deliberately, while I reached up and tangled my fingers in her black hair, pulling her into another kiss. This one was faster, needier. Not just chemistry, but momentum.

"You are an unexpected pleasure, Bobby Santos," she whispered against my lips.

She took my hands and brought them around behind her head, guiding them to the zipper. I pulled it down in one smooth motion. The dress sighed off her body like it was relieved to let go. She stood there, unashamed, more powerful in her nakedness than most people are in armor.

Then she turned and walked to the window unit. Adjusted the dial until cold air roared into the room.

"That might cause shrinkage," I said, as goosebumps climbed my skin.

She stepped back to me and began helping me undress.

"No," she said with a sly smile, "it won't."

Chapter Five
Saturday

The day started off better than it had any right to. For someone who drank like I was trying to drown something and stayed up far past a reasonable hour, I woke early. Too early. No hangover, no dry-mouth carpet-tongue, no pounding skull screaming for water and forgiveness. Just clear eyes and a body that felt like it had been rewound to factory settings. Whatever Amelia gave me last night was less of a "remedy" and more of a miracle. If someone bottled it, they'd make a killing in Vegas or Mexico. Probably both.

She was already gone by the time I opened my eyes. Not surprising. Amelia struck me as the type who never stayed longer than she intended. She took what she wanted, left before the silence could ask questions, and didn't apologize for any of it. The only evidence she'd ever been there was a single red chili pepper left on the pillow next to mine. A warning memento.

She was a character, no question. Smart, self-assured, sharp enough to shave steel. And she had that rare thing talent of possessing humor without cruelty. A dying art in a world where everyone's locked and loaded with opinions, most of them loud and useless. In a place like

Three Days In Hell

Helman, that kind of humor wasn't just charming. It was survival.

After a hot shower and a shave that made me feel almost human again, I grabbed yesterday's clothes that still carries the stench of smoke, sweat, and other sins, and headed to the motel laundry room. The sun was only starting to stretch across the horizon, casting long, tired shadows across the cracked asphalt. A debris of beer cans, confetti, crushed hats, a lonely maraca littered the lot from the previous night's festivities. A couple slept in the bed of a pickup truck, limbs entwined, their socked feet sticking out the back like some kind of domestic sculpture.

The laundry room light buzzed overhead like it had a grudge. Inside, a little girl sat on one of the folding tables, legs swinging, a book held open in front of her like a shield. She couldn't have been more than seven or eight with dirty blonde bobbed hair, eyes like a polished river stone, and skin the color of scorched sugar. She looked up just long enough to clock me. She had no fear, no curiosity, just awareness, and then dipped back into her book.

There were no clothes in any of the machines. They were dead quiet, except for the sound of turning pages. I started a wash cycle and fed a few quarters into the vending machine for dryer sheets, trying not to disrupt the fragile peace of the place.

The girl said nothing. She didn't need to. Her silence was louder than most conversations I'd had in the last twenty-four hours. Maybe she came here to escape the noise. From the dancing, the shouting, the fireworks, the chaos from the night before, that kind of quiet was probably worth its weight in gold.

I didn't ask questions. Not yet.

Some things introduce themselves without a word.

She stared at the pages like they held a secret only she could decipher. I couldn't quite make out the cover, so I leaned in a little.

"Whatcha reading?" I asked.

She didn't answer right away. Just closed the book slowly and held it out for me to see. It was the kind of Bible you find in every motel nightstand, courtesy of the Gideons and whatever shred of moral scaffolding still clung to America's underbelly. But this one had been desecrated and scratched up like some angry drunk had a bone to pick with the Good Book.

"Can I see that a second?"

Too used to doing what adults told her, she handed it over without a word, which said more than anything else could. I flipped through it. Pages had been torn out and passages underlined in red or circled with manic energy. Someone had jammed crude and violent drawings in the margins. If anyone had tried to find salvation in these pages, they'd have gotten lost halfway to Leviticus.

I handed it back. "You like that?"

She shrugged. "I don't have anything else to read."

That landed like a weight in the gut. I gave her a nod and stepped outside.

The morning light had finally crawled over the motel roofline, casting long shadows across the parking lot. A mess of last night's excesses littered the ground – spent fireworks, plastic cups, ashtray guts, half-eaten ribs swarming with flies. But the car was untouched. Thank God for small miracles.

I popped the trunk. Five banker's boxes of Bibles were stacked neatly inside, still sealed with packing tape. A folding card table leaned against them, my portable altar, if you could call it that. I cracked open a box and pulled out a fresh copy, the binding crisp, the gold trim still catching the light like a promise.

Back in the laundry room, I handed it to the girl.

"Here. Try that."

She took it cautiously, her expression somewhere between suspicion and reverence. She flipped it open and gasped softly at the immaculate pages, untouched by ink or idiocy.

"I can have this?"

I nodded. "Might as well make it a clean copy."

She clutched it tight. "Thanks."

"Not many people read the Bible," I said. "Especially not kids."

She didn't disagree. "I don't mind it. I don't always understand it. I used to go to church school on Sundays. They explained the stories."

"But not anymore?"

She shook her head. "There's no more school."

"You from Helman?"

She nodded.

"Do you know what happened to the church?"

Another shrug. Maybe she didn't know. Maybe she just didn't want to say.

"You excited for the Festival?"

That sparked something. Her eyes brightened like a match struck in the dark.

"There's nothing else to do but wait for the Festival."

"If you don't go to school, what do you do all day?"

She gave a non-answer that was somehow more telling than the truth: "Nothing."

"That's a long day to fill."

She offered a half-hearted gesture. "I just wait."

"Wait for what?"

This time, she paused. Thought it over carefully like she hadn't been asked the question before. Then her small face lit up again with that strange mix of innocence and something older.

"The Festival."

I checked my watch. Ten minutes left on the wash, another thirty for the dry. I figured I'd let her keep her quiet and wandered back toward my room.

"Maybe I'll see you there," I said.

She looked up. Her eyes were bottomless and too knowing for someone still losing baby teeth. She held the book out again, as if maybe she wasn't supposed to keep gifts.

I shook my head. "Keep it. That book's tough enough without the dirty pictures and satanic graffiti."

She smiled. Not a childish smile. Just a little curve of the lips like she understood something I didn't.

I laid my second suit across the other bed like I was prepping for a wake. Shirt next to it, creased and clean. Then I stepped outside to check the inventory in the trunk. Five boxes of Bibles, still untouched. I found a half-crushed pack of cigarettes behind the jack and lit one, the first drag chasing away the morning damp.

I hadn't met Helman yet. No nod, no handshake, no official blessing. Which meant I was still a foreign body in Helman's bloodstream. Working the Festival without his green light could be dangerous, but I'd worked worse odds. Local laws were like local gods; some demanded tribute, others were just names etched in a stone nobody bothered to read anymore. But in this town, everything revolved around that one man, and I wasn't interested in waiting around for royal approval.

Three Days In Hell

That meant I'd have to push my Bibles guerrilla-style. No razzle-dazzle. No song and dance. No bait before the hook. I'd hit quick and talk straight. Simple people like simple words, and out here, subtext was just another word for bullshit. You didn't pitch morality with poetry. You pitched it with grit and a smile that didn't ask for trust, it took it.

I figured I'd head back to the faces from last night and set up next to the beer tent. If Helman didn't like it, he could find me and tell me himself. I'd learned a long time ago it was easier to ask for forgiveness than beg for permission, especially when nobody wanted to look God in the eye without a drink in their hand.

In towns like this, religion and alcohol went together like snake oil and faith healers. Even in the so-called dry counties, there was always a bottle tucked away under the pew or behind the altar. People didn't like their sins exposed; they liked them baptized in bourbon and whispered behind closed doors.

A woman stepped out of the motel office, her shorts riding high enough to remind me of why sunblock exists. Her legs were the color of refrigerated lard. She sipped motel coffee and chewed on a donut like a cow working over cud.

That reminded me that Woody served a Continental breakfast in the office. I followed the scent of burnt coffee beans and sugar back inside.

It was a grim little spread. A folding table offered shrink-wrapped donuts, off-brand bear claws, and a chrome coffee urn that dispensed something dark enough to be called coffee but light enough to pass for tea in the right light. Around the table milled the usual suspects; tourists with boiled ham faces, drawn like moths to the neon promise of fried food, cheap thrills, and moral absolution sold in ten-minute bursts.

These people weren't visitors. They were scavengers. Strip-mall pilgrims looking to root through the garbage of spectacle.

I poured myself some coffee and watched as a man in a fluorescent beach bucket hat fought with a plastic muffin case. He looked like someone who'd lost a bet with a can of whipped cream, his nose streaked with zinc oxide, his fingers too bloated to finesse the tab on the container. He struggled like a chimp trying to crack a safe.

Another man took pity on him, popped it open, and walked away. Bucket Hat smiled, grabbed a couple muffins, and caught me watching him. He flashed me a grin that made me wish I hadn't made eye contact; he was a vacant man, sun-fried, and doped up on life's small victories.

I sipped my coffee and turned away, already calculating the angles I'd need to play once the sun climbed a little higher and the town's conscience loosened in the heat.

"Hey there, fella," he said, speaking around a mouthful of muffin. "Pete Junkersfield. Pleased to make your acquaintance."

I wasn't sure what I'd done to earn the honor, but I took his hand anyway. It was sticky with glaze, and I wiped my palm on my pants the moment the shake was done. "Bobby."

"Ain't nothing like the Chili Festival, am I right?"

"I'm giddy like a schoolgirl, Pete. Even without the pigtails."

He burst out laughing, cheeks wobbling. "That's a good one. I gotta remember that. Now, just between two new friends, are you a regular, or are you a virgin?"

Three Days In Hell

I gave him a sly wink. "Let's just say I'm glad there's no volcano nearby."

The confused look on his face cracked into wide-eyed realization. "You got a serious funny bone, my friend! Hey Gally! We got ourselves a virgin here!"

A woman – possibly wife, possibly sister, probably both in spirit – turned and grinned, flashing a smile that was one canine short of complete. She blushed, gave a doughy thumbs-up, and went back to her donut.

"You're in for a treat, my friend. The missus and I've been coming for years, and trust me, it only gets better."

I smiled and looked for the nearest exit, but Pete stepped in like a bouncer guarding a sacred rite.

"You competing or spectating?"

"Come again?"

"*El Fuego en el Agujero.*" Pete relayed in bastardized Spanish. "Fire in the Hole. You know, who can eat the hottest chili and still walk away without needing last rites."

I laughed politely. "I think I'll pass. I'm new, remember? I'd rather not light both ends of my digestive system on fire."

Pete roared, loud enough to turn heads. "Ain't that the truth! That's what makes it great! You want to know a secret? I've been training. *Serranos. Jalapeños.* Like popcorn. I'm not folding in round one this year. Ten big ones are on the line, and brother, I need every one of 'em."

I turned out my jacket pockets like a vaudeville hobo. "Right there with you, Pete."

He chuckled. "You should put twenty on me to win. I've lit up our toilet like the Fourth of July, but it's been worth it! My mouth could swallow a handful of hot coals and suck 'em like gumdrops."

Judging by his wife's approving nod, I didn't need proof.

As soon as the energy between us dipped, I made my move. "Well, Pete, been a pleasure. Gotta grab some sunscreen before the sun turns me into leather."

He grabbed my hand again and pumped it. "Pleasure's all mine, Bobby. Don't be a stranger now."

I paused. "You wouldn't happen to be from around here, would you, Pete?"

"Nah. Why?"

"Just thought you might be in the market for a Bible."

"A Bible? Why would I need that?"

"To open your next muffin pack."

He didn't get the joke, but he grinned anyway. There was a blueberry stuck between his teeth so dark and round it looked like he'd lost a molar.

"You be sure to holler for ol' Pete!" he said, winking like a kid learning how. "And don't let me catch you on that stage, now. I turn real competitive. We may be friends now, but come the chili gauntlet? I go full dog-eat-dog."

I nodded and caught the distraction I needed when Gally asked him something about spice levels. I slipped past him, only to bump straight into Bins who had half of a donut crammed into his mouth.

I shook my head disapprovingly. "The food's for guests," I said.

Bins grinned, powdered sugar falling from his lips. "Everyone knows Woody puts out a nice spread on Festival morning."

I scanned the sad table. "Must've missed that in the guidebook."

"Anyway," he said, picking up someone else's abandoned coffee and taking a swig, "this isn't a social call. I'm here to collect you."

"Collect me? Helman?"

He looked around, suddenly nervous. "No need to broadcast it. Yes, Helman. Told me to fetch you pronto. Amelia bent his ear about you. Now, let's get going."

He snapped up the last of the donuts on his way out the door. We walked to my car, and he waited for me to open it. Outside, people had started to congregate. They steadily filed out of their hiding places with the mindlessness of sheep corralled together, waiting for further orders from the shepherd. They milled about, waiting until their numbers swelled before moving down the street toward the center of town. It was a strange collection of people, a gathering of misfits that found solidarity in the ceremony of capsicum.

Moments later, one of the bands started up, filling the increasingly heavy air with the bleating of brass horns.

It was nearly seven-thirty in the morning. The Festival had started.

***

We took side streets and back alleys to get to the Helman house. The town had closed off its two main intersections three blocks in every direction from the center, making cross-town travel a logistical headache. As we zigzagged through the clogged arteries of Helman, we passed packs of festivalgoers dressed in every shade of red or draped in chili-themed gear ranging from shirts, earrings, sunglasses, hats, to even inflatable pepper costumes. They looked like cultists on their annual pilgrimage, dragging along equally-decked-out rugrats, all whooping and hollering for the day ahead. It was Mardi Gras with a Southwestern twist, less sequins, more spice.

Bins lit a cigarette and offered me the pack. I took one and lit up, thinking over the unexpected detour.

"What do you think he's going to say?" I asked.

"How should I know?"

"Humor me."

He exhaled slowly and smoothly, letting the smoke drift out the window. "Beats me. But he's going to want to see a return on investment."

"There's not much profit in this."

"You'd be surprised how much blood Helman can wring from a stone. Besides, you're a new face."

"What's that supposed to mean?"

"That makes you interesting. And JB likes interesting people."

"Why?"

"You don't get to be top dog without knowing who's sniffing around you."

I looked at the river of red-flecked humanity flowing toward town center. "So, why am I so special? You telling me that Helman knows all their names?"

Bins laughed. "They're cattle. Not people. Not the way you are, at least. New people are questions to JB. And he likes to know the answers. You're not in town twelve hours, and you and Amelia are already playing kissy-face? He notices that kind of thing. Like it or not, that kicks you up a few pegs. It also means you can't hide."

That didn't make me feel as important as it probably should have. Last time I made myself known, Shank made sure I'd have the scars to show for it.

"He ever take a closer look at you?"

Bins smirked. "I've put in some work for Helman. Nothing major. Run a few errands. Carried some weight over the border. But that's it. If he gets an itch, though, you'll feel his fingernails. He doesn't invite many new faces into his house. Some, but not many."

We pulled into the semi-circular driveway. I got out and tossed Bins the keys.

"Here we are," he said. "The Tower of Power. When you want me back?"

"How long do you think this'll take?"

Bins glanced toward the rising hum of the town center and shrugged. "What say I take her for a wash and swing back?"

I listened to the distant thrum of the crowd, swelling like a wave about to crest. "Just meet me at the Festival. Set up the table near the vendors."

Bins hesitated. "You think that's smart? What if JB says no?"

"If this doesn't go well, an unsanctioned Bible table won't change much. Either way, I'm out."

"Suit yourself."

He then pulled away, leaving me facing the Helman estate: white stucco walls, red-clay-tiled roof, wrought-iron balconies that looked like they hadn't heard laughter in decades. I got a clearer view now than I did yesterday, back when it was just a curiosity. This time, it was the destination.

The left wing had a private patio, walled high and tight with concrete. The right side was all floor-to-ceiling windows, likely a sitting room for sunlight and cocktails. In the middle, a grand fountain shot water arrogantly into the air, Helman's middle finger to drought concerns and public opinion.

Both gates to the wraparound driveway stood open, like arms stretched wide in expectation of my arrival. Outside, the property buzzed with movement. Delivery trucks idled. Workers scurried, erecting canvas structures and threading long strands of colored lights between poles and trellises. The town wasn't the only one getting a makeover for the Festival; Helman's estate was going full carnival.

I walked past the chaos and knocked on the thick front door. It felt dense beneath my knuckles and solid enough to hold off a battering ram. After a couple of minutes and another round of knocks, it opened. The man on the other side looked as though he'd spent the last twenty years failing to sleep. His eyes sagged like sandbags, and he wore a heavy coat better suited for a Rocky Mountain winter than a Southwestern morning.

"Yes?" he croaked, his voice dry and craggy, like he'd been gargling gravel.

"Bobby Santos," I said, smiling. "Mr. Helman's expecting me."

He gave me a long, withering look before stepping aside and opening the door just enough to let me in.

Inside, I took stock like I always did. First impressions matter in my line of work; people's homes say more about them than they realize. This one couldn't decide what it wanted to be. One room had a hand-carved table topped with a two-dollar kiln-blasted clay vase. Another featured designer furniture resting on a worn, local throw rug. Opulence met rural kitsch like two drunks slow dancing, awkwardly but earnestly.

Hallways branched off from the two-story foyer like capillaries, each leading to rooms spacious enough to park a car. Ten-foot ceilings. Expensive tinted windows that softened the light while cutting the heat. But despite the architectural bragging, what really hit me was the cold.

It was freezing. Nipple-prickling cold.

Now the butler's coat made sense.

"Jesus," I muttered as the chill bit into my skin.

He didn't blink. "Follow me."

I did, trailing him down the main hall. We passed through rooms like a tour of "Clue" brought to life: billiard room, conservatory, formal dining area. I half-expected Miss Scarlet to strut out with a vintage cigarette holder and bat her lashes at Professor Plum.

Each room was occupied by beautiful men and women reclining in various poses of calculated disinterest, like just existing in this place drained them. In one, a woman with a jet-black bob and sweat-slicked cheeks stared into space, her expression toeing the line between bored and broken. Around them, service staff moved with surgical focus, threading garlands and setting up place settings like they were prepping a five-star dinner party instead of a chili-soaked town festival.

Finally, the butler dropped me in the kitchen, and what a kitchen it was. A chef's temple.

Exposed white brick gave it a rustic glow, but the appliances told a different story: three natural gas ovens with split-level burners, industrial hoods humming overhead, copper pots dangling from ceiling racks, knife blades gleaming on magnetic strips. There were two full-sized fridges and matching standalone freezers flanking a pair of deep farmhouse sinks. Two oversized islands offered enough butcher-block real estate to host a cooking show.

Everything sparkled. Everything shined. Every surface looked like it had been wiped down five minutes ago by someone terrified of fingerprints.

I found Helman at the lowered section of the island, which had been built for a smaller person or one consigned to a lifetime in a wheelchair. His bony hands worked methodically through a pile of red peppers so ripe their juice pooled like little blood puddles. He looked different from the night before, more vulnerable, more exposed, trapped in that metal frame in a kitchen so vast it made me wonder if anyone could even hear him scream if he fell out and needed help.

Ever since my brother's fight with MS, wheelchairs unsettled me. No matter how much power someone held, that contraption always made them look like a victim. FDR might've been president four times, but he still needed help to wipe his ass. In the city I'd once lived in, homeless men in wheelchairs were easy prey, robbed for the tithes they'd gathered or tortured for kicks. Some managed to find peace in the cage. My brother wasn't one of them.

"Sit, sit," Helman barked without looking up.

I slid onto a stool at the island. Around us, a swarm of caterers unpacked crates of produce, meat, and vegetables. He waved them off like flies.

"Chili Festival means chili time," he said. "Best in the state. Though if I'm being honest, every day's chili day around here. Hell, today we just put a blue ribbon on some lucky bastard and call it special."

"And a nice chunk of change, from what I hear," I said.

He glanced up, blade paused mid-slice. "You heard about that, huh? Yeah, I back the people's hard work with a little something. Trick I learned from the greats: give the have-nots a shiny ball, and they'll play with it all day, forget what hurts."

He rolled his chair to the stove and dumped the peppers into a simmering pot. They sizzled loud enough to make me want to stand closer just to steal some heat.

"You a chili man, Mr. –?"

"Santos. Bobby Santos."

"Santos," he repeated, smiling thinly. He stirred the pot, the wooden spoon clinking softly against metal. "Amelia tells me you're handing out Bibles. I hear that right?"

"Yes, sir."

He stopped stirring, gave me a look. "Not much revenue in that, I imagine."

I laughed. "Hardly any."

Helman poured the shots and pushed one toward me across the table with a practiced ease that said he did this sort of thing often, pulling people into his confidence, making them feel seen, until they forgot which parts of themselves they were supposed to keep hidden.

"I asked about your tomorrow," he repeated. "What does it look like? Not the one in your planner. The one that shows up after you close your eyes and the world gets real quiet."

I studied the glass. The liquor inside was the color of old varnish and smelled like something that came in a dusty bottle from a locked cabinet.

"I haven't looked that far ahead," I said.

"That's a lie, son," Helman replied, lifting his shot but not drinking it. "Men like you don't get out of bed without thinking three steps forward. You've been thinking about tomorrow since yesterday. And I'd bet good money it don't look like Bible sales and cheap motel sheets forever."

I didn't argue. Helman was the kind of man who liked to draw his own conclusions. Interrupting that process was like putting your hand between a dog and its chew toy.

"I'll tell you what I see," he said, finally taking the shot. He winced a little, let the burn work through his chest, then fixed me with a grin that didn't touch his eyes. "I see a man who's run from something for so long, he doesn't know how to stop even when he's standing still. I see a man who's too smart for the game he's stuck in but too proud – or too damned stubborn – to walk away from it."

He leaned forward.

"And I see a man who, despite what he tells himself, is still looking for a way out. That about square with the truth, Bobby Santos?"

It did. Too much. Which meant I couldn't say so. Instead, I threw back the shot. It burned like the house's cold seeped into my bones and lit a match. I welcomed it.

"You ever play cards?" Helman asked, idly shuffling the deck with impressive speed.

"A little."

"Good," he said. "Because you just sat down at the table. And I don't let men leave the game once they've been dealt in."

I stared at the empty shot glass in front of me, wishing it was a black hole I could crawl into. I didn't look at Helman. I didn't have to. I could feel his amusement thick in the air like cigar smoke.

"I didn't know," I said finally.

"No," Helman replied. "You didn't. But now you do. So, the question becomes, what are you going to do about it?"

I didn't answer. Because there wasn't one that didn't make me look stupid, guilty, or dead.

Three Days In Hell

Helman leaned back in his wheelchair and swirled his drink, eyes on the ceiling like he was trying to decide if the chandelier had always been crooked.

"She tells me everything," he said. "She's loyal like that. And smart. Got the nose of a goddamn truffle pig when it comes to lies. That's how I know she hasn't told you about her situation. Yet."

He let that hang.

"Now, maybe that's because you're just a charming drifter with a few sweet nothings and a pocket full of paperbacks. Or maybe it's because she's testing me. Seeing if I still got the juice. Either way, I figured I'd meet the man who's got my wife curious enough to keep secrets."

Still, I said nothing. What was there to say? "I didn't know" didn't sound any better the second time around. And "It didn't mean anything" would've insulted them both.

Helman finally looked back at me. His eyes weren't cold, they were *alive* like something behind them had just woken up and remembered it still had teeth.

"You're not the first man to make her forget herself. But if you're smart, Bobby, you'll make sure you're the last."

He knocked back his drink and set the glass down with a clink.

"I'll give you your table. You can sell your Bibles. Maybe you even save a few souls along the way. But don't go thinking this is charity. It's a bet. And between us? I don't place bets I can't win."

Then he wheeled himself back to the stove, like we'd just discussed the weather, and the weather had been favorable.

I stared at the paper, the half-grainy, half-glossy mug of *El Mochomo* sneering out from the front page. The kind of face you see only twice: once when he's making a deal, and once when he's sealing your coffin.

The picture was old, but the eyes were still alive and coiled with hunger, like something barely restrained behind bone and skin. I'd read about the way his people made examples out of rivals, stuff even seasoned enforcers wouldn't whisper without downing a bottle first. Now here I was drinking with his baby sister's husband after accidentally crawling into bed with the Devil's kin.

My skin itched. My scalp tingled like it wanted to crawl off my skull and run for the border.

"So, what now?" I asked, voice flatter than I wanted. "You going to tell her to keep her distance from the drifter peddling Bibles?"

Helman chuckled again, that dry crackle of leaves catching fire. "Tell her?" he repeated. "Boy, if I started telling Amelia what to do, I'd be buried in the garden next to the last man who tried."

I didn't like the way he said that. Past tense and all.

He rolled back to the stove, stirred the pot like nothing had just been said that could ruin a man's life. The smell of peppers and cumin filled the cold air. It should've been comforting. It wasn't.

"You're lucky," Helman said. "She must've seen something in you. She doesn't bring just *anyone* home."

"She didn't bring me anywhere," I said.

"You sure about that?"

I wasn't because I didn't know what he meant by that remark.

He poured himself another drink, and didn't offer me one this time. Just stared at the glass like it was a crystal ball and maybe he could see how long I'd last if he nudged things the wrong way.

"I like you, Bobby," he said finally. "You've got some bad decisions in you. And bad decisions make good stories. Just remember something. Around here, stories don't always end where you think they should."

"Are you threatening me?" I asked.

Helman smiled. "Son, I'm trying to keep you *alive*. That's about as generous as I get."

The kitchen fell quiet except for the bubbling pot and the soft clink of ice settling in his glass.

"Set up your table," he said. "Sell your Bibles and do whatever it is you do."

I stood up, legs stiff from sitting too long in the cold. Or maybe it was fear. Hard to tell the difference these days.

"You think Amelia sent me here?" I asked. "To test you?"

He shook his head. "No. She sent you here to *see* you. I think she's still figuring out what kind of man you are. So am I. But don't flatter yourself thinking you're playing the game."

"What am I doing, then?"

"You're the piece she's *moving*."

Helman leaned forward on the island, his elbows digging into the lowered butcher block like it was a confessional altar. The glow of his cigar flared for a moment before the ember dimmed into a faint pulse.

"It's a give and take, Santos," he continued. "To be fair, the town was on life support. My family's town. My legacy. Amelia showed up at my door one day with a short, one-piece red dress that swirled just right when her hips swayed. She pitched me the plan. *El Mochomo* would keep the town running in exchange for serving as a weigh station for the cartel's products. Not a distribution center mind you, I don't have the stomach for that, just a place to receive merchandise and prepare it for shipping. The town had an image to uphold after all.

"The Iguana's her baby. A side project where she runs all of the extracurriculars there. I make it look legitimate on paper. After all, she is from south of the border, and some things just sit better with the locals when they have a familiar name to go with a place."

He removed a cigar from his shirt pocket and rolled it around in his fingers. "Her brother gets his monthly cut of the proceeds. Business is business. But don't get me wrong. I'm no flunkie like that shit-heel Dupree. I had power once. But when push met shove, her fingers go deep into the well, and I'm just a guy in a metal chair with wheels."

"Why are you telling me this?"

"Because you're a serious man, Bobby Santos. I can see that. Now so can Amelia. Serious men are rare in places like this. They have a way of being harbingers of change. Sometimes good, mostly bad, to the establishment. Why do you think Amelia sought you out so quickly? She wanted to know just how serious you are. And so did I. We might have had different reasons for doing so, but I think we both got the same answer.

"Now, I know what you're thinking. 'Helman, you're trying to pull the wool over my eyes.' But that's not the case. You'll see for yourself. I'm just the face of the town, Bobby Santos. I'm the name on a sign. A historical data point, nothing more. For now. But after last night, me and you have something in common I think, which is why I asked you here. "You're tied to Amelia in a way no man wants to find himself tied, my friend. I should know. I am too. We're just like Robert Parker or that Oliver Cromwell fella. Selling our souls to a beautiful devil. Only in my case, that deal's run its course.

"Oh, I used to think I could control her," he said, voice soft now, almost lost in the hum of the freezer motors. "Tried money, tried guilt, even tried love, if you believe a man like me capable of it. But that woman doesn't love anything she can't break. So, instead, I learned to make myself useful. Like any loyal dog."

He took a long drag on his cigar and exhaled slowly, the smoke wafting toward the overhead hood. "But you, Santos. You're not useful. Not yet. You're *interesting*. And that's more dangerous because it's got potential."

There was that word again – *useful*. It seemed that was the characteristic people around here liked best. I shifted on the stool. The liquor was sitting heavier now, like a brick in my gut. I wanted to say something, maybe about walking away, about leaving town before sundown and forgetting this whole misstep. But we both knew that was a fantasy. You don't walk out on the devil once she's danced with you. Not without paying the band.

"You know what happens to useful men around here?" Helman asked.

I didn't answer. He didn't wait.

"They get offered choices that don't feel like choices."

The cigar hit the ashtray with a quiet clink. Helman rolled back slightly, his eyes losing focus for a moment, drifting, maybe remembering who he used to be.

"You asked why I told you all this," he said. "It's because I'm tired, Santos. Tired of being a puppet prince. Tired of pretending this frozen palace of mine means something. And maybe… maybe I just wanted to talk to someone who didn't look at me and see a goddamn chair. Tell me, and I want you to be honest. What do you think of our town's future?"

I stared at the empty glass in my hand, as if staring long enough might turn it into something else, something that made sense. My breath clouded the air, white and shallow, like I was barely here. His eyes were still on me. Watching. Measuring. I felt sick. Not just in my stomach, but deep in my bones like something rotten had taken root inside me and was finally pushing to the surface. My hands were damp, clammy with fear or shame or both. I didn't know. I couldn't tell anymore. The chill in the air pressed in, but all I could feel was heat rising behind my eyes.

"It's bad," I said finally. I had to stand up from the table to collect my thoughts. Helman had bombarded me from all sides, and I needed a breather. "But it's not the first place that's gone under. I'm sure some big-money developer will gladly steamroll this place and put up a mall or gated community with a golf course or something."

Helman's face got stone serious. He lowered his cigar and looked at me through squinted eyelids. "But my family didn't come to these parts to build a golf course, son. They made a decision, and made a deal, and were one of the first people here, and they started making things happen. My people helped build this town. And yeah, when the mining went away, we were the cause of that as well. But now things are out of hand. I don't like being prostrate to these cartel wahoos."

He sighed heavily with a couple more puffs. "This town can be something again. Not the way it was, maybe, but better than it is now. Only Amelia's people make out by keeping this town down. A dying town attracts little attention, savvy? Especially from the powers that be. And can I be frank with you? You're also a man of low scruples. Now, don't take offense to that. That is a plus in a town like this. It opens doors and opportunities."

"What kinds of doors?"

His eyes narrowed. "The kind most men don't want to walk through, but those that do, find a very fucking profitable return on the other side."

And so Helman cast out his own line to see if I'd take the bait on the hook. "What exactly do you want from me?"

"Ain't that obvious to a man of your perception and intellect? I want you to get rid of my problem. I did you a favor, now I want one in return."

The force of my laugh startled even me.

"You want me to eliminate the cartel? You must have mistaken me for someone a few sandwiches short of a picnic. I like my neck where it is. Pristine and uncut and without my tongue sticking out of it."

Annoyed that I didn't understand him, he waved me off. "No, no, no, I don't expect you to take out the cartel. Her, boy. Just her."

Helman's face didn't twitch an inch as his eyes scrutinized my reaction. Mine did the same to him, checking if he was serious or just having some fun.

When I determined humor wasn't his strong suit, I shook my head. "Now I know you lost your mind. You're asking me to kill a woman who has done nothing to me."

"No, son. I'm asking you to rid the town of cancer. One for the sake of many, so to speak. Come on, Bobby. You've been around the block enough to know that good pussy doesn't belong to good women. That's why we love 'em so much. But that doesn't make them healthy for us. We'd walk on a razor's edge with bare feet just for a whiff."

"Look, I'm sorry I slept with your wife. But I'm no killer."

"Not a killer, or you don't kill women? There's a difference, you know."

"Yeah? What's that?"

"A reason. Let me ask you something. You have a temper, Bobby?"

"About as much as anyone else."

"No, I mean, you ever have something that sets you off? Someone gets you all riled and seeing so much red that you just want to hurt it? Anyone ever get under your skin like that??"

"Yeah."

"So, what'd you do about it?"

"I fucked his wife."

Helman laughed. "Well, there you go, son. What'd I tell you? Don't bullshit a bullshitter. Just because you can't find a reason doesn't mean there isn't one there."

"You telling me you can't find someone desperate enough to pull a trigger? No offense, but this town isn't exactly steeped in virtue."

"I can't do it for obvious reasons. I also can't look like I had a hand in it for those same reasons. But you, a stranger, that blows in and out of town without so much as making a ripple? No one knows a man like that. A quick love thing gone awry. Maybe she tried to cheat you or blackmail you, and you gave her what was coming. It doesn't matter. Either way, you're gone before the body's found, and no one's any wiser. But someone will be richer. A lot richer."

I paused. He found my Achilles heel and strummed at the tendons like guitar strings. "How much richer?"

Helman grinned at that, tight-lipped and hungry. It was the kind of smile a man wore when he knew he'd finally pulled a lever inside you, when the click echoed in your chest and you couldn't pretend you hadn't heard it.

He wheeled himself closer again, the leather of his seat creaking as he leaned in like a conspirator. His voice lowered, not because he was afraid someone might hear, but because he knew lowering it made it carry more weight. Made it feel *sacred*.

"Fifty thousand. Cash."

The number hit like a sucker punch to the gut. Not because it was too high or too low, but because it was *real*. Tangible. Immediate. Enough to disappear off the map and start over someplace where people didn't ask too many questions.

"You have that kind of scratch just lying around?" I asked.

Helman chuckled. "You think I wear this chair for fun? Nobody pats down a cripple. I've got cash stashed in more nooks of this house than I've got feeling in my legs. And I keep it liquid, just in case."

I turned away from him, walking over to the industrial sink. I let my hands grip the cold steel edge. For a long moment, I just stared down into the drain, watched a tiny bead of condensation drip from the copper pipe above and disappear into the grate.

"It's not just about money," I muttered. "That kind of thing stays with you. Whether you get away with it or not. You look in the mirror and you'll see her face. Every. Damn. Time."

Helman's voice followed me like a shadow. "That's only if you think she's a person. You still do, don't you?"

I turned around. "She's a lot of things. But she's not *nothing*."

"That's where you're wrong, Santos. She *is* nothing. Nothing but a bloodline that answers to the Devil himself. You think this ends with a club and a few backroom deals?

Think again. She's the tip of the spear. A living, breathing blade those cartel fucks stuck into the flesh of this town."

He tapped his chest. "You think I'm the villain in this story? I was *trying* to keep the peace. But peace doesn't last with vipers. Eventually, they bite."

I didn't speak. I couldn't. He saw that same hesitation on my face, the war inside me grinding its gears. And he did like all good businessmen do when they want to grasp the brass ring.

He took another puff from his cigar and blew the smoke toward the ceiling. "The only question is whether you're the kind of man who leaves behind regrets… or the kind who buries them."

I stood there, listening to the tick of the kitchen clock and the soft rattle of the vent above the stove. Somewhere in the back of the house, a woman laughed. Someone clinked glasses. The Festival was starting.

And somewhere outside that door, the Devil waited. Beautiful. Dangerous. Waiting to see if I'd dance again.

"You're a drifter, Bobby Santos," he continued. "Drifters drift. And I'll get you the fifty to keep those winds blowing you in whichever direction tickles your fancy. No trail for anyone to follow."

I lost my poker face, and it showed. That was a number with a lot of power. In the right place, that money had legs; it could walk into any room and make people listen, make them forget their principles and remember their hunger. It wasn't just a number; it was a doorway. A shimmering, treacherous invitation to step off the path I'd barely managed to stay on. I felt how easily it could change everything. Pay off every debt, silence every regret, maybe even buy back a piece of who I used to be. My heart pounded, not from fear but from the thrill of it, the weightless anticipation of jumping without knowing if there was ground on the other side. I wanted to say no. I should have said no. But I was already imagining what yes would feel like.

"Oh, look at you. Christ, Bobby. I'm just messing with you. I'm playing a mental game with you. What do you call it? A thought exercise." He flashed a smile that was anything but friendly. "All right, son, why not get down to the Festival and see if you can unload some of those Bibles? How many you got to get rid of?"

I told him. He made a face and shook his head.

"I don't mean to be the bearer of bad news, but I hope you brought yourself a few changes of clothes. I think you're going to be here a while. Don't get long in the face. We're all prisoners of this town in one way or another," Helman said. "Doesn't have to be that way, but it is what it is."

Helman's voice trailed behind me like smoke as I slid the door open and stepped out onto the patio. The blast of desert heat slapped me in the face, a blessed reprieve after the walk-in-freezer chill of his kitchen. The air smelled like dust, old chlorine, and the faint aroma of grilled meat carried in from somewhere farther down the hill.

I didn't look back.

Maybe he'd meant it as a joke. Maybe not. But that number – *fifty thousand* – had a way of worming its way into your ear and nesting there. He'd dropped it like an anchor into my thoughts, and no matter how far I walked, I could still feel the chain pulling taut.

I made my way through a gate that opened onto a winding stone path toward town. Voices grew louder the farther I went, the laughter, the live music, the echo of a microphone check were melding into a boisterous cacophony.

The Festival was in full swing.

Chapter Six

Bins still had my car, so I decided to hoof it to the center of town. I hadn't gotten two blocks before the familiar weight of sweat clung to my shirt, making it feel more like soaked canvas than low thread-count cotton. The contrast in temperature to the Helman house was palpable. I took off my suit jacket and slung it over my shoulder to alleviate some of the heat as well as to hide the spreading sweat patch growing on my back. I didn't know dick about meteorology, but I figured it had to be at least in the mid-nineties, and it was only a little after ten o'clock in the morning.

Booths lined Main Street like teeth, each one manned by some weathered local hawking their wares with greasy smiles and sunburnt pride. Smoky meat curled into the air alongside the scent of hot oil, spices, and a little desperation. Banners flapped lazily overhead: *Annual Chili Festival – A Town Tradition!*

I found an empty spot at the far end, near a shaded bench where the crowd thinned out. A few kids were playing with balloons. An old man napped under a tree.

This would do.

I set the crate down and opened the lid. Inside were the Bibles. Neatly stacked, leather-bound, black as night. They looked heavier than they were, symbolically, maybe. Maybe literally. In a place like this, a book like that could either save you or bury you.

I sat down behind the crate and waited.

At first, no one came.

Eventually, a few curious glances drifted my way. A woman with her kid. A teenager, eyeing me with that mixture of suspicion and boredom. A man with a chili-stained shirt gave me a polite nod but kept walking.

The sun beat down. The day wore on. I sold a couple. Not many.

And through it all, I felt her.

Not saw, *felt*.

Amelia. Somewhere in the crowd, in the stalls, in the shadows. Watching. Maybe testing. Maybe plotting.

Helman was right about one thing: *everyone* here was a prisoner.

Some just wore better clothes.

The street shimmered under the heat, and in that moment, the whole town felt like some godless purgatory masquerading as a community. I found Bins in the concession area. He looked up at me, squinting through the haze of smoke and pain. His shirt collar was stained with sweat, and what looked like salsa. His face was flushed, whether from heat, embarrassment, or whatever had just happened to him, I couldn't tell right away.

"You look like shit," I said, crouching beside him.

"Nice to see you too," he mumbled, grimacing as he dabbed the bloodied cloth against his temple again. "Didn't expect a mosh pit at a chili cook-off."

"What happened?" I asked, already scanning the crowd for signs of who or what might've caused it. The card table lay belly-up like a dead beetle, legs splayed. Some of the Bibles had landed in a slick of melted snow cone syrup.

Bins took a drag off the cigarette and shrugged. "I don't know if you know this, but some people don't like what you're pushing."

I surveyed the carnage. It was like a tornado had touched down and torn through the display. "Who?"

Bins winced as he removed the cloth and inspected it. "The damn *cholos* over there."

He gestured across the street where a group of bikers congregated, drinking beers around their motorcycles. One of the larger men caught me staring and held up one of the Bibles he had taken and tore it in half in front of my eyes, daring me to do something.

"Stop-stop-stop-stop!" I cried out, rushing over to him. "What do you think you're doing?!"

The bikers laughed at me as if I was a kid pointing a pop gun at them.

"Get us more beer or get lost," the large man said, daring me to retaliate. His vest was covered in a series of patches equivalent to medals on a soldier. Only the monikers that decorated the breast – *Unholy Ones*, *Filthy Few*, and one featuring the *Ace of Spades* – signified specific acts of confirmed depravity.

"Fuck him up, Gator," a smaller biker said. He was the size and bore the look of a weasel who seemed very comfortable hiding behind the larger members of the pack. Gator had a buck knife visible on his left side but made no motion for it. He obviously didn't think he needed an extra advantage with someone of my stature, and he was right.

"Forget about it," I said, turning around to head back to Bins.

The bikers erupted in laughter, making derogatory comments as my unfortunate ally slinked away to collect what was left of my stock off of the street.

"Who would have thought that bikers didn't want Bibles?" Bins joked.

I took inventory of what was left. About half of the books were usable; the other half had been messed up pretty badly. They had torn pages from the binders and littered them across the street like confetti. One of the books was strangely damp, and I smelled my fingers.

"Piss," Bins said, before I could ask the question. I wiped my fingers on my pants.

A cold and uninvited thought crept up inside me: *If Helman wanted Amelia gone, why not start with the people who actually controlled the streets? Why pick me? Unless... unless he already had.* And this? This little incident? It was just another shove toward the edge. Another page in the "thought exercise."

"Come on," I said. "Let's find a new spot. Somewhere out of sight, out of mind."

Bins scooped up a few more books. "You really think it'll make a difference?"

"No," I said flatly. "But it'll buy us some time. And I have a feeling time's about to get real expensive."

He took a drag off the cigarette as he found his way to his feet. He tucked the rag into his back pocket and helped me relocate the setup a block further down. We arranged it to showcase the Bibles in as good a display as he could manage with the resources at our disposal. It was no-frills, purely functional, but it was better than trying to draw in foot traffic to window shop the back of your trunk.

Three Days In Hell

I regarded the flow of sweaty red faces, looking for a viable mark. They moved like a pink, fleshy swell, swirling in eddies and spreading slowly over the streets in random directions. They looked like tormented souls condemned to be trapped in their flab and gluttony, poked and prodded as if Satan himself stoked the fires around them. Seeping from kiosk to kiosk, they stuffed their fat faces with hot stews and dry tortillas, only to move on to another that would seduce them with fried fats, sugars, or alcohol.

Every so often, the sound of broken glass punctuated the rise and fall of chatter, and the static spurting out of the system speakers dispersed throughout the town blocks.

"Say there, fella. What's this all about?" a breathy, female voice said behind me. It had a thick undertone of a deeply southern accent not from around this region.

I turned from the sweltering mess behind me to face a woman whose round, ruddy face was flushed and glistening like a roast under heat lamps. She was pushing fifty hard with bleached-blonde hair fried from too many drugstore dyes, sweat-smeared makeup melting into creases carved deep by years and hard luck. Her hot pink tube top clung for dear life to rolls that didn't care for modesty, and her shorts looked ready to surrender altogether.

She looked at me, half-bored, half-bothered, swiping her forehead with the back of a meaty hand.

"What's what about?" I asked.

"This," she said, waving a hand like she was parting cigarette smoke. "What're you sellin'?"

It didn't take much, maybe a moment's read, the kind I'd practiced for years. My one party trick. I could sniff out a person's temperature and tailor my words to match. Call it instinct. Call it survival.

I gave her a lopsided grin, careful not to show too much teeth. Teeth made people nervous. Especially teeth sharpened for lies.

"Me? Sellin'? Bite your tongue." I laid on the charm like molasses on a hot day. "Salesmen are slick, cold-blooded types. The kind of thing you'd scrape off your shoe. I wouldn't sell water to a salesman on fire. No friend, I'm not a seller. I'm a giver."

She chewed her gum slowly and hard, like a cow working cud. Her eyes lit just a flicker.

"That a fact?" she said, suspicion flickering like a blown fuse. "Well, what're you givin,' then?"

I caught Bins watching from the side like a hawk pretending to be a pigeon. I gave her a wink and reached for one of the Bibles, dusting it off like it was a prized antique instead of a trunk-find wrapped in pleather.

"Books," I said, turning the cover to catch the light.

Her face twisted like I'd handed her a dead fish. "Oh," she said. "Thought it was somethin' good."

"They're better than good," I said, quick to pivot. "Finely made. Bound with care. Let me ask you somethin': you know your way around a kitchen?"

"I do," she snapped, chest puffing up like a marshmallow ready to pop.

"Then you know the magic that happens when you cook with love. Making a book's the same. You knead dough, fry chicken, bake up a cobbler, you put your heart in your hands and your hands in the work. Same with this book. Someone stitched this together with love. You can feel it."

She squinted, eyes fighting the sunlight or just her own doubt. "Looks expensive."

Three Days In Hell

"Only in soul," I said. "To you? Free as air. It'll feed you longer than a freezer full of casseroles."

She snapped her gum again. Loud. "Maybe. But I don't read much."

"That's where you're wrong," I said, switching gears fast. "Most people see a big book and think 'school.' Homework. Headaches. But that ain't this. This isn't a chore; it's a feast. You don't gulp it. You savor it. Let it drip slow, roll around your tongue, like the first bite of something sweet you never knew you were craving."

Whether she understood or not didn't matter. The sale was in the show. You dressed the pitch up nice, made it shine, made 'em feel like they were the ones doing you a favor.

"You sure make it sound tempting," she said, catching her breath.

"No, ma'am," I said smoothly. "Temptation is for the slick devils in seersucker suits. Me? I'm just the delivery boy. The goods speak for themselves."

She worked her jaw, chewed the idea like her gum, and then her face cracked open into a grin. Yellow teeth, crooked and tired, peeked through like old tombstones.

"Alright, you got yourself a deal," she said, offering a hand like a slab of ham. "I'll take one."

I handed her the Bible, slow and reverent, brushing the last speck of dust from the cover like it was a relic. I let my hand linger on hers just long enough for the trust to settle. In this game, remorse came fast. You had to make 'em feel like they'd been touched by something bigger, not duped by a smooth talker.

"Thank you kindly, Ms…?"

"Appleton," she said. "Delores Appleton."

"That's a lovely name," I said, letting the flattery drop smooth and casual. "You wouldn't happen to be related to the Kingsbury Appletons, would you? Finest bakers in all Calamet County."

Delores lit up. She didn't know the name, of course. Or the county. Both were as fake as a three-dollar bill but being tied to something warm and golden made people feel like they belonged somewhere better. That was the trick. Identity was a loose thread, and with a little tug, most folks unraveled just fine.

"I don't believe so," she said, brushing a hand through her brittle hair. "But I sure know my way around a pie crust."

"Of that, I've no doubt, Ms. Appleton." I dialed up the grin a notch.

"The name's Delores," she giggled, trying to sound shy but leaning into the attention like a moth on a porch light.

"Delores, then. And may I ask you a quick question, Delores?"

"Okay."

"If you're not from Calamet, where do your feet call home?"

Her mouth cracked open again in a wide smile, all gums and neglected enamel. "Why, right here."

"I knew it," I said, clapping my hands softly. "I know good people when I see 'em. Let me guess, you must live in that big house on the hill?"

She laughed loud enough to draw a look or two. "Me? Oh, heck no. I live in Yellow Rose."

"Yellow Rose?" I echoed, cocking an eyebrow.

That was Bins' cue. He leaned in just enough to be heard, breath smelling like the ghost of lunch and cheaper beer. "The trailer parks," he muttered.

"How wonderful," I said, turning back with the same honey tone. "Well, do let your neighbors know about our little chat. Send 'em our way if they get curious about your new treasure."

She nodded, eyes bright with pride she didn't own five minutes ago.

"Oh, Delores?" I called after her, hand raised. "One more thing. You wouldn't, by chance, be entering one of the contests today?"

Her face flushed from pink to crimson. I thought for a second she might keel over. "The chili eating contest," she admitted. "I can down ten bowls in ten minutes. It's kind of my thing."

"Well now," I said, leaning in like we were co-conspirators, "I know where to put my money if there's a bookie around."

She waved a hand, flattered but dismissive. "I hardly win anything. It's just good fun."
I nodded to the Bible tucked under her arm. "Looks to me like you already won."

That grin again, the same one, and something about it crawled under my skin. Gave me a shiver I couldn't shake. The kind of chill that doesn't come from cold, but from something deeper. Something off.

Delores waddled off into the crowd, her body folding into the flow of the fair like a drop of oil in a greasy stew.

"Okay, now that was slick," Bins said, sparking a cigarette with his crooked Zippo. He watched her go, then turned to me, admiration laced with unease. He handed me the cigarette, lit another for himself. "I saw what you did there. Damn, man. I've known some smooth talkers, some real grifters. But you –" he shook his head. "You're the goddamn whisperer."

I took a drag and let the smoke curl out slow.

"How'd you know what to say?" he asked.

It was too hot for a full sermon. Too hot to explain that it's not about words. Not really. You could have all the lines, all the angles, all the silver in your tongue, but if you couldn't read the room, if you couldn't smell the hunger in someone, you were just noise.

I scanned the crowd. Laughter, sweat, the smell of fry oil and sugar. A whole sea of marks. All of them wanting something, even if they didn't know it yet.

"Simple rule in this business," I said. "Don't give anything to anyone who doesn't already want it."

"Well, how do you know they want it in the first place?"

Bins was as persistent as a dog under the dinner table. The kind of guy who pressed his nose to the bakery window and drooled, not just for cake but for the knowledge of how it was made.

"Everyone wants it," I said. "They just don't know it yet. Doesn't matter what it is – Bibles, drapes, fungus cream, miracle polish. The trick is sniffing out the trigger. Find the itch, offer the scratch. You hit that nerve, say the right words, and squeeze."

I looked at him. "But that comes with time. A mountain of practice and a graveyard of failure."

"Yeah, but –"

"Watch and learn, Bins," I said, shutting the conversation down with a flick of my wrist. "Watch and learn."

Three Days In Hell

And I did what I always did best: I worked the crowd like a surgeon with a scalpel. Every pack of wanderers was a herd of sheep waiting for the wolf. I didn't need them all. Just one or two from each group. Pick off the weak, the weary, the curious.

The first was a rake-thin scarecrow of a man, barely filling out his oversized muscle tee. He had the kind of patchy, almost-mustache you get when puberty taps you on the shoulder but doesn't stick around to finish the job. Balding early, poor bastard. He trailed behind a woman a foot taller and a hundred pounds heavier; could have been his girlfriend, wife, maybe mother, hard to tell. A guy used to taking orders, not giving them.

He was an easy mark. I fed him a line about conviction. About standing up to the invisible weight crushing the spirit. He grabbed the Bible before I even offered it. Hook, line, and the most important information, address – Bins took it down in his notebook.

Next was Esmerelda. Hispanic, late forties maybe, swallowed by her own family. You could spot the pecking order a mile away. She wasn't the queen hen. Her sisters or cousins were, giggling and chirping like parakeets on uppers, clawing for attention in a language that spilled over itself like a waterfall.

I waited for the band to start playing, then called her over, gently, with a crooked smile and my shaky high-school Spanish. She came, like a moth half-expecting the flame to be kinder this time.

Her clothes looked like they came from a tablecloth clearance bin. She had a mole on her cheek that sprouted wiry hairs, and eyes that flinched when you looked at them too long. Perfect.

I didn't say much. Just opened the Bible slowly, like it was a sacred relic. Let her hold it. That's all she needed. Some people were scared by the weight of it. Others, people like Esmerelda, felt it anchor them. Her fingers curled around the spine like a hawk gripping prey. When she walked back to her family, there was a sway in her hips that hadn't been there before. A little victory tucked under her arm.

Another name. Another address.

Then came Randall Foster.

Randall was the kind of cocky small-town roach who thought the world was his ashtray. Early twenties, face still cratered with acne scars. Walked like he owned the street. Chewed tobacco like it made him dangerous and spat like he wanted to offend God Himself.

He had the wallet chain, the shaved head, the attitude. Probably hadn't left the county since birth, and yet he looked at strangers like they were trespassing on *his* dirt.

I didn't go to him. You never chase a dog that bites. You let it sniff around, circle, try to mark its territory. And when it's close enough, you feed it just the right kind of poison.

After watching me hand out the seventh Bible, Randall strutted over, boots heavy, like he wanted the ground to remember him.

"What the hell you got in those things, marijuana?" he asked, grinning, brown spit trailing down his chin like molasses.

"Marijuana?" I said, quick with the wink. "Hell, I wish. I could use a bowl or two to get through this heat. You got some?"

That stopped him. You could see the gears grinding behind his eyes. He wasn't ready for a counterpunch. Took him a few seconds to recover.

"You a cop?" he asked. "You *gotta* tell me if you are."

I didn't tell him that was a myth. Cops lie for a living. But with Randall, truth wasn't the weapon of choice. Ego was.

"Do I look like a cop?" I gestured to the table, the stack of Bibles in the sun like bricks of salvation.

He leaned back, narrowed his eyes. "Wouldn't be the first pig thumping a Bible. Same difference far as I'm concerned."

"I get it," I said. "I got my own gripes with the badge crowd. And just so you know, just 'cause I *got* Bibles don't mean I *thump* 'em."

"That so?" He spat again, just shy of my shoes. "And what's the difference?"

"I embrace vice," I said. "I don't pretend to erase it."

Randall chewed that over with his tobacco, eyes darting between the book and my face. He didn't trust me. That was good. Trust was dangerous. What I needed was curiosity.

And he was damn curious.

"I have my own issues with the boys in blue," I said. "And for the record, just because I *got* them doesn't mean I *thump* them."

"So, what're you supposed to do with these things, then? Swat flies?"

I let out a well-practiced chuckle. "That'd be like taking a flamethrower to an ant." I flipped open the Bible, letting the pages flutter like confetti. "You run out of toilet paper, you've got a thousand sheets at your disposal. Here, give it a feel."

I tossed him the book, and Randall scrambled to catch it. It landed heavy in his hands. He looked down at it, then up at me, wearing the kind of crooked grin you'd expect from a kid who just found something dead in the woods.

"Heavy as fuck," he said. "But this paper'd shred your asshole to ribbons. How's anybody read this thing?"

"Insomnia," I said. "Crack a passage, lights out guaranteed."

He smirked. "I wasn't much for Scripture anyhow."

I leaned in, as if telling a secret. "Who is? Am I right?"

"So, why you trying to pawn 'em off on everyone?"

"Christ had his cross," I said with a shrug. "I got my boss." Then I turned up the weary act, my voice dropping into that slow burn of a man who's been pushed around one too many times. "Between us? I don't move inventory, I don't get paid. It's like commission, but with freebies."

I plucked the book from his hands before he could argue. "Truth is, I'm sick of pushing something nobody wants. And let's be honest. This book? This ain't for folks like you and me. It's for people behind big fences in big houses."

That hit him.

Randall straightened up, chest puffed. "Whatcha mean by that?"

Bingo.

I raised my voice a notch, putting a little vinegar on it. "You said it yourself; you're not much for Scripture. And I'm wasting the time of good folks like you just so some pencil-neck in the office can push me around with a paycheck!"

"Take it easy, man. No need to get riled."

"I *am* riled!" I snapped, adding a bit of theatrical heat. "It just makes me mad as hell."

Randall looked off to the side, spit again. "Well... you said I didn't have to read it, right? Said I could use it for other stuff?"

"That's true," I said, calming my tone. "You do what you want with it, long as I get your name and address. I mean, it's not like my office is checking in. No Bible quizzes. But really, why would you want it anyway? Seems like more of a nuisance than anything else."

Randall shifted on his boots, kicked a patch of dry dirt. "Now see, I don't like someone telling me what I can and can't have. That sort of thing puts me off."

"Even if they're doing you a favor?"

"Mister, that's what the government always says, and I don't like *them* much either."

I threw up my hands. "Well, paint my ass red and call me a baboon. You're dead right. My bad. I didn't mean it how it sounded."

"How's it *supposed* to sound?"

"I'm just saying, you're smart enough to know what you want, and I let my beef with my boss get the better of me. That's on me."

"That's all right. We've all had those types of bosses."

"You know something? Use it however you want. Start a fire, roll a joint, wrap a sandwich. I don't care."

"I *can* read, you know. Can write my own name, too. I'm not some idiot."

"Exactly. And only an idiot tries to give a man something he doesn't want. And believe me –"

I paused, waiting for him to speak..

"Randall. Randall Foster."

"–believe me, Randall Foster, I'm no idiot either. I'd be one if I didn't give *you* a copy, no strings attached."

He jabbed a finger at the box. "One of the new ones. I ain't taking your floor tester."

I grinned, sweat slipping down my back. "Randall, if there are any flies on you, they're payin' rent."

I popped open the box and removed the top layer, pulling from the clean stack buried deep, just so he could see I wasn't playing favorites.

He took it with more confidence this time, let the weight settle in his hands. He flipped through the thin pages, squinting at the print. You could tell the words were strangers to him, but damned if he didn't put on a show, nodding like a scholar, pausing as if the truth had just spoken to him personally.

"That's what I'm talkin' about," he muttered.

Then he shut the book with a snap. "All right, Thumper. And this is really free? No fine print gonna bite me later?"

"Free as the sweat on your brow and the dust in your boots."

He eyed me, then nodded. "All right. Where do I sign?"

I handed him the clipboard and pen. He gripped it like it was his first time and scrawled his name with the determination of a man who wanted to prove something, maybe even to himself.

"Enjoy the Bible," I said. "And enjoy the festival."

That was a win. But in this game, wins were rare birds. The losses, well, they circled in flocks.

For every Delores, Esmerelda, or Randall, there were half a dozen that didn't bite. Some snarled outright, all teeth and bile. Others just gave you that cold hard look unmoved by charm or scripture or even the promise of something for nothing.

You learned to spot 'em. They wore their pain like old boots: broken in and mean. Hardened by too many losses, too many leeches with sweet words and long pockets. You could see it in their eyes: a glint of pure, undiluted malevolence. The kind that wasn't born but *made* – one bitter cut at a time.

And if you weren't careful?

They'd carve a little piece out of *you*, too.

A squat, round tree-hugger with a tangled beard and bug-eyed sunglasses watched me from across the street. He stood with three other activists, all of them chanting for the masses to ditch meat in favor of plant-based chili. His T-shirt screamed *GRASS FED HUMAN*, as if daring carnivores to make eye contact.

Problem was, he didn't look like a man fueled by kale. His jowls sagged over his collar, and his forearms looked like they'd been stuffed with pork shoulder. Still, he stood arms-crossed, a meatless martyr amid the smell of sizzling beef and pork. When I looked back at him, he didn't blink; he just stared, challenging me to say something.

I gave him the nod.

He stormed across the street like a barrel on legs and opened fire before his sandals even touched my side of the pavement. Ranted about how I was propping up a religion that had blood on its hands, both human and animal. I didn't engage. There's no reasoning with people like that. Reason's already left the building.

He went for the table, probably aiming to flip it, but Bins intercepted him mid-lunge, catching the man around the middle. He flailed like a toddler having a tantrum, legs kicking, beard bouncing.

Then his friends arrived.

A woman with more metal on her face than a junkyard radiator jabbed a finger at me and started yelling about "institutional lies" and "dead cow bindings." I tried to tell her the covers were faux leather. That just triggered a deeper rant about "the illusion of ethics." Then, as if proving a point only she understood, she grabbed a book and stomped it into the pavement with thick-soled combat boots. The irony of animal-hide footwear on a vegan crusader wasn't lost on me, but it also wasn't worth catching a fist from a ninety-pound banshee.

They circled a bit longer, frothing, poking, screaming. But when I didn't bite, didn't give them what they wanted – *conflict* – they moved on. Eventually. Pin Face left behind a ruined Bible, pages shredded and stained.

Bins walked over, cigarette bouncing between his lips. He glanced down at the wreckage.

"Thanks for the help," I muttered, crouching to assess the damage. No use. The book was done for. I tossed it aside like a lost wallet.

"I'd rather deal with bikers than that crowd," he said. "They're a better class of people."

I scanned what was left of my supply. More than half gone. Between do-gooders, oddballs, and pure destruction, it was dwindling fast. I kept one eye on the crowd now, extra wary of paint cans or more theatrics in the name of "civil disobedience."

"What is *wrong* with this town?" I muttered.

Bins lit another cigarette and offered me one. I took it.

"What do you mean?"

"I mean everyone here either needs a shrink, a prescription, or a padded cell." I paused. "Or all three."

Three Days In Hell

Something moved in my periphery, a flicker fast enough to warn me. I sidestepped just before it hit.

A soda cup, half full, exploded at my feet. Sticky brown spray painted my pant legs and shoes.

I spun toward the crowd, scanning faces, but there were too many. Too much movement. Too many people doing their best to look innocent.

"It's hell, man," Bins said with a smirk, exhaling smoke. "Ain't it great?"

Then she came.

A woman slithered through the street with the casual menace of a jungle cat. Her arms swayed high above her head, making her crop top ride up just enough to flash the under-curve of her breasts and the glittering stud in her navel. She was moving to music only she could hear – drunk, high, or floating somewhere between both.

Her skirt was barely linen and barely legal, clinging to hips that swayed like bait. Her hair was black, streaked with purple and long enough to curtain her sharp, angled face. High cheekbones, a fox's nose, and almond eyes that flashed red when the light hit them just wrong.

She didn't walk. She *hunted*.

And if I believed in past lives, I'd bet everything she once had wings and lured men into the sea.

Viviana wasn't like the others.

She didn't just wander by and happen to notice our slapped-together stand shoved between slicker, more polished kiosks. No, Viviana *made for us*. Like a child who'd heard a juicy rumor and wanted to see if it was true. There was intent in every step.

She disarmed me before I could speak, lifting one of the Bibles by its spine and fanning herself lazily with its pages.

"A man in a suit. In *Helman*," she said, her accent strange, unplaceable. She sniffed theatrically. "And you *reek* like one."

"Oh?" I asked, amused despite myself. "And what exactly do outsiders smell like?"

"Sterile," she said with a curled lip. "You stink of antiseptic."

I opened my mouth to respond, but she pressed a finger to my lips. "Why don't you come with me?" she said in less of a question and more a command. "We'll drink beer. Listen to music. Make love. All day. All night."

Out of the corner of my eye, I saw Amelia. She was near the competition tent, locked in a heated argument with JB. Her hand jabbed the air, eyebrows like daggers. JB looked ready to explode. I couldn't hear them, but the body language was all fire. Everyone around gave them a wide berth.

Viviana caught my glance and turned my face back toward her, then kissed me: wet, fast, unapologetic.

"Shall we go?" she said.

"As tempting as that is, I've got work."

She followed my gaze toward Amelia, then gave me a look like a mother scolding a distracted child. "Is *her* name work? Unusual name for a woman."

"It's work," I said, flatly.

"Selling books?"

"Giving them away."

"Giving books away is a *job*?" she asked skeptically.

"All the glamor is mine. I wake up every day feeling blessed."

"I'd like to know more. That's why I'm here," she said. "Wondering what it would take for you to put your hands on my hips and pull me close. Like this."

Her mouth opened. Her tongue flicked past mine and vanished just as quickly. Her eyes stayed locked on mine.

It was a *good* kiss, the kind that starts in your gut and makes promises your brain tries to ignore. Her hands were all over me, confident and practiced. I finally caught her wrists and held them still.

I looked again at Amelia. The sun caught her white skirt just right. She looked unbothered by the heat keeping cool, composed, and in complete contrast to the human inferno gripping my collar. There were women who were *gorgeous*, and then there were women whose beauty drew you back for second, third, fourth looks. Viviana was the former. Amelia was the latter.

Viviana didn't care about subtlety. She wielded her sexuality like a crowbar, which was effective, brutal, and meant to *bend*. She didn't worry about the result. The reaction was all that mattered.

"What's wrong?" she asked, pouting. "You don't like girls?"

I picked up a Bible and gently placed it in the hand that had undone two of my buttons. "You're no girl," I said. "Girls don't kiss like that. You're all woman. But work comes before pleasure."

She looked at the Bible, shrugged, and let it drop onto the table with a soft *thud*.

"It's too hot for books," she said. "Come drink with me, and I'll tell you what I can do – what *only* I can do."

I turned to find Bins; he was gone, of course. That man had the timing of a bad magician.

"It's a little early for me," I said, scrambling for an exit. Viviana's tactic was as old as desire: keep talking until resistance cracks and all that's left is surrender.

And honestly? She almost had me.

I considered it. One hour, one day, a week ensconced in whatever Viviana promised. It would've been easy. It would've been *fun*. And if this day was any indication, I wasn't offloading these books anytime soon.

But Amelia was still there. And not just in my thoughts. She was *watching*. Not with jealousy. With interest. With something like *amusement*. There was a smirk playing on her lips, like this was all a game she already knew the rules to.

Viviana, sensing my stall, tilted her head and offered one last seductive sigh.

"I'm going to drink," she said. "Probably too much. You should come. But you won't. I may be a woman, but *you* are not a man."

She stared deep enough that I felt it in my gut. Then she smiled, turned, and walked into the sunlight. Her sheer dress caught the light. No panty lines. No modesty. She left nothing to the imagination.

That's when Bins returned, holding a beer, watching Viviana's hips melt into the crowd.

"Why is it," I said, "that every time I actually *need* you, you vanish?"

"Seems like you were handling that just fine. So, how are we looking here?"

"Ugly."

"I told you Helman was going to be a tough sell."

"Yeah, you and everyone else I talk to."

"Sucks to be you then."

"Yeah. Sucks to be me."

I took advantage of the pause to watch Amelia. She was sitting alone at a table near the competition tent. Helman had rolled off, wherever it is Helman rolls off to. For a guy in a wheelchair, he moved like a ghost.

An old man with an apron brought her a drink on a tray, with a side bucket of ice cubes. A couple of bystanders watched, envious, as she dipped her hand in and popped ice into her mouth like they were hush puppies.

"Shit," Bins muttered. "Don't mean to rain on your parade, but you got trouble coming."

He elbowed me and nodded to the left. I turned and saw them.

Two men in their late twenties swaggered our way. Cartel. Their clothes were loud, their posture louder. The tall one had slick, greasy hair and the build of a starved rooster. A lazy eye made him look slow, but the twin teardrop tattoos at the corners of his eyes told another story. The sun caught his silver grill when he smirked, he revealed more steel than teeth.

The shorter guy walked a pace ahead. Baby face. Round belly. A sick paisley shirt in gray and blue satin, buttoned over his gut. His snakeskin boots looked like they had a rap sheet of their own.

"*Él Mochomo's* boys," Bins muttered. "Cartel."

They stopped in front of the table. The Little Guy sized us both up, then decided I was the one to talk to.

"What are you doing, ese?"

"Nothing," I said. "Just minding my business."

He picked up a Bible with two fingers and flipped it like it offended him. Then tossed it to his buddy, who caught it and sneered.

"This don't look like nothing," Silver Teeth said. "This looks like a whole lot of *something*."

"Please," I said, gesturing to the grime on his hands. "Try not to ruin it."

He nodded, then casually threw it into the street. It landed hard, then got run over by a pair of pickup trucks.

"I got permission to be here," I said. "From Helman."

"Oh, from Helman," the Little Guy said. "Where is it? I don't see no permission slip. You see any permission slip, Eduardo?"

Silver Teeth bared his metal smile. "Nope."

"Where's your money, *cabrón*?" the Little Guy asked.

"What?"

"Your money, *ese*. You sell, they buy. You pay."

"I'm not selling anything."

"No?" he said, glancing at his partner. "Then how you gonna pay us? Everyone pays. *Tamales, churros, cervezas*... Everyone. You don't sell books? Fine. Still gotta pay."

He nodded, and Silver Teeth pulled back his shirt, revealing the butt of a handgun tucked in his waistband. It wasn't a bluff. These guys didn't bluff. They just skipped to the consequences.

"I talked to Helman this morning," I repeated. "He said we could set up here. Ask him."

"You giving us orders, gringo? You calling shots now?"

My heart kicked into overdrive. "What? No. That's not what I meant –"

They laughed. Sudden, loud, barking laughter.

"Relax, man," the Little Guy said. "Life's too short, eh? Give us what you got now. Rest after the Festival."

"I told you. I don't have money."

Three Days In Hell

He leaned in, squinting. "You're not kidding. You really *don't*. That's bad. That's *very* bad."

Silver Teeth leaned in, whispered something. The Little Guy pulled his gun and jammed it under my chin.

"Who you work for, ese? Police? *Federale*? Speak up!"

His breath was a toxic cocktail of cheap tequila and spoiled meat.

"Hank Twohy," I said.

"Hank *what*? Who's he with? Aryans? Barbarians?"

I kept eye contact, hoping he wouldn't pull the trigger.

"Fellowship Ministries."

He blinked. "Who the fuck is that?"

Bins jumped in. If he didn't have bad timing, he'd have no timing.

"Fellas! This isn't what you think. This guy's legit. Swear."

Silver Teeth moved fast. Brass knuckles, one punch and Bins crumpled. Then he loomed over him, ready to end it.

"Hey! Hey! Hey!" I yelled, desperate. "I'm just giving out Bibles. That's it. No sales, no profit, no turf war. Just the Word of God."

The Little Guy squinted. "*Offerings*? You talking code? What's that? Speed? Molly?"

"I swear – just books. Just God's word."

Silver Teeth looked to the Little Guy for the go-ahead. I could see it in his eyes – he *wanted* it. He *loved* this part.

"*La palabra de Dios*?" the Little Guy said, mocking me. "There's only one word that matters here, *gringo*."

He nodded. Silver Teeth grinned.

I saw Bins close his eyes. Maybe he was praying. I wasn't. All I saw was Luanne, smirking at the new guy she flirted with the day I walked out.

Not exactly what I wanted to flash before I died.

But before the trigger pulled, a voice cracked through the air:

"*¡Qué pedo aquí? Alejate, cabrón!*"

Amelia.

They froze.

Amelia marched over like she owned the street. The crowd parted instinctively. Little Guy and Silver Teeth shared a look. It was pure *concern*.

"Nothing," the Little Guy said quickly. "Just a couple pendejos. They owe us money."

"*Money?*" she said, ice in her voice. "For what?"

"He's here. He pays to be here."

Amelia stared them down. "This is a *Festival*, cabrón."

The Little Guy shrugged. "So what? No one cares."

"I *care*," she said. And that was all it took.

Something changed in him. A tremor. He lowered the weapon. "Okay, okay."

He looked at Silver Teeth. "*Escuchaste a La Negra, capullo. Déjalo.*"

Silver Teeth spit on Bins as he walked past. I helped him up, got him seated against the car.

The bystanders slowly drifted back to their food and drinks like nothing had happened.

But now they knew.

Amelia wasn't just beautiful.

She was dangerous.

Amelia turned to me, searching for any visible wounds. "You alright?" she asked me.

"I think I have to change my pants."

At first, Amelia looked confused but then understood my sarcasm. "It's good to show humor," she said. "True men shouldn't get rattled."

I watched the duo disappear into the crowd. "They friends of yours?"

"My brother's. I've known them since we were kids."

"*La Negra*," I said. "What's that?"

"My hair," she said. "My nickname since I was a little girl."

Bins muttered something about getting cleaned up. Amelia smiled brightly as if the past ten minutes hadn't happened. "A beautiful day and a beautiful Festival."

"Where's your husband?" I asked, trying to judge her reaction.

And just as quickly as it had appeared, her smile disappeared for a second before it reappeared. "You know."

"I do now," I said. "You never said anything last night."

"Would it have mattered?"

"It might have."

She laughed. "No, I don't think it would have. You are a person familiar with other men's women, I think."

"What makes you say that?"

"A woman knows. We sense these things. We see a look. Maybe a gesture. It is not like you have the nerves of a priest, and even they are not unmalleable.

"I should be insulted."

"It's not meant to be an insult. Just an observation. An observation and an understanding. You don't lead your life that way."

"And how do I lead my life?"

"By instinct. Feeling. Or am I wrong?"

She wasn't, and when she saw I didn't have a rebuttal, she smiled again, and I felt any resolve in me slowly crumble. I tried to regain my position. "You never answered the question," I said. "Why didn't you tell me about Helman?"

Her face got pouty. "I don't want to talk about him."

"I do." I reached out and touched her arm. Her skin was soft and warm, and I wanted to keep my fingers where they were, but she shrugged them off. "I saw him this morning. At the house. Your house."

If this news surprised her, she didn't show it. She kept looking at something in the distance. "What did he tell you?" she asked stiffly.

"Nothing," I lied. "Just asked what my business was in Hellman."

A skeptical gleam flickered in her eyes; the uncertainty was too quick to conceal. They held me with doubt but gradually softened in a temporary acceptance.

"Come," she said, with the kind of voice that didn't ask.

She led me through the dust and heat to a canvas tent that looked like it had seen better wars. Inside, a long table stretched like a firing line, each station armed not with bullets but bowls of hellfire. They called it the *Fire in the Hole Challenge* – the main event, the siren call that dragged the hopeful, the broken, and the plain stupid into the dead heart of Helman.

On paper, it was a pepper-eating contest. In practice, it was masochism in a hundred-degree oven, a crucible for pain-junkies who confused torment with glory. Still, there was a twisted kind of nobility to it, like outlaw gunslingers facing down in the street, their weapons replaced by crimson pods that burned like damnation. You didn't win by drawing first. You won by not flinching when hell took your tongue.

The table was set for six, each place a throne of agony. Bowls brimming with chilis in every size and hue, each tagged with a placard that listed its SHU, Scoville Heat Units, for those too naive to know that oral pain could be measured. This wasn't about stuffing jalapeños in your face like a frat boy on a dare. This was professional-grade sadism. *Triple-A* stuff. Big league misery.

Five competitors were already there, sweating through their shirts, skin toughened by sun and sin. Faces you wouldn't trust in a dark alley, or a bright one. I spotted Pete Junkersfield, a clown around here, or at least, a cautionary tale, depending on who was telling it. He saw me, grinned like a cracked mirror, and clapped me on the back.

"Didn't think I'd see you here," he said, his voice greasy with charm. "Ten grand'll do strange things to a man. Just remember, there's no shame in folding before the Reaper comes knocking."

The other two weren't men at all, at least not by the kind of dainty standards you'd find in polite company. They were women in the biological sense, sure, but something about them screamed harder, meaner. Carved from the same granite as the others only sharper around the eyes. They weren't here to flirt. They were here to conquer.

"This is only for the *mas macho*," Amelia whispered, steering me away from Pete like a dealer shielding a mark from a rival. She tapped my chest with two fingers, light but deliberate. "This kind. Right here. So many tough guys think they've got it. Most don't make it past the third bowl. Even those two she-wolves got bigger stones than most of the men lining up for this gauntlet."

The bowls read like a fiery *Book of Revelations*.

The first peppers were *Serranos*. Child's play. 23,000 SHUs and worth fifty bucks. Just enough to wake you up and let you know you were in the wrong place.

The second batch was a bit more worrisome. Thai chilis. 100,000 SHUs of pure, creeping madness. Two hundred dollars to bite into a heat so sly it slid behind your teeth and stabbed from within.

The third was just a no-no. *Habaneros*. Neon-orange death blossoms worth $750 a bowl. 350,000 SHUs of citrus-scented cruelty. These weren't peppers; they were flare guns that went off in your skull.

Fourth? *Ghost chilis*. Wrinkled red nightmares at a million SHUs. A thousand bucks for the chance to meet your ancestors in a hallucination while your organs debated mutiny. The kind of pain that stripped away your soul, then made you watch as it burned.

Then came the *Carolina Reaper*. The Fifth Horseman of the spice Apocalypse. Two million SHUs and three grand that came with a side of existential despair. It looked like something that crawled out of the underworld and decided to stay. One bite and your teeth remembered every sin you'd ever committed.

But the final selection wasn't a pepper. It was prophecy. *Pepper X*. Three million, one-hundred thousand SHUs. Five grand to stare God in the face and not blink. Rumors said it was made in a lab, or a hellmouth. Even the placard seemed ashamed to announce it. They said it could melt gloves. That it had been used in war crimes. That it wasn't a pepper so much as a final judgment.

I found out later that no one ever ate it all. Not clean through. Not standing. But if you did, if you made it to the end with lips cracked, tears running, stomach seizing, you'd walk away ten grand richer. Or you'd be carried out on a stretcher, one step closer to becoming a local legend or a footnote in a cautionary tale nobody would tell with a straight face.

I looked at the table. I looked at the people. Then I looked at Amelia, whose eyes glittered like glass in the sun.

"Still want in?" she asked, voice low.

I didn't answer. I just stared at the bowls and waited for the devil to pull out a chair.

"Ten thousand? For that kind of pain? That's a sucker bet," I said.

Amelia didn't flinch. She just looked at me like I'd missed the point entirely. "That's more money than some people make in a year around here."

"Yeah? You know what that kind of heat does to your insides?"

She turned her gaze toward the five poor bastards lining up; they were five meat sacks with sweaty, cracked lips, and nerves jangling under sunburned skin.

"Five people seem to think it's worth it," she said. "People are driven by different things. Some want money. Some chase fame."

"*Fame?* For this?" I asked, raising an eyebrow.

"How could there not be? You're doing something most people wouldn't touch with a ten-foot pole. Do it well, and you're remembered. In a town like this, that's as close as anyone gets to immortality."

I gave a nod, slow and dry.

"Immortality," I echoed.

She turned those dark eyes on me, and it felt like a hand slipping inside my chest and taking hold of something tender.

"Everyone wants something, Bobby Santos. Even you. Question is, what are you willing to do to get it?"

"And what is it you think I want?"

She smiled the way a wolf does when the lamb finally sits still.

"You want out of this town. I can make that happen. Or I can make it worth your while to stay. There are so many… rich possibilities. And they're all yours. If…"

"If what?"

"If you win."

I gave her a smirk and shook my head.

"I don't know what they're putting in the water around here, but it's making people crazy."

Amelia stepped closer, voice a velvet knife.

"And yet… you haven't left. You say you've got a debt to pay. But what's so important it's keeping you stuck in this sunburned graveyard, handing out books nobody asked for? You got someone waiting back home? A girl? A job? Both? Neither? None of that sounds like a reason to stay."

"Why not?"

"Because you have both – right here."

"I'm not interested in staying here selling Bibles."

"*Giving* them away," she said with a teasing smirk.

She didn't have to lean in, didn't have to say another word. It was already happening – the pull. That look, that body, that way she *moved* like gravity was hers to command. There's a specific madness that strikes a man when a woman that dangerous looks at him like she's already decided how it ends. It makes you stupid. It makes you reckless. It makes you jump at a chasm that's got *final* written all over the bottom.

She turned her head, and her black hair flowed like ink in water, hypnotic and slow. I felt the pull in my gut again, sharp and stupid. The kind that leads to burned bridges, bad choices, and sometimes, if you're lucky, a good story.

"Enter the contest," she said, "and win. Beat the rest, you don't even have to finish the whole line. Do that, and I'll give you whatever it is you want most."

"Anything?"

She nodded once, smooth and deadly.

"Is that a fair deal?"

I narrowed my eyes.

"Then I want answers. And I want the *truth*."

"Of course."

"You might not like the questions."

She smiled again, that smile that always made me feel like I was three steps behind in a game I didn't know I was playing.

"Which one is that?" she asked. "Why I slept with you when I had a husband... or why he asked *you* to kill me?"

Just like that, the floor dropped out. The element of surprise I was nursing like a warm drink got yanked right out of my hand. She didn't even give me the chance to respond. She just turned and led me forward, like a showgirl escorting a condemned man to the center of the stage.

"Win the challenge, Bobby," she said. "Then we'll talk."

And there it was.

We hadn't known each other for a day, and already Amelia had dissected me, peeling back my layers like a manila folder full of dirty secrets. She cut through me with the kind of casual sadism reserved for surgeons who'd long since stopped caring about the oath they swore.

I should've walked away right then and there. Should've told her I wasn't interested in being anyone's hired trigger. It's not every day someone asks you to kill their wife. But Amelia's reaction to that little bombshell? It wasn't shock. Wasn't fear. It was amusement, pure and unfiltered. Her lips pursed like a kid learning how to burn ants with a magnifying glass. And I, apparently, was the next ant.

That was the danger. The kind I always found myself crawling back to. Not the bruised-and-battered damsels some men liked rescuing. No, I was a moth for married women with a taste for blood and chaos. It was the taboo, the thrill of running the razor's edge. I told myself I'd walk away when it got too hot. I always told myself that. But the problem with fire is, it doesn't warn you before it catches.

I glanced at the five competitors circling the table like starving goblins. Pacing, mumbling, running calculations in their heads. Trying to convince themselves that it wasn't madness, just another challenge. But you could see it in their eyes, the glaze of desperation. Some looked related. Maybe they were. Helman felt like the kind of town where the family tree was more like a noose – tight, twisted, and ready to snap. Even ol' Pete Junkersfield looked less human and more like some degenerate troll under a bridge, waiting for a reason to explode.

Jesus, this town.

I'd been through a dozen pit-stops across the southwest, but Helman? It was something else. The air felt cursed. The people wore their misery like it was a second skin. They moved like sleepwalkers, talked like parolees, lived like ghosts. And it wasn't hard to imagine myself among them, just another soul swallowed up by the dry rot. Amelia was right. There wasn't a damn thing waiting for me back home. Just Shank, and another errand designed to keep me in debt till my bones turned to dust.

I couldn't run. Not forever. Sooner or later that monkey was gonna wrap both hands around my throat.

"Do we have a deal?" Amelia asked.

There was urgency now, tightening in her voice like a snare. Her eyes locked onto mine, and when I tried to break the stare, her hand snapped up, fingers curling around my jaw, keeping me in place.

"Yes or no?"

I didn't answer with words.

I just turned and walked.

The competitors caught sight of me, and instantly I was the intruder. The outsider. They glared like I'd walked in wearing a badge or holding the deed to the place. I planted myself beside Junkersfield, who just chuckled and shook his head.

"I warned you," he said, grinning. "Hope you brought the good toilet paper. The stuff they got at the Indigo is like John Wayne: rough, tough, and don't take shit from nobody."

Before I could fire back, the tent shook with a voice that sounded like it belonged to a man three times the size of the one it came out of.

"*¡Buenas tardes!*" the emcee bellowed.

All eyes shifted to him.

He was gangly, rail-thin, and dressed like a snake-oil salesman who'd lost a bet with a vaudeville act. His coat barely hung on him, and his pants stopped short, revealing dirty, sockless ankles. But what he lacked in dignity, he made up for in charisma. The mustache was too thick. The teeth too white. The voice? Too loud by half. He spun around the tent like a preacher selling salvation out of a trunk.

"*Están borrachos, muchachos?*" he shouted, and the crowd roared back in slurred approval.

"The sun is hot, the ground is hot… but the chilis?" He grinned devilishly. "The chilis are *ho-hot-hot!*"

More whoops and whistles.

He basked in it. Swam in their noise like a prophet bathing in prophecy. His hand swept dramatically over the bowls of peppers like he was introducing the cast of *Dante's Inferno*.

"Fifteen seconds, muchachos. That's all. In the hand, in the mouth, in the belly. You wait thirty seconds. Then you move on. If there's more than one left at the end, guess what? We keep going."

He held up a *Habanero* like it was cursed gold, then flinched and fanned his fingers in mock agony. The crowd howled. He was the main event before the main event.

Then he made his rounds, nodding at familiar faces, smirking at the seasoned freaks. But when he got to me, his whole vibe shifted. Smile gone. Eyes sharp.

He counted on his fingers theatrically, then pointed right at me like I'd farted in church.

"*¿Quién es este? Un policía? Un sicario? Un profesor de matemáticas?*"

The crowd laughed harder.

Then he looked at me, dead serious. "Who are you?"

I straightened. My throat was dry, but the words came anyway.

"Bobby. Bobby Santos."

The emcee's face lit up like a lit fuse.

"*¡Bienvenidos, Bobby Santos! El Santo del Fuego!*"

The tent exploded in applause.

He ushered us to our seats. I was last, and as I sat, a server placed a single *Serrano* on a paper plate in front of me – green, innocent, and already smirking.

Pete leaned over, whispering like we were old pals at a funeral.

"I warned you," he said again, voice full of mirth. "This place ain't right. And it sure as hell ain't fair."

The emcee raised his arms and the crowd fell silent.

"You know the rules," he barked. "Eat the pepper, or you're *terminado*. If your mouth ain't clean, or your stomach ain't strong, guess what?"

He patted me on the back.

"Stay out of the chilis."

I waved him closer.

"How many people have finished this thing?" I asked.

He laughed like I told the world's worst joke.

"He wants to know who's *finished* the challenge!"

"*¡Pocos!*" the crowd thundered back.

The emcee grinned, shrugged.

"Not many. But hey, don't worry. No one thinks you'll make it past the *Habanero*."

"*Jalapeños* too low-brow for this festival?" I asked.

"*Cálmate, ese*," he said, grinning. "Don't shoot the messenger."

He pointed to a wiry man in the back corner scribbling names, taking money, handing out slips.

"That guy sets the odds. Takes the action."

"And what are my odds?"

He gave me a look full of mock sympathy. Then he clicked his tongue and smiled like a dealer handing over a busted hand.

"Far, *amigo*. Very far."

The emcee patted me on the back like a man sending another poor bastard to the gallows. "On my count! Three... two... one – ¡*Comer!*"

We each grabbed the chili by its stem and tore it free with our teeth.

Serranos were slick little bastards. At first bite, they played nice, crisp like a Bell pepper, with just a whisper of grassy warmth. But it was a lie. The moment the seeds hit your gums, the heat bloomed like a flare behind your eyes. Still, this was the easy part. A polite handshake before the slaughter. A gateway drug with just enough kick to fool the uninitiated.

The emcee moved down the line, inspecting mouths like a dentist with a stopwatch. He grinned when no one failed the inspection.

"One down, *cinco más!*" he shouted.

The crowd whooped. The servers moved like pit crew, slamming down the next round – small, fire-red Thai Bird chilis.

No rest. No water. No reprieve. Just forward momentum and pain.

"Three, two, one –¡*Comer!*"

I bit down, and the heat didn't build; it *hit*. The Thai chili was a sugar-coated switchblade. Sweet up front, then *slice*. Smaller than the *Serrano*, sure, but that only meant it was meaner. Hotter. Nastier. A mouthful of wasps.

My sinuses emptied like a dam breach. My eyes stung. My lips pulsed like fresh bruises. I chewed on, teeth grinding through fire, and my hand reached for the milk like it had a mind of its own, but I stopped myself just in time.

The crowd smelled hesitation. They pounced. A wall of jeers rained down, chanting my name in a singsong of mockery.

Three Days In Hell

"Saaaaaan-tos... Saaaaaan-tos..."

I didn't tap.

"Five seconds... and stop!"

We opened our mouths on cue, tongues out like whipped dogs. Everyone was red-faced, glazed in sweat, snot, and drool. Even the seasoned freaks were reeling. Junkersfield looked like he'd been steamed in a pressure cooker with his cheeks blotchy and eyes leaking. But we all held the line.

Then came the third round: Habaneros. Not just any, the Red Savinas. The nuclear option.

The second that devil touched my tongue, my entire body went to war. Citrus, smoke, and pure chemical hell. The inside of my mouth felt like a coal chute, and my gut clenched as hiccups broke through my diaphragm like depth charges. The chunks I was chewing turned into shrapnel. I tried to swallow and ended up inhaling some of it. The burn seared my throat like a drag off a lit flare.

And then Junkersfield cracked.

He let out a half-cough, half-retch, and painted the table in a violent explosion of pepper-colored puke. It was a Jackson Pollock of failure. He grabbed for the milk like it was holy water, chugging one glass, then another, and still couldn't put the fire out. The waitstaff moved with surgical efficiency, mopping up the technicolor mess and escorting Pete out like a disgraced general after a failed coup.

I finished chewing. Somehow. Tongue out. Teeth clenched. I didn't look at Pete as he stumbled past.

One down. Five of us left.

The emcee didn't even pause to mark the milestone. No breath. No mercy. He waved for the servers again, who dropped the next bomb on our plates:

Ghost Peppers.

I heard someone mutter, "*Chinga tu madre*," like he was cursing a demon before exorcising it. The woman to my right flinched, her hand shaking as she reached for the capsaicin grenade. She looked like she was preparing for a firing squad.

The *Ghost Pepper* didn't hit like the *Habanero*. It waited. Lulled. It started with a fake-out sweetness, like a candy-coated cyanide pill. Then the burn came slow and thick like molten tar flooding your mouth. The kind of heat that didn't spike so much as it *settled in,* expanding like a gas leak in a locked room.

But here's the truth: by that point, we were already cooked. Our tongues were ruined meat, our mouths smoldering ruins. A jellybean would've tasted like battery acid. Everything hurt the same.

I looked at the crowd.

Their faces blurred, fused together in one obscene, leering mass. Eyes gleamed with anticipation. Not joy, cruelty. These were not spectators. They were vultures. They didn't want to see who *won;* they wanted to see who *broke*.

Same kind of people who threw stones at witches or clapped when the switch got flipped on a man in the chair. Mob morality. Fluid ethics. They'd cheer for you one second, then roast you alive the next.

This wasn't about peppers anymore.

It was a bloodsport. A reckoning.

And I was still in it.

Through the stinging sweat, I scanned the crowd for Amelia, but all I saw were smudges, faces blurred by tears and heat. But one blur resolved itself. JB Helman sat calmly in his white hat and wheelchair, sipping from a glass filled with ice that *should've* melted hours ago in this sun-blasted town. He didn't wave or call out. Just gave me a single, crisp nod, like a man acknowledging a horse he'd bet on. Maybe he had. Hell, maybe *everyone* had.

But Helman wasn't the biggest thing on my mind. Right now, it was the *Ghost Pepper*, this malformed, mean little devil with a skin like an infected wound. Pocked. Warped. As if nature had tried to kill it halfway through growing and it said, "Try harder." Some people called it the Devil's Tear. Fitting. It was angry, it was red, and it didn't forgive.

"*Tres... dos... uno!*"

I didn't think. I just bit. The whole damn thing.

Two chews in and my face lit up like someone had doused it in lighter fluid and tossed a match. There was *nowhere* in my mouth that didn't hurt. Not the tongue. Not the gums. Not even the *teeth*. It felt like the capsicum had chewed through the enamel and was now burning straight into the roots.

The obese woman next to me gagged and spit the pepper out, nearly knocking her milk over in the scramble. Her fat fingers clutched the glass like a lifeline and *poured* it over her mouth, letting it run down her chin like holy water. But when the milk didn't work fast enough, she grabbed *my* glass and drained it in three desperate gulps.

"*¡Terminado!*" the emcee belted, pointing like a judge at the gallows.

She fled, waddling toward the trash cans, mouth agape and eyes wild.

The tweaker beside her didn't fare much better. She hadn't even finished chewing when she rubbed her eyes, spreading the oil across her face. Her scream was high, sharp, and wounded like a rabbit in a snare. She bolted, clawing at her face, the pain blinding and all-consuming.

Two attendants hauled her away as she spit out curses between howls. They sat her down and dropped a wet towel over her eyes while she thrashed in the chair.

And just like that, three remained.

You think courage is getting up after being knocked down every day?

Try this.

Try enduring fire so intense that it melts the lining of your mouth, blisters your tongue, and hollows out your guts like a shotgun blast from the inside.

My whole face throbbed like I'd dipped it in boiling oil. Sweat poured off me in waves. My mouth was a warzone. My jaw clenched involuntarily, and I slammed my palm onto the table just to remind myself I could still move.

"¡*Abierto!* Open up!"

I sucked in air like a drowning man. The heat outside was nothing compared to the inferno in my mouth; it was practically refreshing. My tongue felt like raw meat on a grill.

The servers didn't wait.

They brought out the *Carolina Reapers* like holy relics that were wrinkled, red, and gnarled like the devil's own thumbs. The *Reaper* was a legend. It didn't just burn, it *punished.* It was a weapon. A trap. Sweetness at first, like a final kiss, then the blade in the back.

The crowd groaned.

They'd seen this before. Seen people survive the gauntlet only to be undone by this last trial. Most people didn't make it past the *Reaper*. It wasn't about endurance anymore; it was about breaking the soul.

I could feel my pulse in my teeth. My stomach churned like it was filled with lit charcoal. My shirt clung to me like plastic wrap, soaked through. I looked feral. Maybe I *was* feral.

The older guy beside me was halfway gone already. Eyes shut, snot streaming, forehead glued to the table. Maybe praying. Maybe dying.

A server handed me a towel, and I pressed it to my face like a baptism. Brief relief. Not enough.

The emcee fed on our pain like a parasite. He strutted up and down the stage, hands in the air, voice booming though I couldn't hear a damn word. My ears rang like someone had slapped the side of my skull with a frying pan. The world around me throbbed red.

We were falling apart.

And still, there was still one more pepper.

Before the next round could kick off, the old man lurched to his feet like a marionette with its strings snapped. He wobbled, nearly ate dirt, but one of the servers caught him before he faceplanted. He'd tapped out; bone dry, and with nothing left in the tank. Two others dragged him off, his boots carving desperate tracks in the dirt like a man being pulled from his own grave.

That left two of us.

My last rival looked fresh out of juvie; he was young, twitchy, trying to wear a mask of menace with those coal-black eyes. His tank top used to be white but now wore the color of crime. The neckline plunged low enough to reveal a pit bull inked onto his chest, teeth bared, like it was ready to leap off his skin. His gut let out a gurgle, a warning siren, and he tilted sideways, lifted a cheek, and let one rip. The smell was a chemical crime scene: sulfur crossed with sewage. Hit me hard. I gagged. Reflex. Couldn't help it.

He laughed, that high, sharp laugh of the damned, but even he yanked his shirt up over his nose. Guess he wasn't immune to his own brand of mustard gas.

"This is it, muchachos!" the emcee barked, stepping up like a carnie at the end of the world. "Fortune! Fame! Everything you ever dreamed of, right here on this damn table!"

The crowd howled like junkyard dogs, thirsty for blood.

"Who will it be?" he roared. "The Saint or the Dog?"

"Dog! Dog! Dog!" they chanted, a low, rabid rhythm. It pumped up my opponent, gave him a shaky edge, even though he leaned to one side like his guts were trying to crawl out of him. In the back, the bookie scratched new odds onto a grease-stained posterboard, the Dog pulling ahead by a nose. I wondered if he'd still favor the punk if he'd caught a whiff of that devil's breath a minute ago.

Then came the *Reapers*.

We each picked up one of these blackened crimson things that looked like they'd been plucked from the devil's own garden. My fingers trembled. Couldn't help it. Two million Scoville units of pure hate. Twice the heat of the *Ghost Pepper*, which had already sent two poor bastards into the arms of Saint Peter. But this? This was just the warm-up. *Pepper X* loomed next, waiting like a final boss.

"*Listos?*" the emcee called. "Three... two... one..."

I caught the heat before it even touched my lips and an invisible inferno that curled my nose hairs and whispered threats to my soul. I had to will it into my mouth, muscle my jaws into action. Even my teeth balked, like they knew better.

They didn't.

Three Days In Hell

You'd think after tasting hellfire itself, your body would shut down, its nerves fried, pain centers nuked into silence. Even Jesus got a moment's mercy, maybe, when the pain blurred into something else. But a *Reaper* doesn't show mercy. A *Reaper reaps*.

The moment my teeth pierced the skin, it was like biting into a live grenade.

Boom.

Hot relentless tears came, relentless rivers cutting down my cheeks. My eyes went red, vision swam. The heat sank in, grabbed me by the short hairs, and yanked hard. My balls curled into themselves like they were trying to escape the blast radius. White light burst behind my eyes, so bright it blinded me before the darkness swallowed me whole.

And you know what?

If this was the tunnel to the other side... I wasn't gonna fight it.

Chapter Seven

I never believed in angels. Whether they came with wings or sounded like that old sap from *It's a Wonderful Life*, they always seemed like the fever dreams of desperate minds and people clinging to the idea that someone upstairs was keeping tabs. We had one stuck on top of our Christmas tree when I was a kid, all golden curls and vacant smile, and my grandmother had plaster saints on her bedroom wall staring down like they knew something I didn't. People used to talk about guardian angels, little whispers in the dark, some holy, some hellish, but to me, they were just stories. And stories were smoke. Nothing you could hold.

But when I opened my eyes, I would've sworn I saw one.

The world came back in smears, like someone had wiped my vision with a greasy rag. Everything swam in the haze, everything except her. Her face cut through the fog like moonlight on broken glass. Smooth. Untouched. The kind of face sculptors try to get right but never do. Eyes like dark velvet, full of something close to mercy, not the soft kind, but the kind you see in someone who's seen too much and still chooses to care.

She smiled when I stirred. It said one thing: *you made it*. And right then, maybe I believed in angels after all.

She didn't speak. Just lifted the lip of a bottle to my cracked mouth and tipped it slowly. I drank. Of course I drank. That water hit like salvation, sliding down past the fire that still clung to my throat like a bad memory. My vision sharpened, and I recognized her finally. She was one of the girls from the old mine. Later I'd seen her at the Iguana, eyes wide, voice quiet. She didn't belong to this town. Not really. She was just passing through the wreckage.

"Thanks," I rasped, voice like broken gravel.

More water. The world started returning in pieces. The crowd was gone. The sun had dipped low and bleeding gold into rust across the sky. Whatever chaos had gripped this twisted little town earlier was gone, faded to a dull, mean hum. Before I could ask her name, I heard a sharp, feminine, voice I knew too well.

"Get up. Move along."

The girl didn't argue. Fear slipped into her face like a shadow crossing a wall. She vanished without a word, and then it was Amelia standing over me.

Her face filled my view like a loaded gun.

"What happened?" I asked, accepting the glass of milk she shoved into my hands like it was penance.

"You won, Bobby Santos," she said with a smirk full of smoke and secrets.

"I did? I ate the *Pepper X*?"

She laughed, and not kindly. "Don't be ridiculous. You didn't even make it past the *Reaper*. But you stayed upright longer than your competition. That makes you the victor." Her smile turned a little wicked. "How's victory taste?"

My stomach lurched like a bad bet. Fire still burned deep, not just in my gut, but in every nerve that had survived the heat.

"Like I'm gonna regret it in an hour," I said, already feeling the revenge my intestines were plotting.

The tent was nearly empty. The madness had drained out, leaving only paper cups, trampled confetti, and a band that sounded like they'd given up midway through the chorus. The Chili Festival had burned out, leaving behind the stink of sweat, spice, and stale beer, and was the perfume of a town that lived for the brief moment between chaos and collapse.

Amelia dabbed my forehead with a towel the angel had left behind, her touch soft but calculated, like everything she did.

"They're resting for tonight," she said, voice slipping into a purr.

"What's tonight?" I asked, already regretting the question.

She gave me the look a woman gives a man who's always three steps behind. "The Festival's not over, Bobby. There's music. Dancing. Shows." She leaned in, her voice a silk thread. "Real music. Real dancing. Like I do."

Then she shimmied with a slow roll of hips and a sly smile that said she knew exactly what she was doing and why.

I got to my feet, slow and clumsy like a boxer who'd taken one too many shots to the ribs. My legs held, which surprised me. On the table was a glass of milk, and I grabbed it like a drowning man does driftwood.

"I'm gonna have to pass on that," I said, draining the glass in one go. Lukewarm. Shame. I would've sold my soul for something cold enough to bite back. I scanned the area, looking for the nearest port-o-john in case my stomach decided to turn state's witness.

"I've got a hot date," I muttered. "With a pillow and the bathroom."

Amelia pouted like it was rehearsed. "You can't," she said in a half-demand, half-seduction. "You're the Chili Champion. You have a place of honor."

"I'm not going to be in... ideal condition," I said, trying not to paint her a picture of what was likely to happen in the next hour. "In case you missed it, I ate things that were basically war crimes."

She dismissed my protest with a flick of her wrist. "You're fine now. Besides, you have questions. I have answers. Let's get you cleaned up and refreshed. You'll feel better, I promise."

Amelia was always full of promises. That was her game – make you forget the past, ignore the facts, and think only about what *might be*. She had that look, like trouble dressed in silk. You knew there was a price for getting close, but that never stopped anyone.

She offered her hand like it was a deal I hadn't already agreed to. I took it, because of course I did.

Her ride was a two-seater sportster, a sleek, low car that hugged the pavement and dared you not to look twice. I dropped into the passenger seat like a sack of regret and leaned back. My bones ached in languages I didn't even speak.

We didn't talk. We didn't need to. She drove with purpose, cutting through the dusty outskirts of town until we hit the RV park that contained a dusty grid of trailers and temporary setups just outside the Festival's noise radius. It was a pop-up village of coolers, tarps, and the hope that the fun hadn't already ended.

"This place has a pool," she said. "One of three in Helman. JB had it put in and figured it'd keep people around. More time, more money."

The pool was a blue rectangle of despair and barely big enough for a dozen people, let alone the fifty who swarmed it like animals at the only watering hole for miles. It overflowed at the seams, slopping water onto the concrete like it was trying to escape the mess it had become. Sunburned kids, drunk dads, women in stretched-out bikinis. It was less a swim and more a slow boil.

"If it's all the same to you," I said, watching a Band-Aid float past a man's chest hair, "I'm not up for a swim."

Amelia chuckled, low and close, her breath grazing my ear like she was handing me a secret. "I don't come here to swim," she said. "I've got an errand to run. Then we'll talk."

She walked like someone who never asked permission. The crowd parted for her the way it did for fire or violence. I followed.

We cut through the sweat-soaked bodies to an old ice cream truck, or what used to be one. The wheels were long gone, replaced with cinder blocks. Paint peeled from its sides like sunburn, and the pictures of cartoon treats had faded into ghostly outlines. The name – *HOODS* – barely clung to the metal, bleached out by too many unforgiving days.

A squat man lounged in a beach chair beneath the awning with a cigarette stuck to his lower lip like a parasite. His eyes tracked Amelia the way a wolf watches a rabbit that walks straight into its den.

Whatever errand this was, it wasn't going to be about sprinkles and sundaes.

Three Days In Hell

The man perked up when he spotted Amelia. If you could call what he did *perking up*. He was the kind of heavy that made chairs look like they were doing time. The frayed polyester sagged beneath him like it had already given up. His Hawaiian shirt was something that belonged on a discount rack in hell and hung open, showing off a wife-beater that had once been white but now bore the evidence of every bad life choice he'd ever made. Grease stains, cigarette burns, and time.

A straw fedora sat too high on his oversized head, like it was trying to escape. His sunglasses, the oversized kind usually reserved for aging starlets and unstable celebrities, made his face look like a windshield for flies. Under all that mess was a day's worth of scruff that threatened to eat his pencil-thin mustache alive.

He was mid-bite into something that looked vaguely like a burrito, or at least some brown, steaming concoction masquerading as one. When he saw her, he stood too fast for a man his size and wiped his free hand on his pants like it made a difference.

"*Negra,*" he grinned, voice like gravel in a beer can. "You're early."

He offered his so-called clean hand. Amelia didn't take it. She never took what didn't serve her.

"Business looks good, Armando," she said, nodding toward the chaos by the pool.

"More warm bodies, more greenbacks," he shrugged, like it was all math and no morals.

"Which is why I'm here."

He let out a chuckle. "Tax collection time."

He clambered into the husk of the old ice cream truck. From inside came the sounds of metal cabinets slamming like angry ghosts. He returned holding a fat envelope. Whatever was on it made it glisten in the sunlight, and not in a good way.

Instead of taking it, she gave a lazy nod in my direction. He turned to me and shoved it into my hand like it was radioactive.

"This is Bobby," she said. "Bobby, meet Armando. He manages this circus."

Armando gave me a once-over, sizing me up like a bet he wasn't sure about.

"*Qué onda, wey?*" he said, grinning through stained teeth. "You two wanna stick around for the mud fights? Kicking off in a half hour."

"Mud fights?" I raised an eyebrow.

"Yeah, man. I hose down that patch over there, and two people go primal. Throwing mud, wrestling, biting sometimes. It's stupid, but the crowd loves it. People'll bet on *anything*."

Amelia cut in, sharp as a blade. "My time's short, Armando."

"*Bueno*. You know where to find us when you change your mind." He winked, then disappeared back into his grease-stained kingdom.

Amelia gestured toward a couple of rocks that overlooked a dip in the mesa. I followed orders. It was quieter here with just the wind, the distant slosh of the too-full pool, and voices carried by the breeze. They didn't sound like joy. More like the resigned muttering of folks who'd come for something better and ended up with a sunburn and a bad decision.

I looked out over the landscape. It was barren, a stretch of nothingness that could double as the moon if you were filming on a budget. Sand. Scrub. Sun. A wasteland with just enough life to make you wonder why it bothered.

Then she was behind me, her voice soft but firm.

"Here," she said. "Try this. It'll help your stomach."

I took the paper-wrapped offering and squinted. "You're always handing me things to fix what's wrong with me."

"And they've worked, haven't they?"

"So far."

"This will too." She peeled the paper off her own and took a slow bite. It was an enticing scene, cherry red, bright against her lips.

I eyed mine. "What is it?"

She gave me a look that could melt asphalt. "Ice cream," she said, voice like the first drag off a cigarette. "What else would it be?"

I tore open the wrapper like it might bite me back and gave the thing a cautious sniff – chocolate. I ran my tongue over it, slow, tentatively. Just a fudge sickle. But after the third lick, I didn't care. I bit deep, and the cold rushed in like salvation. The rich, frozen chocolate soothed the battlefield of my mouth and quieted the lava still bubbling in my gut. For a second, I remembered what comfort felt like.

Amelia licked her fingers, slow and deliberately, catching the cherry juice before it dripped down her wrist.

"So, what do you want to know, Bobby Santos?"

There was only one elephant in this room. And it was big. "Why does your husband want you dead?"

She didn't answer right away. Just stared out over the mesa like she was watching the past roll in with the dust.

"Relationships are complicated," she said finally.

"This one sounds like it went straight to hell with no stops along the way."

"Ours was never about love. It was a handshake between devils. My brother and JB struck a deal over power and protection with a pretty ornament to hang off JB's arm to sweeten the arrangement."

"And that ornament was you."

She nodded once. "JB gets to keep playing king of a ghost town, and my brother gets a safe haven. No one looks twice at Helman, and that's just the way they like it."

"Still doesn't explain the part where he wants you six feet under."

She looked at me then, something hollow behind her eyes. "What happens when a prisoner gets tired of the chains that bind him? When a man starts to wonder if the trophy he owns might slip off the shelf and break?"

"What are you saying?"

She looked at me sadly. "JB is in a wheelchair, but he's still a man. And he still can exert his will when he wants, where he wants."

"He hits you?"

"Just enough to leave a memory. Just enough to remind me my last name is his. If not by his hand, then there are several others willing to do his bidding."

I clenched my jaw. "So, why not leave?"

"I've tried," she said, voice flat. "But I'm not just a wife. I'm a piece in a bigger game. My brother needs the marriage. JB is leverage, and if I walk, the whole balance goes up in smoke."

"Then what? Your brother sends men after you?"

"Worse," she said. "He sends *family*."

"You're his sister."

"We don't share the same last name. Not anymore. He wouldn't lift a finger to save me. Hell, when JB hit me the first time, my brother bought him a new watch. Said it was for 'keeping time on his temper.'"

"And you're just waiting around? Letting them decide who buries you first?"

"If I run, my brother drags me back. If I stay, JB gets bored enough to finish what he starts."

I stared at her. She looked away.

"You're not telling me something," I said.

"I like it here," she whispered.

I blinked. "What?"

"I know it sounds crazy, but I do. I like the people. The dust. The quiet. It reminds me of home. Not the home with my brother. The one from before. When things were… simpler."

"That's a hell of a reason to stay in a place that might become your grave."

She gave me a soft smile, but it didn't reach her eyes. "Graves are everywhere, Bobby. At least here I know the plot."

I took another bite of the fudge sickle, more out of habit than hunger. The silence stretched between us like a noose waiting for a neck.

"You could always find someone to do it," I said carefully. "A hit. Quiet. Quick."

She shook her head. "They'd never touch JB. They fear my brother too much. They'd rather die than cross him, and he'd make sure they did. Along with their kids, their cousins, their dogs."

"So, it'd have to be a stranger," I said. "Someone with nothing to lose. No ties. No trail."

"Someone like you," she said. "You are an unknown. He needs you. And so do I."

She didn't need to spell it out. That look – part invitation, part challenge – said it all. Her eyes burned, low and dangerous, like cigarette embers at the bottom of a glass. She wasn't asking for help.

She was offering a choice.

"Oh, no," I said, shaking my head. "Not me."

"I need help."

"And I'm sorry about that, but I can't do what you're asking me to do."

"And what exactly *am* I asking?" she said, eyes narrowing just enough.

"The same thing *he* asked me to do."

"But that's okay?" Her voice didn't rise; it cut, smooth and cold.

"I didn't say that."

"You don't have to be a killer to kill for the right reasons," she said.

"And what are those? Enlighten me."

"A good reason. A just one."

"Such as?"

She leaned in. Her scent was sun-warmed sweat and faded perfume. "Helping a vulnerable woman escape a cage. A frightened woman. A woman you like. A woman you could learn to love."

I pulled back. "You think that's enough to put a bullet in your husband?"

She looked at me flatly. "Are you going to put one in me?"

"What? No! Of course not!"

"But *he* thinks you will. That's the corner he's painted you into. So, when you don't, when you can't, what do you think *he'll* do?"

I had no answer. I hadn't thought it through, and now it was too late. I saw Dupree again in my mind, leading me into those old mines. I shivered.

"I've been in Helman two days," I said. "And already I've got two people asking me to kill each other. That's not exactly normal."

"I don't know if it's that different from anywhere else," she said, gazing out toward the dust-choked horizon. "People live. People hate. People kill."

"Just when I think I've figured this place out, it throws me another curve."

"Helman is what you make of it, Bobby Santos," she said. "If you have no ambition, it won't suit you. But no place would."

She touched my face, her fingers cool and soft like silk run through cold water.

"What did he promise you?" she asked.

"Money. Fifty thousand dollars."

A flicker crossed her face, not quite a flinch, but close. "So, that's all I'm worth. A stack of bills. Don't tell me the amount. I don't want to know how cheap I came."

I didn't say anything. I thought about Luanne. About trust and where it led. I'd fallen once already. I wasn't looking for a second drop.

"And what's JB's life worth?" I asked.

Her eyes held mine and didn't let go. "A promise. Of something better. JB is offering you to walk away with a few dollars in your pocket. Or you stay."

"Stay?"

"Stay and have everything JB had. His house. His name. His power."

She took my hands, slowly, and placed them against her chest. Her skin was warm beneath the cotton.

"His wife," she added. "That's the start of something better."

I stared at her. At us. I couldn't believe how quickly this tangle of choices masqueraded themselves as destiny.

"I don't think I can stay," I said. "This is too much to think about."

"Is that your idea of freedom?" she asked, voice low. "Always moving into different spaces?

I turned away, staring out at the jagged horizon. Dust clouds danced in the distance like ghosts with nowhere to go. Maybe I was one of them.

"Running isn't the worst thing," I said finally. "At least when you run, you get somewhere else."

"Do you?" she asked. "Or do you just find a new motel with the same broken light above the bed?"

Her words cut deep because they weren't wrong. Every stop I made felt more temporary than the last. Just a different shade of beige on the same peeling walls.

"You think staying here is better?" I asked. "This place is built on rot."

She smiled, just a little. "But rot feeds new growth."

"Now you're a philosopher?"

"I'm a survivor."

She stepped in close, and I didn't move. Her voice dropped to a whisper, soft enough to pass for a breeze.

"You don't have to decide now," she said. "But don't pretend like the road you're on leads anywhere better. Here it could be different. Better."

I didn't answer. Couldn't.

She leaned in and kissed me – not desperate, not demanding. Just a press of lips that felt like a quiet question: *Could this be something else?*

When she pulled away, I was still silent.

"What are you ambitions, Bobby? What do you really want?"

I turned away from her gaze. It cut too deep, too fast. "You don't know me."

Her voice hardened. "People have started with less and ended with more."

She reached out, cool and calm, and turned my face back to hers with fingers that could either console or kill.

"What do you want, Bobby?" she asked me again.

"I told you. I don't know. Whatever everyone else wants, I guess."

"And what's that?"

"Do we really have to do this?"

She shook her head, jaw tight. "Answer the damn question. What do you want? Really want."

Her focus pinned me to the floor like a nail. I squirmed.

"Come on, Amelia…"

"You don't know?" she snapped. "Never thought about it once?"

"It's not like that —"

"Then tell me," she hissed. "The world's yours. What does it look like?"

"Freedom," I offered weakly.

"No." She slapped that word out of the air. "You have that. If you wanted it. So, what is it? Tell me. What do you really want?"

"Money," I blurted. "Enough that I don't have to worry about not having any."

The words hit the air like a cheap confession. Honest, but flimsy.

Amelia's eyes flared. She slapped me, hard. A flash of heat bloomed on my cheek.

"Better," she said, voice low. "That's more real. But it's not *everything*."

She stepped in. Slapped again. My head rocked.

SLAP!

"What do you want?"

SLAP!

"What do you *want*, Bobby?" she pressed me angrily.

The blows came quickly and sharply, and I stumbled back, arms up, trying to shield myself. Her nails sliced under my chin delivering hot pain, and a quick bleed. She paused like the sight of my blood proved something.

"What do you want?" she whispered.

"Jesus, Amelia…"

She feinted, and I flinched.

"Okay!" I shouted. "Okay – I want to be left alone! To –"

SLAP!

"Wrong answer."

"Amelia –"

SLAP!

"WHAT. DO. YOU. WANT?" she screamed into my face.

And that was it. The dam cracked. I saw stars, memories, ghosts. I was a little boy again playing with matches and punished by a mother's fury and hands like thunder. I was crying, snot-faced and broken. But not out of fear: out of rage.

And this time, I wasn't the same kid.

I didn't scream. Didn't roar. My words came low and rough, each syllable dredged from a place I kept locked up tight.

"You want to know what I want?" I said, staring down at my blood-streaked fingers. "I want everything. Everything I've never had. Everything I couldn't keep. I want money. Power. Sex. Control. Vindication. I want to stop *losing*."

Silence fell between us like a knife sliding into soft flesh.

Amelia stepped close and kissed where the tear had cut a line down my cheek.

"Then take it," she breathed.

And this time, I kissed her back like I meant it. Not just heat; hunger. Not just passion, but permission. I felt her breathing break in waves against me, fast and shallow. A live wire buzzed between us, and for the first time in years, I *felt* something that wasn't numb.

When the kiss broke, she was smiling. Dark. Dangerous. Knowing.

"You kill him," she said softly, "and there will be nothing you will ever want for again."

"And what about your brother? Won't he come after me?"

"No."

"Why not?"

"Because you'll be here. With me. The new face of Helman. The man who took the throne. My brother deals in outcomes, not emotions. Kill JB, and he'll do business with whoever's left standing. That's just order, Bobby. Not murder."

"And I'm the one sitting on the throne?"

"It's always been you. Can't you see that?" Her voice was velvet and gasoline. "Your life led you here. This moment. The only question is, do you take what's yours?"

Her cherry popsicle hit the dirt. Red against red.

"JB's just the whitewashed mask. My brother uses Helman's image to hide what it really is. A nowhere town for nobodies. That's the power of it. Forgotten things don't get watched. That's how money grows in the cracks."

"What kind of money?"

Her eyes glittered. "The kind that burns holes in suitcases."

She grabbed my hand and pressed it to her cheek. Soft, but burning hot beneath the surface.

"You were sent here for business. What happens if you don't go back?"

I didn't even blink. "Nothing. They'd be probably happy I never returned."

She paused. Just a beat. Long enough to let that word echo.

Then she said, "You know what I wish?"

"What's that?"

"I wish you were JB. That we lived in that house. Swam in the pool. Fucked four times a day on any surface we wanted. Sang. Danced. Drank. Got rich and stayed that way."

It came out raw. Like a piece of her had cracked loose.

"That sounds good," I said.

"You'd like that?"

"Yeah. I would."

"Then kill him," she whispered. "For me. For us. And there'll be nothing in our way."

She smiled, but just barely. Like she was joking. But not quite.

That's when the cold hit me. First one since I got to Helman. Not fear. Not excitement. Something older. Deeper.

Three Days In Hell

She leaned in close, her breath hot on my neck. Her body pressed against mine. Nature did the rest. And I wanted her right there and then and would do anything to have her.

"When?" I asked.

"Tonight," she said. "The party will be chaos. Think of a rave in a warzone. That kind of noise. No one will see it coming. But you'll be there. *We'll* be there."

She kissed my eyes. My cheeks. But paused at my lips.

"Forget whoever broke you before. She's not here. I am. I'm the future, Bobby Santos."

She slid my hands up her shirt and placed them where she wanted. Her gaze held me – smoldering, heavy-lidded, infinite.

Then she kissed me like it was the last thing we'd ever do before everything changed.

And just like that, she broke the kiss and walked back through the dust, past the peeling truck, past the sounds of children yelling by the pool that smelled like bleach and sunburn. I watched her go, my mouth still tasting faintly of chocolate and fear, feeling the heat cling to my back and the uncertainty of what was to be done tonight coil around my ribs like smoke:

***

I came to Helman for atonement. Or maybe just to give some fat cuckold his pound of flesh. A final show of guilt and penance before vanishing. It also dropped an albatross on my lap and put me into tight space between a rock and a hard place.

For killing Amelia, I'd get a windfall and a first-class ticket out of this ghost-town sinkhole. I could go someplace quiet. With beachfront. Somewhere far from consequence and hard to reach. A new name, maybe. A tan.

For killing JB, I'd have a big house in a small, shitty town. But I'd also have the kind of money that made misery manageable. And a woman like Amelia at my side and all the sex, secrets, and cigarettes I could consume.

As much as I didn't want to admit it, Amelia was right. Killing isn't hard. Anyone can do it. You just need a reason. A reason on a sliding scale – love, hate, fear, lust, vengeance. Anything will do if you push it hard enough. And somewhere in all that, I was drifting between two motives, two marks. Caught between a man and a woman who both thought the other had it coming.

Amelia drove me to the Indigo and dropped me off with a look that lingered just long enough to leave a bruise.

"I'll send Bins for you tonight," she said. "Get some rest. You're gonna need it."

All I wanted was a shower, a hot, scalding rinse to wash the grime and rot of the day off my skin. Maybe even scrub some of the guilt down the drain with it.

Out front, the parking lot buzzed. A few families had clustered like wild dogs. Someone had a grill going, and the smell of flame-charred meat clung to the thick evening air. Helman's version of community: sunburned strangers grouped together in a pack, laughing too loud, drunk on cheap beer and shared decay. If incest had a soundtrack, this was it.

A pudgy kid in a grease-stained yellow shirt charged at me with an ice cream cone melting down his hand. He let out a noise – part pig grunt, part fox-in-heat – then collapsed into a wheezing belly laugh as I flinched. His fat jiggled under that shirt like a balloon full of pudding. I kept walking.

Three Days In Hell

The sun was down, but the kids were still ramped up, tossing junk near the street and trying to set it on fire. The flames sputtered and spit while they shrieked and egged each other on. A few turned their gazes on me, their eyes glassy with too much sugar or not enough supervision. I quickened my step, suddenly afraid they'd latch onto me like bored animals discovering fresh meat.

"It won't end well," a voice said behind me.

I turned. A woman leaned against a doorframe, smoke curling from her lips. Her body looked thirty, tight and lean, but her face – her face had stories etched into every line. One eye was slashed by a vertical scar, like someone had tried to erase her past and failed. She stepped into the porch light. The scar gleamed.

"What won't end well? What are you talking about?" I asked, eyeing the chaos behind me.

She smiled without humor. "What are *you* talking about?"

I shrugged. "Guess it doesn't matter."

"Exactly," she said, dismissing me with her eyes. "No one listens anyway."

"The scar..." I nodded at her face.

"Cost of knowing things."

"Knowing what?"

She took a long drag, then exhaled like she was venting poison. "Everything. You can know every damn thing there is, and people still won't believe you. That's the curse."

"Knowing too much?"

She nodded slowly.

"You must be fun at casinos."

"I could give you the numbers," she said. "You wouldn't play them. I could tell you not to cross the street, and you'd still get hit by a car. I could tell you to run, and you'd stay."

"Try me."

She locked eyes with me and said, "Stay. Don't leave tonight."

"I'd like to," I said. "But I've got plans."

She gave a dry, cracked laugh. "What did I tell you?"

She turned and walked toward the vending machines, hips swaying like she'd done this warning dance before – and lost every time.

Then it happened.

A blast of light behind me. A kid screamed. One of the little fire-starters had caught his pant leg. He ran howling down the street, flames licking up to his knee, while his friends collapsed in laughter.

I didn't move. Just watched. And thought maybe the old woman was right. Maybe she always was.

I walked to my room. The key turned easy. Too easy. The door was unlocked. Something it wasn't when I had left that morning.

That was never a good sign. Nothing good ever comes from an unlocked door; not cash, not diamonds, not a medium-rare Tomahawk steak. Just trouble. Trouble that's already made itself comfortable.

"About time you showed," said a voice I knew. "Thought maybe that last chili finally did you in."

I flipped the light. JB Helman sat by the table like he'd owned the place forever. TV on, volume down. A bottle of good bourbon and two glasses on the table, waiting. He looked perfectly at ease, a man who enjoyed catching others off guard and watching them squirm.

"Sure," I said, closing the door behind me. "Come right in. *Mi casa* es *tu casa*."

"Congrats," he said, grinning. "You made it farther than last year's champ. That guy folded at the same spot you did. Honestly, I bet five grand you'd go earlier. Guess I'll eat that one. In the spirit of sportsmanship, of course, since we're not officially partners yet."

He poured three fingers of bourbon into a glass and gestured to the room.

"I own this dump," he said. "Figured you knew. I'd have done this chat at the house, but the party's at full tilt. Not the right setting for real conversation." He slid the glass toward me. "Snort?"

"Pass," I said, a hand on my gut. The fudgesicle had done more than soothe my stomach, maybe Amelia laced it with something. Either way, I wasn't in the mood to push my luck with liquor.

"Oh, come on. You downed enough chili to make a goat puke. This'll settle your gut. Trust me. Bourbon's medicinal."

I took the glass. Sipped. No explosion. No fiery regret. Just warmth spreading through my belly like a soft flame. JB watched my face and chuckled.

"See? Like magic."

He topped off his own glass.

"So," he said, "what'd you think of our little fiesta?"

"It was hot."

He laughed. "No shit, wiseass. Look where you are. You get your work done? Peddle enough Bibles to make your bosses happy? Serve your penance?"

"No," I said. "Didn't give enough away."

He nodded, savoring that answer like a sip of bourbon. "Might want to get yourself a room in town then.

Cheaper than this fleabag. Sounds like you're stuck in Helman a while."

"Looks that way." I drank.

"Doesn't have to."

That's when he brought it out, a snub-nosed revolver with a black grip. Shiny. Compact. Mean. He laid it on the table like a calling card and studied my face for a flicker of fear.

"You know, Bobby," he said, "I'm old. Not stupid. And you're neither."

He downed his drink and stared at me like he was trying to read the fine print on my soul.

"You wait for me to talk," he said. "Stay quiet, stay still. That's the mark of a thinking man. Also, the mark of someone I wouldn't trust with a dime."

"You think I'm untrustworthy?"

He smiled. "Everyone is. That's how things get done. Money passed in silence, paperwork shuffled at midnight, a handshake in an oil field. That's real business. Honest men don't last in business. They die broke or bitter. Even when both sides profit, someone's always on top."

"Is that what we're doing? Business?"

"No, son." Helman leaned back, that old-man smirk curdling into something meaner. "This is a parlay. A proper one. The kind that leads to business."

He poured another two fingers and stared through the bourbon like it held secrets. "I made you an offer this morning. Now I'm waiting for an answer. Or a counter."

This Helman wasn't the same man I'd met earlier. The soft-spoken cripple was gone. Replaced with something sharper. Meaner. The kind of animal that doesn't get weaker when it's wounded, just more dangerous.

That, and the fact that he was pointing a gun at me.

"This town ain't for everyone," he said, casual as hell. "It's crazy, sure. Messy too. But that's the way we like it. One hand scratches the other, and maybe you walk out with a suitcase full of cash to scratch whatever itches you've got left."

"Just a regular philanthropist."

He grinned, but there wasn't anything friendly in it. "What can I say? I'm a people person."

He saw me glance at the revolver. "Go ahead. Pick it up. Tell me that doesn't feel smoother than a saucer full of cream."

I picked it up. Light. Sleek. Deadly. I cracked the cylinder, eight shiny chambers, empty. Smith & Wesson's finest.

"Ain't she pretty?" he said. "That's to handle that little problem we discussed this morning."

"And if I say no?"

"Then I leave here hurt. Offended. Then you meet Dupree. And trust me, you don't want to meet Dupree in that way. He's less… friendly."

He slapped the table. When he lifted his hand, two bullets sat gleaming in the lamplight.

"And these are for you," he said. "Use 'em, or they'll get used on you. Either way, brass gets spent tonight."

"Why not give me the full eight?"

He let loose a laugh that sounded more like a wheezing bark, like a wolf with pneumonia. "I want her dead, Bobby. Not turned into soup. Two shots should do the trick, don't you think?"

"Tonight? At the party?"

"Why not? Think anyone'll notice a murder in my house?" His laughter got darker. "This isn't some chili-eating, taco-snorting, mariachi-blaring backyard cookout. This is Babylon meets Sodom and Gomorrah. Booze, food, music, women... and chaos. No one notices anything in chaos."

I didn't answer. I didn't need to. The weight of the revolver in my hand said enough.

"So, we understand each other?" he asked.

"It doesn't seem like I have much of a choice."

Suddenly, his smile vanished. His eyes went flat and dead. "Lose the sour puss, son. Everyone's got a choice. You chose to come here. You chose to screw my wife. It was all choice."

"I don't know if I can kill a woman."

Helman stared at me like I was a child talking about Santa. "How the hell would you know? You haven't tried. Besides, pulling a trigger ain't killing. That's a video game. You want real killing? That's face-to-face. That's watching the light go out. That's looking into their eyes while you take everything."

I knocked back my bourbon, refilled. My hand shook. I hoped he didn't notice.

"That's an awful lot weight for me to carry," I said.

"Bullshit. Anyone can kill. Even you. Especially you. Don't let the tits and perfume fool you. Amelia's cold. Ice cold. She'd run over orphans and nun vans if the money was right. And she's done worse."

"She says you're behind the trafficking."

"Of course she did. What'd you expect? Truth? You don't want the truth, Bobby. You want the version that lets you sleep at night."

I drank again, hoping the bourbon would blur the look on my face. He saw through it, but he was kind enough not to say anything. He refilled his glass.

"Look, I'm not innocent," he said. "But don't be a sap. Don't think she is either."

He downed his drink. "So, fifty grand. We good?"

I nodded slowly. "What do *you* get out of this?"

"Just what I always wanted. My town, my rules. No sharing. Not the money. Not the power. All mine. That's how it was when the Helmans first rolled in. We didn't give out handshakes, we took what we wanted. And now you expect me to split with a bunch of beaners across the river? That never sat right. Still doesn't."

"And her brother?" I asked. "He's packing more firepower than the Texas National Guard."

Helman gave a dry chuckle. "For the triggerman? Yeah, it'll go sideways. But for me? He'll grit his teeth and stay the course. Money's a jealous mistress – take your eyes off her, and she'll find someone else. He might send a few *cholos* to sniff out his sister's killer, but he won't go full vendetta. Not when business is booming. The day he plays cowboy is the day they find him in a ditch with buzzards picking his teeth."

He leaned in, his voice a low drawl. "But you? You're a ghost. A rich one. You ride the wind. No prints, no trail to follow. You vanish. Where's he gonna look, Bobby, if you don't wanna be found?"

"You make damnation sound like a Caribbean vacation," I said.

"It's simple math, son. Plusses in one column, minuses in the other. When the scale tips, the choice ain't hard; it's obvious. Around here, we call that clarity.

"When you strutted in here with that Bible and preacher voice, I thought, 'JB, that's a sign from a higher place.' Then I saw you chew down those chilies without breaking a sweat, and I knew. My personal savior. You got steel in you, Bobby. You just need a reason to use it."

If I pulled the trigger for Helman, he got to play rooster in the henhouse. Whether he ran the town better than Amelia didn't matter. Either way, it was still hell, just wearing a different hat. And I didn't have to stick around for the fire.

If I took Amelia's offer and snuffed Helman instead, I'd be handing her and her cartel brother a brand-new leash to choke this town with. Maybe Helman was the only thing keeping *El Mochomo* from turning this place into his personal blood farm. If so, killing him was a green light for expansion.

A husband and wife both asking me to be a Black Widow to the other. Either way, someone died, and the town kept bleeding.

That's when I heard the rumble of Detroit steel snarling outside my door and saw headlights flashing like a wink from the beyond. Then came the knock.

"Time's up," Helman said. "You ever see a ventriloquist work a dummy? Hand shoved up its ass, flapping the lips? That's me. I'm the dummy. Amelia's the one moving my mouth. And let me tell you, Bobby, I'm damn tired of it. Dog-tired. She's a cancer. Bet you figured that out today. She fed you lies, and I suspect you saw the bones poking out."

His chair snagged on a table leg. I crouched and tightened a loose screw, gave the rest a check too. He watched with a tilted smirk.

"You know these contraptions?"

"My brother."

"What's he got?"

"Had," I said. "MS. Lived in that chair until he took a gun to his mouth. Said it was better than becoming dead weight."

"Heroic," Helman muttered. "Takes guts to pull your own plug."

"Some call it cowardice."

"Those are the leeches. The ones who cling. I should know; I married one."

I helped him to the door.

"The party's the place," he said. "No rules, no brakes. A buffet of sin. Music. Booze. Women. Men. You name it, it's there. One more stiff on the floor? No one's counting, savvy?"

Outside, the motel was turning into Mardi Gras with a death wish. Wild eyes. Painted faces. Bodies grinding to music with no melody. The kind of crowd that wanted to burn something just to watch it scream.

Dupree leaned on Helman's convertible, smoke curling from his cigarette like a devil's whisper.

"How you doing, Penny?" Dupree sneered.

He opened the door and out stepped the girl, my angel who resuscitated me after the chili challenge. She was sweet and small. She shouldn't have been there.

She flinched from his hand, head down, and walked to me. Her fingers brushed mine as she took the chair. Cold, scared fingers.

"She'll take it from here," Helman said. "I'll see you tonight, Bobby. You'll do what I asked. And if I don't see you… well, you know who'll come knocking."

He nodded toward Dupree.

Then he motioned, and the girl pushed him toward the car like a lamb leading the devil back to his throne.

Chapter Eight

Not long after, Bins called and said Amelia wanted me picked up in an hour. That gave me just enough time to stand under a cold shower and try scrubbing the day's grime off me. Not just the kind you can see. The kind that sinks under the skin and lives there. Some stains don't lift – not with soap, not with time. The best you could do is learn to live with them, like scars from fights you half-won.

Helman had left me the bottle, like a parting gift or a warning. I poured another splash and walked to the window.

Outside, the parking lot had swollen since Helman left, a carnival of lost souls buzzing like drunk fireflies. More families had joined the crowd, dancing in circles that led nowhere. Others passed in costume, heading toward Helman's mansion like it was some kind of cathedral of sin. The whole thing stank of bad omens like the damned lining up at the river Styx, waving empty pockets at the ferryman.

Helman had offered me money and a clean slate. The kind of deal that says: "Disappear. Start over. Forget all this."

Amelia promised something else. Something softer. A future. Roots. The idea of not running. Of building something that lasted. Only problem? I'd never been good at staying put. I always told myself I was a drifter by choice, but the truth is, I just never found a place that wanted me to stay.

And maybe I didn't trust futures I couldn't hold in my hand. Cash in the pocket beats promises in the wind, a bird in the hand and all that.

Back when I used to knock on doors for a roofing outfit, we'd sign folks up with a little money down, and payment due on completion. I was paid a commission for my sweat, and four jobs in one town was good money. Then a couple of folks in the panhandle stiffed me and called the law. Turns out they were kin, and the whole town turned against me. My boss called me incompetent and cut me loose. Another notch, another town, another lesson.

Amelia's pitch felt like something shiny, dangling just out of reach. She knew what strings to pull. Maybe she thought I'd chase a dream if it included her. Or maybe she figured I was still nursing wounds left by a woman who'd carved her initials into my ribs. Maybe she wanted to be the proof that it could be different this time.

Both Amelia and Helman had made their cases. Laid out their offers like cards on a table. Both expected me to choose them. And I still didn't know which card to play.

Only thing I did know? If neither one of them ended up in a box before sunrise, I probably would.

That's when the knock came.

I opened the door and let Bins in. The music outside had thickened into a pulse, throbbing through the streets like blood through dying veins. The city, once flatlined, had a heartbeat again thanks to Helman's party and Amelia's schemes. It was dancing on its own grave.

Bins clocked the bourbon on the table like it owed him money. He tossed a garment bag on the bed, then made a beeline for the bottle.

"Mind if I help myself?" he asked.

He didn't wait for an answer. Just poured into the same glass Helman had used, like we were all drinking from the same poison well.

Where the hell've you been?" I asked.

"Nice to see you too," Bins said, his voice soaked in sarcasm. "Festival, same as you."

"You have a bad habit of disappearing."

"I watched your suicide-by-chili stunt, if that's what you mean. Wasn't really my scene. Watching folks melt their guts for a couple thousand bucks doesn't do it for me. Not when there's women around."

I unzipped the garment bag he'd thrown on the bed. Inside was a white jacket bright as a bleached corpse and emblazoned with a sequined red phoenix, or something trying real hard to be one. The sleeves were decorated with chili peppers, also sequined, like a fever dream stitched by a colorblind showgirl.

"What the hell is this?" I asked.

"Your attire," Bins said, downing his drink and refilling like he owned the bottle. "Helman's request."

Not long after, Bins called. Said Amelia wanted me picked up in an hour. That gave me just enough time to stand under a cold shower and try scrubbing the day's grime off me. Not just the kind you can see. The kind that sinks under the skin and lives there. Some stains don't lift – not with soap, not with time. The best you could do is learn to live with them, like scars from fights you half-won.

Three Days In Hell

Helman had left me the bottle, like a parting gift or a warning. I poured another splash and walked to the window.

Outside, the parking lot had swollen since Helman left, a carnival of lost souls buzzing like drunk fireflies. More families had joined the crowd, dancing in circles that led nowhere. Others passed in costume, heading toward Helman's mansion like it was some kind of cathedral of sin. The whole thing stank of bad omens like the damned lining up at the river Styx, waving empty pockets at the ferryman.

Helman had offered me money and a clean slate. The kind of deal that says: "Disappear. Start over. Forget all this."

Amelia promised something else. Something softer. A future. Roots. The idea of not running. Of building something that lasted. Only problem? I'd never been good at staying put. I always told myself I was a drifter by choice, but the truth is, I just never found a place that wanted me to stay.

And maybe I didn't trust futures I couldn't hold in my hand. Cash in the pocket beats promises in the wind, a bird in the hand and all that.

Back when I used to knock on doors for a roofing outfit, we'd sign folks up with a little money down, and payment due on completion. I was paid a commission for my sweat, and four jobs in one town was good money. Then a couple of folks in the panhandle stiffed me and called the law. Turns out they were kin, and the whole town turned against me. My boss called me incompetent and cut me loose. Another notch, another town, another lesson.

Amelia's pitch felt like something shiny, dangling just out of reach. She knew what strings to pull. Maybe she thought I'd chase a dream if it included her. Or maybe she figured I was still nursing wounds left by a woman who'd carved her initials into my ribs. Maybe she wanted to be the proof that it could be different this time.

Both Amelia and Helman had made their cases. Laid out their offers like cards on a table. Both expected me to choose them. And I still didn't know which card to pick up and play.

Only thing I did know? If neither one of them ended up in a box before sunrise, I probably would.

That's when the knock came.

I opened the door and let Bins in. The music outside had thickened into a pulse, throbbing through the streets like blood through dying veins. The city, once flatlined, had a heartbeat again thanks to Helman's party and Amelia's schemes. It was dancing on its own grave.

Bins clocked the bourbon on the table like it owed him money. He tossed a garment bag on the bed, then made a beeline for the bottle.

"Mind if I help myself?" he asked.

He didn't wait for an answer. Just poured into the same glass Helman had used, like we were all drinking from the same poison well.

Where the hell've you been?" I asked.

"Nice to see you too," Bins said, his voice soaked in sarcasm. "Festival, same as you."

"You vanished."

"I watched your suicide-by-chili stunt, if that's what you mean. Wasn't really my scene. Watching folks melt their guts for a couple thousand bucks doesn't do it for me. Not when there's women around."

I unzipped the garment bag he'd thrown on the bed. Inside was a white jacket – bright as a bleached corpse – emblazoned with a sequined red phoenix, or something trying real hard to be one. The sleeves were decorated with chili peppers, also sequined, like a fever dream stitched by a colorblind showgirl.

"What the hell is this?" I asked.

"Your attire," Bins said, downing his drink and refilling like he owned the bottle. "Helman's request."

The thing looked like Liberace died and got buried in a Tex-Mex billboard. The phoenix wasn't even rising; it was nosediving, wings crumpled like it was blackout drunk and plummeting from a whiskey-sick sky. Whoever stitched it up either didn't understand the myth... or understood it too damn well.

I tossed it onto the bed like it was radioactive. "I'm not wearing that," I muttered. "I look like Liberace's gayer brother."

Bins let out a low, gutteral laugh like a man who knew better than to be surprised by anything anymore.

"That's the tamest thing you'll see tonight, trust me." He slouched into the chair, boots on the table like we weren't adrift in the weirdest purgatory this side of Revelation. "Every so often, someone like you shows up. Drifter. Got that shimmer in the eyes. Makes people here sit up, start hoping again. Fools."

"Other drifters like me?"

He shrugged. Casual. Careless. Cowardly. Like he hadn't said anything at all. "There have been a few."

"Keep talking."

"When new blood rolls in, JB and Amelia start twitching. You've seen it. They become excited."

"Excited, how?"

"Hell, if I know. Like you've got something they lost. Or want to lose again. They're collectors, man. Packrats of the soul. Helman, Amelia – they pick people up like trinkets at a yard sale. Use them. Then toss what's left behind the shed."

"How many before me?"

He scratched at something invisible on his arm. Didn't meet my eyes. "I didn't count. Some drifted off. Some didn't. Some are still here, in ways you wouldn't expect. Point is, I've seen this story play out. Doesn't end with credits and curtain calls."

I pulled the last of my clean shirt and pants from the closet. Slid them on like armor. The jacket went over the top like a shroud; it was heavy, stiff, and thick enough to sweat through standing still. Felt like it was trying to crawl inside me.

"I'm going to roast in this thing."

"You won't," Bins said. "Trust me."

I walked to the window, drawn to the glass like a moth. Another wave of partygoers spilled past. They were half-naked, half-mad, draped in feathers, vinyl, face paint, and sin. The air vibrated with bass and perfume and something older. Something rotten. Women danced like they'd been unshackled from morality, like memory had been burned out of them with gasoline and drumbeats. The town was alive, but wrong. Like a body that keeps twitching after the soul's moved out.

"What the hell's wrong with this town?"

"You'll have to be more specific."

"This morning it was deader than disco. Now it's the goddamn Apocalypse Parade. I get it – 'The Festival' – but I've never even *heard* of it. And I've been around."

Bins gave another shrug. But this one dropped like a verdict.

"That's what happens when you live somewhere time forgot. This town should've died a hundred times: lost industry, fire, flood. But it didn't. It just stopped *aging*. Like it made some deal no one remembers, and now it won't lie down."

"Why?"

He drained the last of his drink, winced like it bit him going down, and stood slow and deliberate like a man getting ready to walk into the lion's mouth.

"Because *being here* is the punishment. Nobody leaves, not really. Even if they get out, they don't stay gone. The road looks like it goes somewhere, but it just loops like a noose tightening in slow motion. You think you're passing through. But the truth is…"

He looked at me.

"…the town's already passing through you."

Then he grabbed the doorknob.

"Now suit up, cowboy. You don't want to be late."

***

As we drove, the costumed partygoers wove through the streets like shadows wearing borrowed skin. If not for the garish, glittering fabric clinging to their bodies, it would've been hard to tell them apart from the darkness that ruled every corner the streetlights didn't reach, or to which they had long since surrendered.

In a town drowning in gloom, the Helman house burned like a fiery beacon. Perched at the far end of town like a monarch surveying his decomposing lands, all roads led to it, or away, depending on how you looked at things. Whether you took the main drag or one of the broken, skeletal side streets that cut past boarded-up businesses and sagging homes, the flow of people all surged in the same direction. They scuttled down alleyways and cracked sidewalks like ants returning to their queen.

Bins had been right. The town might've looked like a dying man wheezing through his final hours, but tonight it pulsed with something close to life. Not joy, not celebration, something fouler. Excitement's darker sibling. A frenzy lit by something malignant and hidden. It wasn't just Festival energy. It was as if the storm had circled back around and this was the worst of it, the backside. The calm before had passed. The reckoning had arrived.

The car crept through the crowd. Now and then, a drunk would stagger up and smear their painted face across the glass, leaving streaks of greasepaint like crying clowns in a nightmare. Whether I wanted to be or not, I was part of this spectacle now, folded into something that felt ancient and mean. Whatever happened tonight, I wasn't walking away unchanged. And honestly, I didn't want to know ahead of time what that change might be. It was better to meet it in the dark.

Bins stopped to let two prostitutes cross the road. They were dressed like yin and yang; one in white, one in black. Angels, if angels wore six-inch heels and lingerie that barely clung to them. They froze in the headlights, their body paint catching the light in jagged ways. The black one, a chubby little devil, lifted her shirt and flashed us, her triple-pierced tongue wagging like a warning. The white one hiked her skirt and bent over just enough to flash the crack of her ass. Then they cackled deep, wet, smokers' laughs and vanished into the dark like a magic trick no one wanted to see.

I helped myself to Bins' cigarettes, lit one, and blew the smoke out into the wild night.

Helman. For all his bark and muscle, he was still just a man in a wheelchair. And I knew how my brother thought, how most people thought, if they were honest. A man in a chair has nothing but his mind, his money, and whatever grudges he's kept fed and sharp. They always had something to prove and nothing to lose. Their comfort was temporary. Their safety was rented. An eight-year-old with a zip gun and no conscience could walk up and put one between his eyes, and that'd be the end of it.

So, what was he really holding on to?

And what did he think I was?

Amelia was different.

For all her beauty and that stained-glass innocence, she was in a different kind of cage. Her brother and the Cartel made it so. That didn't make her a victim, not exactly. More like a player with her own set of dice. After Luanne, I'd learned that a woman could hustle just as hard as a man, maybe harder. They just hid their motives behind smoky eyes and kiss-me lips.

Yeah, I'd seen Amelia's type before. Sometimes I came out ahead. Sometimes I didn't. But it was a familiar game, and each round taught me a little more. This town was a dump, no question. But if I killed JB, it'd be my dump. Our dump.

And that house? It wasn't some crumbling Miss Havisham pile of gloom. Sure, it had that Mexican adobe flair on the outside, but the inside was sleek, modern, wired, and humming with the kind of wealth that didn't need to flaunt itself. The town was broke, but Amelia and JB sure as hell weren't.

Money couldn't buy happiness, sure. But poverty couldn't buy a damn thing. I knew all about that. I'd hustled too many years chasing a buck. And that game? That was for younger legs and softer hearts.

I was running out of time. And worse, running out of excuses not to choose one of the offers laid in front of me.

I glanced over at Bins. He looked like he was somewhere else entirely.

"What's going on inside that head of yours?" I asked.

"Just wondering, is all."

"Yeah? About what?"

"You and JB. And Amelia. Some weird juju in the air."

"You don't know the half of it," I said.

"And I don't want to," he replied. He leaned on the horn, scattering a pack of drunks like pigeons. "I've lived here my whole life. I know the regulars, and I've seen new faces roll in and disappear just as fast. But I've never seen this kind of stir. Not like this. My two cents? You'd better wise up quick. Because, Bobby? You're walking straight into a situation you can't even begin to imagine."

I flicked the ash out the window. "And what situation is that, exactly?"

He looked over, eyes flat and steady. "The kind where you check in… but you don't check out."

***

The Helman House was lit up like a sinister carnival, and the people funneled through the front gate like performers obeying some unwritten decree. Bright, blood-red chili lights were strung through the trees and draped from awnings and roof trim. Fireworks erupted at random from behind the house, showering the sky with color. The air pulsed with the vibrant spectacle, and because red dominated everything, the house looked like it was burning without fire, without smoke.

Bins parked in the broken lot of a sagging church, where a trio of junkies were huddled around a needle, passing it back and forth like communion. When they saw us, they scowled and slithered deeper into the shadows. Their voices rose in whispers; they were needy, feral, arguing over whose turn it was to fly. Bins saw the look on my face and just shrugged, smiling like he'd seen this scene play out a thousand times before.

We got out. The music was a wall of sound, clashing genres at war with each other, live mariachi bands battling pulsing techno that blasted from hidden speakers. In the distance, the dry rattle of automatic gunfire lit up the night like punctuation.

"Jesus," I muttered, scanning the chaos.

"Right. Jesus. This is a holy time," Bins said.

The Spanish-style concrete walls around the Helman house usually kept the riffraff out, a mute warning that if you didn't belong, you knew it upfront. Spanish in style, maybe, but more English in principle. A nobleman's fortress. The kind that opened its gates once a year so the peasants could glimpse the inside, just enough to stay loyal, not enough to get ideas. Gates, after all, worked both ways. They ensured that the wrong people stayed out on the perimeter. And once closed, they made sure no one ever left.

As we approached the front gate, my heart skipped. What had once been distant silhouettes came into focus, a writhing mass of bodies, packed tight like cattle waiting for slaughter. It wasn't a party. It was purgatory in a red glow.

The front yard teemed with a desperate crowd that made Woodstock look like a quiet night at bingo. These meat puppets pressed together in sweaty, uncertain unity, snaking through the yard in a current that never moved forward. No one veered toward the sides of the house where space opened up, as if they knew their place. Like game show contestants waiting for their number to be called, they lingered, clinging to the fantasy that entry would come if they just kept smiling.

I followed Bins into that erratic stream, and we carved a path through the human slurry to a clearing near a strange collection of eleven statuettes. Each one showed the same man in stages of torment, his body bending with pain until the final figure had him on his knees, face raised toward an indifferent sky.

Around us, people milled with drinks and paper trays piled with food from strategically placed tables which kept the masses fed, drunk, and docile. Just enough to stop them from linking arms and storming the door.

"Are they ever going to get inside?" I asked Bins.

He shrugged. "Depends."

"On what?"

"How they look. What they have to offer. Whether they amuse the powers that be."

"And if they don't?"

"They're stuck, man. We're not. Come on, we need to keep moving."

I watched with morbid curiosity as the crowd resigned itself to the endless loop of walking nowhere, like fleshy golems. Their pink features blurred together in the low light. If they understood their fate, condemned to circle the front porch like dogs waiting for table scraps, they didn't let it show. Some even sat obediently on the steps, staring at the door that would never open. Occasionally, a burly enforcer with a collapsible baton made his rounds, swatting the more desperate ones across the thighs. They yelped and scattered, only to crawl back a few minutes later, eyes glued to the threshold with pitiful anticipation.

"Wannabes," Bins muttered, knocking me on the shoulder to break my trance. He spat at the ground. "Their desperation is disgusting."

"Why?" I asked.

"I was one of them once. Thought if I just showed how bad I wanted it, someone would open the door."

"What changed?"

"I became useful."

He grabbed my sleeve and yanked me toward the side of the house, where a very different crowd congregated. We shoved against the flow of bodies, the current growing more aggressive the closer we got to the far edge of the yard. The press of flesh became tighter. Somewhere along the way, Bins disappeared.

I was alone.

The crowd sensed my isolation like sharks scenting blood. Hands tugged at my jacket, clawing past me for their own gain. I swung an elbow, shoved a heavy body off me, tried to claw forward. Someone grabbed my shoulder. I spun, and without thinking, cracked him in the face. His nose burst like an overripe berry, splattering red across the pristine white of my jacket.

The moment stunned everyone. That opening was all I needed.

I forced my way onto the stone patio that flanked the mansion.

A human wall blocked my path: a towering fat man with the look of a former lineman, now a slab of immovable mass. Despite his size, he radiated the calm confidence of someone who'd won far more fights than he lost. His eyes were small and black, buried in folds of flesh, and his goatee was bound with a rubber band. Hog-leg arms wrapped in faded tattoos hung at his sides. Around him, the ground was littered with unconscious bodies.

No question what his job was. No question he excelled at it.

If the front yard caged the mindless, drugged-out drones, this patio was reserved for a more vicious ceremony of flesh.

A topless blonde towered on one side of a white painted line, her skin slicked with sweat and the occasional smear of blood. Two men tried to cross that line to get to her. Each time they lunged, she knocked them back with cold, clinical precision – a sharp hand to the throat, a knee to the gut, a heel to the knee. Every strike was deliberate. Bones cracked. Blood spilled.

And yet still, they came.

The swell of her breasts. The sway of her hips. Something in her movements numbed their pain and magnified their lust. Every fall fed the crowd's frenzy. Spectators roared with laughter, placing bets, exchanging wads of crumpled bills as bodies hit the ground.

A rush. A knockdown. Another rush. Another knockdown.

When the fight was finally beaten out of them, a thick man dragged their broken bodies off. In seconds, two more eager challengers took their place, eyes glazed with desire and self-delusion.

"They're the worst," Bins said, suddenly beside me again. "Degenerates."

I didn't answer. I couldn't stop watching her.

"She just beat the shit out of two guys twice her size," I said. "You'd think they'd learn."

Bins snorted. "You ever try reasoning with a hard-on?"

"The small head's doing the thinking," Bins said. "All they see is a hot piece they want to lay down with. So, they go for it, and she kicks the ever living shit out of them. Every time. Rinse and repeat."

"Idiots," I muttered.

"This? This is nothing. This is to keep the masses entertained. The real stuff's inside. But you'll see soon enough."

We turned away just as the blonde dropped two more men with brutal precision. Heading toward the backyard, a man in all black stepped out of the shadows and intercepted us. He was thin and sharp-edged, like a desert crow in a thrift-store plague doctor costume. Long, greasy hair. Lazy eye. Pale skin that looked allergic to sunlight. The human version of a virus that never quite cleared.

"Long time no see," he said to Bins, his voice unexpectedly high and nasal. "Where you been keeping yourself?"

Apparently, I wasn't the only person he disappeared on. Bins stiffened. "Around."

"You're twistin' wires, Bins." The Crow Man shook his head like a disappointed parent. "Bein' scarce ain't your play. You keep more balls in the air than a goddamn sorcerer." He mimed juggling with gloved fingers.

"I'll make my payment," Bins said.

"That's music. Your tab's deep, though. And my patience?" He pinched his thumb and forefinger together. "Real thin. My kitties are meowing for their milk."

"Gotta connect the dots. You understand."

The Crow Man smirked. "Watching is a side gig. And you hate the view from the bench."

He turned to me, extending a bony finger wrapped in cracked pleather. "Is this one of the balls you're juggling?"

"Kind of," Bins said.

"He laying green on you?"

"Kind of," Bins repeated.

The Crow Man stepped in close. I could smell the sour sting of tequila on his breath, see the flash of silver where teeth should've been.

"Your face is fresh," he said to me. "What crossed you over here?"

Bins stepped in. "Check the bird. That's Helman's guest."

Crow Man circled behind me. I felt his eyes trace the inked emblem on my back. He clicked his tongue in disapproval.

"Bullshit. I don't buy knockoffs."

"He's wearin' the colors, man," Bins said. "You see the mark."

"Could've pinched it off a corpse."

"But he didn't. You letting us pass, or you want to explain to Helman why you didn't?"

The Crow Man made a face, throwing his long arms up in mock surrender. He stepped aside.

"I vision where you're sittin." We both bow to bigger heads."

As we passed, he called after us: "Two days, Bins. Two days, or you'll be marked. Shadows always creep up and claim their own."

Bins pushed me forward, ignoring him.

"What was that all about?" I asked once we were clear.

"Nothing. I owe him some money," Bins muttered. "But he's strictly minor league."

"His threat didn't feel minor."

"He's trying to make a name. Get his face in front of JB or Amelia. But he's a thug, and they've already got shelves full of thugs. The Crow's going nowhere. No matter how many people he squeezes, he stays small-time."

"You never told me how you know Helman. No offense, but you don't carry a rep that puts people on their back feet."

"I'm what you call a reliable miscreant. I just make sure I'm available when they call, if they call."

"So, why aren't you on payroll?"

Bins smirked. "They haven't handed me a job big enough to grow into my big boy pants. Yet."

The mariachi horns blared their brassy bluster through monstrous speakers at the far end of the acre-long backyard. The crowd throbbed like blood in a vein, more mosh pit than dance floor, bodies colliding with the force of charged ions. Fists flew at every bounce, as if the music itself demanded violence.

Bins jabbed me in the ribs and nodded toward the pool. There, the dirt had turned to thick, black mud. Two grotesquely obese men grappled in its belly, bears tangled in a swamp. Their rolls of fat tore and slapped as they heaved at each other, sweat and sludge coating them like armor. Neither could budge more than an inch under the weight of their own flesh. Still, they charged and slammed with thunderous grunts, a barbaric parody of sumo wrestling, stripped of any dignity or ritual. The crowd roared approval, pummeling them with empty beer cans and broken tequila bottles.

"Bins! Get your ass over here! They're waiting for you!"

Dupree burst through the bodies, nightstick swinging. He cleaved a path like a plow, clearing a corridor of drunkards and junkies.

"You're late!" the sheriff barked, voice booming. "Where the hell have you been?"

"Disneyland," Bins shot back. "What do you think? It's a madhouse out there."

Dupree's face darkened. "It's a madhouse in here."

Bins raised his hands. "Amelia told me to bring him. I brought him. This slag's getting bigger every year."

Dupree sneered at me. "How you like the shindig, Bible Thumper?"

"I thought it'd be bigger," I said.

Dupree snorted. "Wiseass."

Bins elbowed him. "Play ball, you two. I dance to yours, you dance to his."

Dupree spat tobacco juice. "Alright." He turned, and we fell in line behind him.

As we climbed the wide steps to the back porch, hungry eyes followed me; men and women craving what I carried: a promise, a ticket out, a bullet with my name on it. They knew they couldn't snatch it here. Dupree's bulk and nightstick were all the warning they needed. Still, their gazes burned deep into me, asking: *What do you have that we don't? And how can we get it?*

Tonight, they'd see. And they'd learn why some prizes come with a price no one wants to pay.

"Don't mind them any," Dupree muttered, catching me watching two men locked in what looked like the world's slowest torture session. He made a noise in his throat and spat a thick wad of chewing tobacco onto one of the contestant's bare feet. The man flinched but didn't stop.

In a place built on drinking, groping, and bleeding, you'd think more people would be laid back. But everything here was a contest. If they weren't trying to fuck each other, they were trying to break each other. I wasn't sure if the chaos was incidental or a feature of the architecture. More likely, it was both.

The two men couldn't have looked more different. One was rail-thin, the kind of gaunt you get from years of stimulants and bad choices. He looked like a single hard breath could snap him in half. The other had bulk, but the kind that came from ego and protein shakes, not discipline. His muscles sagged like old meat in a butcher's window.

Both sat on the hardwood floor in sit-up position, each with a gold-plated ten-pound weight resting on his chest, more ceremonial than practical. Hovering above them was a man in tight leather and chrome, barking orders like a drill sergeant at a sex dungeon. He circled them like a vulture with a stopwatch, calling for reps with a voice that cracked and snarled.

They rose, slow and shaking, elbows to knees, then reclined halfway and held. Their faces bloomed from pink to wine-dark purple. The BDSM overseer waited until they trembled like wires in a storm before letting them drop to the floor with a thud. Then he added another ten-pound disc. More gold. More agony. More penance.

"Why are they doing that?" I asked.

"They're making amends," Bins said, his voice flat. "The public kind."

"Who'd they piss off?"

Dupree's lip curled. "The skinny one ran the dope flow in Helman before the Cartel set up shop and cut off his balls." He didn't mask the venom in his tone. Whatever history there was, it wasn't just professional; it was personal.

"The Cartel let him operate," Dupree continued, "as long as they got their slice. But he got greedy. Thought he could outfox the wolves. Skimmed when he should've scraped. I told him not to. Told him those boys don't play. But he didn't listen."

I glanced back at the thin man straining under the weight, his chest heaving. Something in Dupree's voice shifted into less anger now, reflecting more disappointment than anything else. That twist in the gut you get when blood betrays blood.

Bins leaned in, voice low. "That's Dupree's brother."

The revelation sat heavy in my stomach. Made the scene uglier. Made the sheriff's silence louder.

"And the other guy?"

"A cautionary tale," Bins said. "Doesn't matter what he did. Just matters that we all see him break."

Dupree stared at his brother for one last beat, jaw grinding, then turned away and spat again, this time hitting some poor bastard square on the shoulder. The man whirled around, fists ready to fly, but one look at the sheriff stopped him cold. The blood drained from his face like someone had pulled the plug.

"Sorry," the man stammered.

The apology didn't matter. Dupree drove his billy club into the man's gut like he was punching a clock. The man folded instantly, coughing bile onto his shoes.

"Come on," Dupree growled. "Showtime's over."

We climbed the broad steps toward the house. Behind us, the crowd moved in again like sharks smelling fresh blood.

The back porch opened up to towering glass with floor-to-ceiling windows that revealed the interior like an aquarium of the elite. Inside was cleaner, quieter, colder. Those on the outside pressed up to the glass, eyes wide with hunger, watching their betters toast with crystal flutes and laugh in the warmth of power. The kind of warmth fire gives off when it's still too far away to burn you.

But not one of them dared cross the line. Hulking bulldogs in tight suits and tighter faces watched the periphery. Their job wasn't just to block entry; it was to remind the uninvited exactly where they stood in the food chain.

And tonight, everyone knew: the rich feasted inside.
The rest begged at the windows.
Or bled in the mud.

Dupree led us inside, through doors that may as well have been the gates of another world. The temperature drop hit like a sucker punch, slicing through the humidity with the precise cruelty of a scalpel. The thick air of the outdoors was gone, replaced by a sterile chill that raised goosebumps and reminded you this wasn't a place for sweat or heat or human error. It was a refrigeration unit for the soul.

Inside, the numbers were fewer, but the egos were larger. These weren't the tequila-swilling degenerates clawing through the muck outside. These were the ones who'd already won. They glided across the polished floors like ghosts at a masquerade, sipping expensive spirits and murmuring pleasantries like the world owed them quiet. They weren't locals. Their skin hadn't been weathered by desert sun or farm toil. It was manicured, moisturized, manicured again. These were people imported from places where sin came with service charges: Manhattan, Nice,

Hong Kong, Geneva, anywhere rich people gathered to congratulate each other.

Their movements were calculated and ritualistic. They clinked glasses with soft smirks, murmured through capped teeth, then moved on, always scanning for someone more worthy of their presence. Every conversation was an audition. Every smile, a transaction. If someone cried out in pain ten feet away, they wouldn't so much as blink unless it spilled on their shoes.

The floor-to-ceiling windows looked out over the chaos below like an aquarium tank, only here, the fish wore Rolexes. Those on the outside could only press their faces to the glass and watch, their breath fogging up the perfect view of everything they weren't allowed to be. Large men with bad tempers and tighter shirts ensured the divide remained holy.

The moment I crossed the threshold, their eyes flicked toward me like motion sensors. First confusion. Then calculation. Then dismissal. Except for a few who caught sight of the bird inked on my back. That one symbol turned heads. A couple whispered behind cocktail glasses. A woman in a pearl-choked dress poked her date in the ribs and nodded toward me. But whatever curiosity I stirred was quickly eclipsed by the next guest's arrival. They moved on, like predators who sensed the meat might be poisoned.

They weren't monsters, at least, not in the traditional sense. No teeth. No claws. But they were worse: anesthetized. Totally numb to anything that didn't reflect their image back at them. Doctors, lawyers, and shell-company barons who moved other people's lives around on spreadsheets. The kind of people who never got blood on their hands because they paid people to bleed for them.

"Wait here," Dupree growled and disappeared down a hallway that hadn't existed that morning.

I stood with Bins, rubbing my hands together in the freezer-grade A/C, thankful for the thick velour of my jacket, even if it made me look like a discount Elvis impersonator. The house itself had changed. Not just in mood, but in shape. The rigid floor plan I remembered from earlier was gone. No longer fixed in place, the walls glided silently on rails, rearranging the architecture like a magician shuffling cards. Rooms expanded, collapsed, unfolded. It was a kaleidoscope of shifting geometry, creating and destroying space on a whim. A living Rubik's cube made from money, arrogance, and design-school hubris.

This wasn't a house. It was a construct. A trap made of style. A statement of control.

I'd learn later the Helman House was both an architectural marvel and a moral abomination. A temple built not to shelter, but to mock. Beauty used as camouflage for rot. At the time, I was just trying to get my bearings feeling like a ghost in a place that wanted me to forget I was ever real.

A glass was shoved into my hand, dark amber liquid sloshing near the rim.

"Welcome to the show," Bins said.

I raised it in mock salute. "Barnum would've given his left nut to run a circus like this."

"You'd probably find it if you looked hard enough."

The guests around us were beautiful in the way predators are beautiful, moving with a controlled, streamlined state with eyes that never blink too much. They looked away when I met their gaze. Not with shame. With strategy. Their instincts told them I didn't belong. That I wasn't part of the game. Or worse, that I might be something they couldn't buy.

"Who are these people?" I asked. "And don't tell me they're locals. I drove three hundred miles through dirt and death to get here. There's no one like this out there."

Bins gave the room a casual sweep, then took a sip from his own drink. "They're not from around here. They're never from around here. They show up once a year. Drink top-shelf for free. Get freaky. Leave nothing behind but ruin."

Dupree's voice bellowed from somewhere behind the shifting walls, summoning Bins like a dog trainer calling his mutt.

Bins drained his glass and snatched another off the tray of a passing waiter. The liquid inside shimmered green. It looked like absinthe or antifreeze, either seemed appropriate.

"Later," he said, vanishing into the labyrinth of luxury.

And just like that, I was alone again, surrounded by people who didn't see me.

"I like your jacket," a woman's voice said from behind me, smooth as silk over a razor's edge. "Birds are my thing. Even the mythological ones."

Her voice matched her look, a rare thing in a world full of contradictions. Pale blonde hair poured over half her face like liquid platinum, styled in a classic cascade that screamed old Hollywood and whispered danger underneath. She stood in front of me in a white gown so sheer it looked like it had been woven from the last breath of a snowstorm. The gown didn't hug her curves; it gave them a stage.

She looked like she had time-traveled out of a 1930s film reel. I half expected her to speak in black-and-white.

She was beautiful in that haunting way like an angel with a switchblade behind her back. I opened my mouth to speak, but my tongue tripped over itself, so I asked the oldest, safest question in the book.

"Can I get you a drink?"

"I'll just have a sip of yours," she purred, plucking the glass from my hand. She kept her eyes locked on mine as she tilted it to lips so delicate that they kissed the rim like it was a secret. "Bourbon."

"Sure you don't want your own?"

She shook her head and handed it back. "Tastes better when it's someone else's," she said, her voice a lazy drawl. "Something about the naughtiness of mingling saliva." Her smile was a scalpel wrapped in velvet. When she saw the color rise in my face, she laughed softly. "You don't strike me as the blushing type."

"Just under the right circumstances."

"Is that what I am?" she said, tilting her head with the kind of smile that had ended wars and started funerals. "Do you want to be under me?"

A lesser man would've melted. I just smiled. "Someone's not shy."

"My daddy always said, say what you mean." She helped herself to another sip. "I don't think I've seen you here before."

"It's my first time."

"A virgin. How quaint." She tasted the word like a fine wine. "What brought you here?"

"I could ask you the same thing."

"You should. But me first."

I studied her eyes. They were sharp, flinty things made for seeing through lies. I couldn't tell if she was playing or probing.

"Helman," I said.

"Yes, it's Helman's soirée," she said, with a flick of her fingers that dismissed the entire mansion like it was old wallpaper. "But I want to know what brought you to Helman – the town, not the house."

"My job."

"You have a job?" she said, genuinely amused. "That's cute. People at this party don't usually have jobs."

"No?"

"They have time to burn and money to keep the fire going."

"And the people outside?"

"They're different," she said, her smile tightening. "They pick up trash, roll greasy burritos, sell scratch-offs to broken dreams."

"But they're still here."

"They have to be. There's nowhere else to go. And no one else wants them."

"So what kind of job brings a guy like me here?"

"I'm listening."

"I give away books. Bibles."

For the first time, her eyebrows shot up in actual surprise. "You're joking."

"I wish I was. I spent all day trying to convince people God still had a business address."

"That's like trying to catch smoke with your fingers," she said, and pantomimed the act with exaggerated grace.

I smiled grimly. "Yeah. Turns out people don't look for salvation where they're drowning in vice."

We both watched the crowd. The men pawed, and the women liked it. It was a theater of excess, bodies rubbing against each other with the slow desperation of the damned.

Her eyes swept the room like a connoisseur picking through a wine list.

"Vice doesn't have a social class," she said. "And our hosts like interesting people. They keep enough animals in the zoo to ensure a decent variety."

"Amelia and JB were ringmasters in the world's most dangerous circus."

She raised a single brow. "That's a unique perspective. You'll find them... accommodating, for a price."

"And if I find the price too steep?"

"Then you'd better pray you never signed the contract. Not out loud, anyway." Her eyes lost their shine. "I'm sure you passed some of the people who didn't pay up on your way in."

"Your advice?"

"If you meet Amelia or JB again, smile. Be agreeable. Don't flinch."

"I already did."

The words hit her like a slap. The mask she wore was cool, seductive, and invulnerable, and cracked for half a second. Her eyes softened. Her breath caught.

"I don't know if I should be impressed by you... or feel sorry for you."

"Why?"

"Because they only invite people who have something they want."

"I do. But I'm not sure I want to give it."

"You won't get that choice."

"What makes you so sure?"

She didn't answer. Not directly. She just smiled softly, sadly, and looked away, as if remembering something better left buried.

"None of us did," she said.

Then, from somewhere deeper in the house, a cheer went up, a primal roar of excitement. It cracked through the frigid air like a gunshot.

Her mood changed instantly. Like a light switch flipping to "game on."

"You like games?" she asked.

Before I could answer, her cool, strong, and insistent hand closed around mine, pulling me through the crowd. We passed through the kitchen, past clusters of perfectly perfumed nobodies sipping poison and whispering lies, toward an adjoining room pulsing with the heavy rhythm of something *else*.

Grunts echoed. Pained, feral. Animal.

I wasn't sure if we were heading toward a card table or a coliseum.

The room was misshapen like it had once been square but lost its fight with time and too many bad decisions. A small crowd leaned forward, breath held, as two men took turns *throwing darts at each other's chests*.

There was no illusion of gamesmanship; this wasn't some barroom macho contest. It was colder. Precise. Ritualistic. Where I'd once seen drunk fools at the Iguana tossing blades for cheap thrills, this had intent. This was *personal*.

Each man bore two blood blossoms on his crisp white shirt, wounds still glistening, soaking through the cotton in slow, crimson halos. White was essential. It highlighted the violence. Made it visible. Made it art.

One of the duelists looked like he'd just stepped out of a black-and-white cologne ad – sharp cheekbones, angled like sculpture, with windswept blonde hair fresh from a regatta. His opponent was the ghost of old Hollywood featuring Cary Grant's square jaw, a perfect part in his slick black hair, and not a whisper of stubble. He stood still, posture military-stiff, awaiting the next strike from Mr. Polo Ad.

The crowd tensed.

Ralph Lauren drew his arm back and flung the dart with the efficiency of a predator. The wet *thunk* of impact was followed by a sharp intake of breath from the man in white. Cary Grant absorbed it without a sound, though a grunt leaked through clenched teeth. That restraint alone earned him a wave of approval from the crowd.

With visible control, he reached up, fingers steady, and *ripped* the dart from his body. Blood flowed freely now, warm and dark against the white. My stomach turned. The crowd surged forward, hungry.

I shook my head.

"Not a fan of sport?" the blonde asked beside me, her voice smooth with mockery.

"That's not sport," I said flatly. "I don't know *what* that is."

"In Helman," she replied, "it's what passes for spectacle."

"I've seen drunk fights. I've seen men throw fists to prove something. But this? This is something else. This is people hurting each other for the applause."

"Who said it had to be fun?" she said, smile thinning. "Some parties, you go to for joy. Others... because you have to. Some last too long. Some never end."

"This one?"

"This one ends," she said. Her tone dropped to something colder. "But what happens here *lasts forever*."

"I won't be here that long."

"You may not have a choice." Her eyes flicked to the jacket I wore, the phoenix pin catching the light. "That says you earned your way here. You weren't *invited*. You were *summoned*."

She wasn't wrong. I had a way of making the wrong decisions at exactly the right time. Walking the razor's edge between good intentions and poor follow-through. I didn't drift toward Helman; I was *pulled*, consequence by consequence. *Sleeping with Amelia* was just the most recent link in a long chain of missteps.

"What can you tell me about Amelia and JB?" I asked.

Her gaze slid back to the duel. Cary Grant took another dart in the stomach and staggered as the pain set in. He held his footing, pride bleeding alongside the wound.

"They're... eccentric," I tried, testing her. "Amelia's all fire and silk. JB's a fossil in a throne. Doesn't match. Two different realities."

"Two different *perspectives*," she corrected.

"My brother was in a chair," I said. "It changed him. Made him mean. Like he was mad at the world for still moving. Picked fights even when there wasn't one to be fought."

"You're talking about *power*," she said.

"Am I?"

"When your brother lost control over his body, he tried to reclaim control elsewhere – *emotionally, verbally, violently*. You said he picked fights. Why didn't you push back?"

"He was handicapped."

"You pitied him."

"Not pity. Empathy. Mercy."

"No," she said, voice sharpening. "You pitied him. And he hated you for it. Because you could walk. You could choose. And he would never get that back. So, he fought you because *power resents mercy*. It wants domination, not sympathy."

She had me pegged. A stranger reading a page I didn't know I'd left open.

"And JB?" I asked. "What about *him* and Amelia?"

"When two people like that circle each other," she said, "conflict's not optional. It's inevitable. Two alpha predators can't share the same kill. But Helman doesn't care who leads the pack. The town survives either way."

"Who runs it now? I mean really runs it. JB? Or Amelia?"

She didn't answer. Just stared at the bleeding man, who dropped to one knee while the blonde one lined up another dart.

"There's always someone in charge," she said. "But the crown comes with a price and the throne bleeds."

The cheer went up again, a savage, gleeful howl from the crowd. And just like that, the mood turned. The blonde beside me changed, as if shedding a layer of emotion.

"You like games?" she asked, too casually.

Before I could answer, her fingers were around mine. Cool. Certain.

She led me out of the room like she'd done it a hundred times, guiding the newest soul through the next level of torment.

The dart room faded behind us, but the echoes remained.

Chapter Nine

Bins was in his element, buzzing from group to group, charming women with disposable chatter, drinking like the wine had a timer on it. He moved with the urgency of a man who knew all oases dry eventually. Meanwhile, I wandered the first floor of the house, past rooms packed with guests performing rituals that looked like leisure but felt like ceremony. No one moved with purpose. They drifted in spirals, caught in some lazy, looping current.

Everything orbited the grand staircase at the center of the house. It spiraled downward like the party was built atop a drain, pulling everyone toward the depths. I let the current take me and found myself at the edge, staring down into the darkness below.

"Don't just stand there," a voice purred behind me. "Head on down."

I turned. Amelia. Dressed in a red cocktail dress so tight it answered questions I hadn't asked. The fabric clung to her like a secret she wasn't interested in keeping.

"I was actually thinking of leaving," I said.

"That would be foolish." She took my arm like it belonged to her, and her lips brushed my cheek with something that felt contractual. "You haven't done what you came here to do."

She pressed in closer, her perfume a sin in itself. We descended like royalty entering a ballroom, but with each step, the air grew colder. The warmth of the upstairs faded. Down here, you could see your breath, and everyone wore it like foggy confessions.

"This jacket suits you," she said, once we reached the bottom. Her fingers traced the phoenix stitched across my back. "The bird makes a statement."

"You mean there were options?"

"Oh yes. A scorpion. A snake. Even a centipede. But symbols have to match the man. Yours burns. "

"I'm fire, then?"

"You're fire that *endures*," she said. "People admire fire. But they fear the ones who carry it without getting burned."

As if on cue, a couple approached, well-dressed, trying too hard. Amelia smiled at them like a queen indulging peasants. When she showed them the phoenix, their guarded demeanor melted. The girl, barely twenty, ran her fingers over mine like she was checking for heat. Her eyes whispered things her mouth didn't dare.

Amelia's arm stayed wrapped around my waist. She stiffened when her hand brushed the butt of the gun beneath my jacket. A beat passed. She recovered flawlessly, smoothing my lapels like a lover, not an accomplice.

"You found a gun," she murmured. "Smart. There are many guns here. One more or less won't raise suspicion."

She guided us across the room, slipping between guests like she belonged to every one of them. We stopped at the far bar.

"The hard part will be getting him alone," she said. "I can help with that."

"Pulling the trigger's easy," I said. "The real trouble starts when they find the body."

"It *has* to be found," she said firmly. "Everyone needs to know. JB must die in public. Symbolically. Loudly."

"And when they start asking who did it?"

"They will," she said. "And they'll catch someone. They have to. And when they do, that person will suffer. Horribly. *If* he's caught alive."

"You've got someone picked out already?"

A sly smile curled her lips. "I do. You do your part, everything falls into place."

There it was. Not a consideration. A promise.

And the way she said *that person* – not *you*, not *me* – made it worse. Because in this town, you didn't need to be guilty. You just needed to be nearby when the flames went up.

She must have seen the hesitation in my face. Her hand touched my arm, gently, coaxingly.

"If my husband lives," she whispered, "we can't happen. Don't you want me, Bobby?"

"You know I do. You're the kind of woman who makes men forget things."

"Only the things they don't want to remember. You want better, don't you? I *do*. I can be more than this. But I need help. Your help. We do this right, we can rewrite everything."

Her eyes searched mine, wide with practiced sincerity. Almost believable. *Almost*.

"Bobby," she said, dropping her voice to something deeper. "A man who sells Bibles in a Godless town is clever.

Strength wins battles. Cleverness wins wars. You've been sent here to fail. A suicide errand by someone who thinks they own you. But you didn't leave. You stayed. Which means…"

"I owe someone," I said, voice grim. "For something I did. Or something I still have to fix."

She nodded, pleased. Like a chess player finally pulling a piece into the right place.

"Good," she said. "Because what comes next… requires a man with something to lose."

"You're not married," she said, voice slow and smoky. "But you're no stranger to what a woman needs. You don't have many lines you won't cross. And I've seen how you look at me. Hunger in your eyes. Like you want me again tonight… and tomorrow… and the day after that… and the day after that…"

Her voice faded into a low feral and deliberate growl, and it wrapped around me like a noose made of silk and fire.

"And when it's all over?" I pressed her. "What happens to *me* then?"

She leaned back and sipped her drink, cooling herself with alcohol while I stood there, laid bare. That tiny and cold pause told me everything. I'd shown my hand, revealed the fear I couldn't keep hidden. And she knew she was holding the winning cards.

Her smile nearly buckled my knees. It was practiced. Powerful. A blade disguised as lipstick.

"There's no *you* anymore," she said sweetly. "Only *us*. Free to be anything we want. We can stay in the big house. Live like lovers. Cook. Run a business. Or do nothing but stay in each other's arms and wonder what the hell we were doing before this. Why it took so long to find each other."

She leaned in again, her breath warm with promise.

"We'll have more money than we know what to do with. *Power?* It's yours. You'll run this town however you see fit. *Women?* You have me. And everything that comes with me. That's not just a good life. That's a *king's* life, Bobby. Your life. And any enemies? Loose ends? Regrets from before?" She snapped her fingers. "Gone. Just like that. How does that sound? How does that *feel*."

It felt good, real good. She had a way of speaking that was so intoxicating that played just the right tune your ear wanted to listen to. But the face she wore then, delicate and unguarded, felt like something painted on. Temporary. I wasn't smart enough to decode it fully, but I knew enough to know it could vanish as quickly as it appeared.

"Alright," I said, and in that moment, the gun at the small of my back seemed to burn against my spine. Heavy. Hot. Like it had been pulled from the coals of a dying forge. Her eyes sparkled as they adjusted again. They were always shifting, always performing. She kissed me lightly, just a breath across my lips. It lasted a second, but it did more damage than a long, devouring kiss ever could. It left me branded.

"You ate the chilis today, Bobby Santos," she whispered, pulling me close. "You have power now."

Good-looking women, *dangerous* women, know exactly what to say, when to say it, and how to coat it in just the right tone. Their timing is music. Their voices, weapons. The best of them make you think you're in control while gently tightening the chains.

Luanne used to try that. But she was a novice.

The garter belts and low-cut blouses she wore were her tools, but they lacked subtlety. Her version of seduction was full-court press: all passion, no patience. Smother you with affection, then rip it away like a spoiled brat who changed her mind.

But Amelia…

Amelia didn't smother. She suffocated slowly. Elegantly. With taste.

Two different strategies. Same result.

I was already halfway to hell.

Amelia took my hand again, and we wove through the crowd like dancers moving toward a darker rhythm. Down a hallway, through a heavy door, into a colder room where pain hung thick in the air.

Dupree stood over a man tied to a chair. Sweat glistened on his pudgy face, his rolled-up sleeves soaked and knuckles slick with blood. He looked up briefly when we entered just enough to acknowledge us, then drove another punch into the man's face.

The man's head snapped back, spraying blood like mist off a wave.

Amelia took in the scene, then calmly closed the door behind us.

"Is that Ernesto?" she asked.

The man's face was pure pulp, swollen and nearly unrecognizable as human. Both eyes were sealed shut by bruises. Blood streamed freely from his nose and mouth. A couple of teeth littered the floor like discarded dice. But the black cassock was unmistakable.

"That's the priest?" I asked.

"Yes," Amelia said. "But don't let the robe fool you. He's no holy man."

Dupree shook blood from his hand like it was sweaty, then grabbed a towel. He glanced at me, then at Amelia.

"He's becoming a familiar face," he said. "What's he doing here?"

"Learning," Amelia replied, moving toward the priest. There was no hesitation in her voice. No second thought. Just cold certainty.

Dupree gave me a longer look this time. Not suspicion, but surprise. Like I was supposed to be a pawn, and now I was standing on the wrong side of the board.

"What'd he do?" I asked, covering my nose. The stench in the room hit hard. It was full of blood, bile, and the unmistakable reek of shit. The kind a man makes when he's broken in body and spirit.

"He didn't listen," Amelia said simply. "He was told how things work in Hellman. He chose not to believe."

"That's it?"

Dupree grabbed a bottle of water, took a long drink, and spat the rest on the floor.

"He thought he had opinions," he said. "Turns out he didn't."

"He going to die because of that?"

Dupree shrugged. "Nah. He'll be patched up. Given a couple days. Then we'll start again. Some people need more than one lesson."

Amelia placed a hand on my shoulder and squeezed just enough pressure to make a point.

"A man who wants *everything*," she said softly, "should understand what it *takes* to keep everything."

"But... he's a priest," I said, the words flat even to my own ears.

Three Days In Hell

She tilted her head. "Would you feel the same if you knew he raped migrant boys smuggled over the border?"

"He did that?"

She didn't answer. Just watched me, eyes unreadable.

"What would *you* do to a man like that?"

Before I could answer, Dupree called in two men. They lifted the chair, priest and all, and dragged him out like a sack of meat. He barely raised his head, and I swear he looked straight at me, pleading with what little was left in him.

And I did nothing.

Dupree wiped his hands with a towel already soaked in blood. He snorted, then stuffed tobacco into his mouth. Spat on the floor.

"Two days ago," he said, "you probably didn't expect to be standing here. I tried to warn you in the diner, Penny. But no one listens. Not really."

He turned to Amelia.

"I could kill him," Dupree said. "Right here. Right now. Wouldn't take much. You don't need this guy."

"Maybe," she said, cool and steady. "But it wouldn't end well for you. You couldn't fill the role. You think you could. But you and I both know it wouldn't last long enough. You couldn't finish the chilis."

Her matter-of-fact delivery cut the sheriff off at the knees. In that instant, she reduced the tough, corrupt lawman into nothing more than a high school bully past his prime, a child, really. His power, such as it was, had always been borrowed, and now it had been repossessed.

"Get cleaned up, Sheriff," she said. "You stink."

Before Dupree could bite back, a knock came at the door. A weasel-faced man poked his head inside.

Amelia shot him a glare sharp enough to shave the smirk off a cat.

"What do you want?" she asked, ice in her voice.

The man raised his hands like he was surrendering to gravity. "Just the messenger," he said, as if answering a question she hadn't asked. "He wants me to bring him the kid."

"Tell JB I'll bring Bobby when I'm ready," Amelia said, dismissive and bored.

But the Weasel didn't budge. He shifted his weight, clearly stuck in a place with no safe footing.

"He wants to see him," he repeated. "Alone."

That changed the air in the room. Amelia froze, her expression sharpening as she zeroed in on the man. He fidgeted like a child under a magnifying glass.

Then, without another word, she took my arm and led me a few steps away. Up close, her face was beautiful, but right now, it looked carved from cold stone. When she smiled, it didn't reach her eyes. Her expression sent a chill down my back.

"He wants your decision," she said quietly. "He wants to know your plan."

"What do I tell him?" I asked.

She didn't answer right away. Her eyes flickered with something alive; strategy, perhaps. Calculation.

"You tell him what he wants to hear," she said. "You tell him not only are you going to kill me, but that you're going to do it with all three of us in the same room. He'll love the bravado. He won't be able to resist."

She paused.

"And when he's comfortable, when he thinks it's all gone according to plan... you turn the gun on him. Two shots to the head. No hesitation."

Then, just like that, she brought me back to the Weasel Man.

"Whatever my husband wants," she said with a wry smirk.

The Weasel nodded and beckoned me along. As he led me out, I didn't look back.

Amelia was right. Killing JB Helman would be easy. The man was trapped in his own body, confined to a chair. Vulnerable. Soft. All it took was conviction.

A strong man could do it.

A man with purpose.

A man who had stopped running.

But was that me? The man was in a *chair*.

I started wondering how long Amelia had been planning his exit. How many other "saviors" she had groomed and discarded like snake skins in the desert. How many were buried out there or locked up in one of these rooms, ghosts who once believed the same lies she was telling me now.

No, Amelia wasn't a victim. She just liked to play one when it suited her. But she was smart. Dangerous. She had cards to spare and knew how to stack the deck.

Her connections south of the border were terrifying, but lucrative. She could make a king out of a drifter. She could build an empire with a man like me... or bury me beneath it.

She was offering me Helman's chair. His money. His name. His world.

I'd spent most of my life driving between nameless towns, pushing cheap promises in cheap suits. The motels all looked the same. The clients all looked through me. At least here, I'd have a stake. A roof. A woman.

There were worse places to be.

Hell, I'd lived in most of them.

But I'd be here. Stuck. In one place. Seeing the same town, the same people, the same goddamn Festival.

And no matter how much gold dust coated the pill in Amelia's hand, that was a hard one to swallow.

Weasel-face led me down another set of stairs, another level deeper into this rabbit hole. This house didn't just go down; it descended. It tunneled. It sprawled like a cancer under the earth. I'd heard of cartel tunnels before: miles long, with lights, rails, even restrooms. But this… this was something else entirely.

The air turned sharp, dry, and cold, practically sub-zero.

We entered a large, cavernous room. No music here. No dancing. No drugs or women or wild laughter. Just a few men standing around, dressed in black and cradling weapons so oversized they looked cartoonish. They smoked and spoke in a language I couldn't place, though something about it tickled the edge of recognition.

"Portuguese," Weasel-face said, catching my look. "Tough bastards. Knife work in the blood. Their ancestors hurled harpoons off wooden ships. Best not to stare. They're like mongrel dogs; direct eye contact's a challenge."

"Where are we going?" I asked.

He didn't answer. Just kept walking.

We passed the guards and came to a heavy wooden door. Weasel knocked with the flat of his fist, hard and rhythmically.

"No need to stand on ceremony!" a voice barked from the other side. "Come in already!"

Weasel opened the door for me but stayed behind. I stepped inside and closed the door.

Three Days In Hell

Helman sat behind a large desk, framed in the glow of a wall of monitors. Each screen showed a different view of the house: rooms, hallways, balconies, outdoor courtyards. A private panopticon.

"How are you liking our little shindig?" he asked.

"It's no corporate team-building exercise," I said. "But it'll do."

Helman laughed a raw, rasping bark. "It grows on you."

He waved me over to the desk. "Come here, Bobby. I want to show you something you're going to like."

I walked over and stood at his side, eyes scanning the video feed. Dozens of angles. Dozens of scenes. Too much to focus on.

"What am I looking at?" I asked.

Helman stuck out a gnarled finger and tapped one of the screens.

"Watch this," he said, almost giddy.

On screen, a man paced nervously inside what looked like an indoor dog run. White tile walls. Steel fencing. A kennel, but cleaner. Or maybe just newer. He looked around, calling out for someone. No audio, but it was obvious from his body language.

Then, he stopped. Stared straight at the camera. Froze.

"He sees them now," Helman said, eyes gleaming. "Oh yeah. He sees them alright."

"Sees what?"

Helman didn't answer. He didn't need to.

The man turned and bolted. And then out of frame at first came two Dobermans, sleek and fast, tails docked to stubs, claws clicking on concrete.

They chased him down the corridor and out of view.

There was no second angle. Just the blur of movement, then silence on the screen.

A cold, nauseous twist bloomed in my gut.

"Why would you think I'd like something like that?" I asked.

"You're the punishment type," Helman said smoothly. "You like giving people what they deserve. Don't say you're not. It's in the eyes, Bobby. It's always in the eyes."

"What'd that guy do?"

"He lied. Said he'd do something. Didn't do it. Dishonesty, Bobby. Big no-no."

"And so you sic dogs on him?"

Helman shrugged. "Well, I don't keep lions, do I?"

Helman howled again, then wheeled over to a massive credenza. He flung open its doors to reveal a black safe, punched in a combination with deliberate flair, and pulled out a hard-sided case. He rolled back to me and held it out like a magician about to unveil his final trick.

"I'm good to my word," he said. "Fifty grand in cash. Just like I promised."

I cracked the case open.

Stacks of crisp bills, banded and pristine, glowed like polished gold beneath the cold lights. It was more money than I'd ever seen in one place. I pulled out a stack and fanned it with my thumb. The breeze it made was cold, but not from the temperature. This was the kind of chill that lived in your bones, money with consequence.

Helman laughed, loud and satisfied. "There it is! I knew I'd seen it before, and now I know it to be true."

"What's that?" I asked, still thumbing the stack.

He pointed two fingers at his eyes. "Alert. Precise. When you see something, you do it. That's who you are, Bobby."

I must've flinched, or frowned, because he was quick to follow up.

"Now don't get all offended. There's nothing wrong with being purposeful. It's the simple order of things. You can wait for opportunity to knock, or you can track the bastard down and kick the door in."

He leaned back and looked me over, calculating.

"Speaking of which, you know where you're gonna do her yet?"

I kept my face neutral. "I have to get her alone. That's tough with people always dropping by, wanting two seconds of her time. You got a spot? Somewhere the three of us could go to set her at ease."

Helman stroked his chin, clearly enjoying the game. "A diversion... That's good. That's real good, Bobby. The three of us, just chatting it up. She won't see it coming."

He gave me a slow, knowing smile. "See? You got it in you. Just needed a friendly nudge."

"I was thinking later," I said. "When the crowd thins out. Fewer eyes."

"No," Helman said, shaking his head. "More noise, more people. That's better. More distractions. But you're right. You need some space to work, but you need more noise not less."

He paused, then leaned in, like we were sharing war stories. "If I offered you my two cents, would you take it?"

"You know your house better than me," I said.

"Damn right," he grinned. "Every year, we end this shindig with a real fireworks display. Not the usual backyard crap, big-city stuff. Starts a little after midnight, when folks are good and liquored up. All eyes to the sky, all ears blown out by the finale. That's when you do it. Bang. Bang. No one'll hear. No one'll see."

He smiled wider. "By the time anyone notices Amelia's gone. A day passes, maybe two, they'll blame it on some south-of-the-border mess. Buy you all the time you need."

He sat back, looking pleased with himself.

"A man who wants freedom," he said, "is a man who can do anything."

Then the door opened.

Helman snapped the case shut, like a guilty kid caught in the cookie jar.

Amelia stepped into the room, cool and poised. She paused in the doorway, letting her eyes take in the scene.

"Am I interrupting?" she asked sweetly.

"No, sweetheart," JB said, grinning, "just telling the chili champion here about the fireworks."

Amelia's eyes lit up with sudden enthusiasm. "He should watch with us. On the roof."

JB paused for half a beat before flashing his smile again. "You know, that's exactly what I was thinking. I guess that's what makes us such a great couple, great minds and all that."

"JB's never shy about handing out credit," Amelia said. "Especially when he's handing it to himself. Okay then, it's settled. Bobby will join us up top. I'd like to freshen up before the big finale."

"Doll yourself up all you want, sweetheart," JB said.

Amelia turned to me, that smile of hers sharpening at the corners. "Yes, Bobby. You should be with us on the roof when the fireworks start. It's the best view to see… everything. Every so often, JB has a good idea."

"I always have good ideas," JB replied gruffly. "Not everyone's smart enough to understand them."

Amelia placed her hand on my arm. "Can I steal Bobby for now? I'm sure he'd like to see more of the party before the show."

"Of course, of course," JB said, waving us off. "I'll see you both up top."

Amelia slipped her arm into mine and led me back into the hallway. As the door closed behind us, her voice dropped to a whisper in my ear.

"For the first time in a long time," she murmured, "I agree with my husband. That's the place, Bobby. Just us three. No underlings. No guards. And the best part? Everyone else will be too busy looking up. It's perfect."

She paused just long enough to let the implication settle.

"Kill him then," she said. "No misses."

We passed a grandfather clock in the hall. It was intricate, hand-carved, something out of a different era. It didn't belong here, not in this underground warren built by criminals.

But it still told time.

And it was telling me that mine was running out.

Chapter Ten

Amelia led us back upstairs to the main level and steered me toward the closest bar. She moved with sharp, clipped precision, teeming with nervous energy. The confidence she usually wore like armor was still there, but thinner now, brittle around the edges. She had made her play, her best offer, but she was still unsure whether I'd take it. That uncertainty showed in how she kept licking her lips and tapping the bar before signaling two fingers to the bartender. He set down two glasses and poured from a fresh bottle.

She knocked back her shot, and I followed. Her hand found mine on the bar, squeezing tight. I couldn't tell if it was for my benefit or hers. Maybe both. But after a few moments, she straightened, collected. The sharp and focused gleam returned to her eyes. It was the old Amelia again. But something had changed.

She looked poised. Beautiful. Deadly.

And I decided then: if I was going to save my neck, I had to get out of there at the first opportunity.

And that opportunity was now.

Less than an hour before I was supposed to be on that roof, standing beneath a sky fat with fireworks and lies.

If I went up there, I wouldn't be coming back down, not as myself, anyway. Maybe not at all.

But if I could get to Bins I might still have a chance. A slim one, thinner than a gambler's last cigarette. But sometimes, that's all it takes. A sliver of luck. A whisper of momentum.

"You're distracted," she said.

"Well, I do have *a lot* on my mind."

"No need to be sarcastic." Her tone was all silk, no warmth. "You've made a plan?"

"I think so."

"And I have mine."

"You found someone already?"

"Yes." She smiled like a knife just before it goes in. "He's perfect for our needs."

Her eyes shimmered with that feverish glee some people get before they watch the world burn from a front-row seat. *This* was the night she'd been building toward. The reckoning. The curtain call.

"What a tremendous night this will be," she said.

Then she kissed my cheek with slow, deliberate lips painted in a red so deep it could've been blood. It was a kiss that brands. It was both a warning and a promise, like a future etched in gasoline and matches.

"I have much to do in little time," she said, already stepping back. "I'll see you on the roof, lover."

And just like that, she disappeared into the crowd, swallowed by feathers, sequins, and sin. The party closed behind her like a wound that didn't want to heal.

Almost on cue, Bins materialized at the top of the stairs, looking like he'd been dragged backwards through the last hour. Shirt untucked, collar askew, hair like a nest of bad decisions.

"Where the hell've you been?" I asked.

He didn't answer, grabbing the nearest glass from the bar and knocking it back like medicine that wouldn't work. The glass hit the counter with a clink that sounded too much like a countdown.

"I *think* you're looking at it," he said, voice frayed.

"I need you sober," I said, yanking the glass out of his hand before he could reach for another.

He waved vaguely at the crowd, a sea of bodies blurring into one long, writhing sin. "Look around. Nobody's sober."

He reached for another drink.

I caught his wrist.

"You can drink your face off tomorrow. Tonight, I need you focused."

Something behind his eyes tightened, like a man realizing the dream he was in had teeth. The party wasn't just wild. It was ritual. And he'd shown up without a mask.

"What is it?" he asked, lower now. Less bravado. More fear.

I glanced around. No obvious eavesdroppers. But with JB and Amelia pulling the strings, the whole room could've been bugged with whispers and smiles. I leaned in close, voice like gravel and grave dirt.

"Come here."

Because what I was about to say couldn't be spoken loud.

Because hell was already listening.

I led him through the throng to a side room with tall French windows that opened onto a balcony. We wove past the guests. Outside, the warm night air felt like freedom compared to the cold dread that hung inside the house.

Below us, the crowd churned like a mosh pit of snakes. Debauchery in motion.

"I need one more thing from you. To get out of here," I said. "Out of this house. Out of this town. Tonight. Before midnight."

Bins gave me a hard look. "That's a tall order. You've seen the crowd out there, right? Besides, you don't want to miss the fireworks. Leave after that."

"I can't. It has to be before."

His eyes narrowed. "How bad of a situation are you in?"

"It doesn't get much worse."

He pulled out a cigarette and lit it with shaking hands, and took a long drag before he spoke.

"JB or Amelia?"

"Both.," I said. And then I came clean with him. "They want me to take out the other."

He exhaled smoke. "I'd heard rumors. That they do this. Take turns trying to kill each other. Like some sick game."

"Hell of a game they play."

Bins shrugged. "Marriage, man. It's not what it's cracked up to be. It's like the moment before a tornado touches down, you know? The air goes still, sky turns black, and the wind sounds like a freight train. Then the debris starts flying, and you're just waiting for that funnel to hit the ground."

"Can you help me out?"

He hesitated. "If they catch wind I helped you? Death would be the least of my problems."

"Just get my car. Park it at the church. I'd do it myself, but I can't get two seconds alone. I'd walk to the highway if I thought I'd make it. Just get the car. I'll do the rest."

Bins looked toward the house. One of JB's thugs stood by the window, watching us. Always watching.

"I don't want to rain on your parade," he said, voice low, "but they're keeping eyes on you. You're being tracked, Bobby. You won't get far."

"If I don't try, I'll have to kill someone."

"Better one of them than you."

"I've done bad things. But I've never murdered anyone."

"Even if it's kill or be killed?" He flicked ash off the balcony. "You've seen what happens to people who disappoint them."

"All the more reason to vanish. So, can you help me or not?"

He took another drag. Thought it over. "I'll be at the church by eleven-thirty. Transportation will be there if you make it."

He didn't say "if you're alive." He didn't have to. That part was implied.

I nodded once.

The deal was struck.

And the clock was ticking.

"Tell me something, Bobby. How does a Bible salesman get into such disarray?"

I gave him a sad smirk. "I don't sell them. I give them away. And what always gets men in trouble? A woman."

"Eleven-thirty," Bins said. "That's forty minutes from now. Don't be late."

I started weaving my way around the first floor, dodging the waiters trying to pawn off their drink trays like poison in crystal. No more booze. No more surprises from smiling strangers. I needed a clear head and a new plan.

I found myself in a side room overlooking the front of the Helman estate. Outside, the crowd was a swirling eddy, dense, frenzied, growing faster by the minute. Through the open windows, I could hear the far-off pop of rogue fireworks being set off in the church parking lot.

My mind started assembling a rough timeline. Bins would need ten minutes to get to my car. Another fifteen to fight his way through traffic and the street chaos. Maybe another fifteen to deal with whatever else this night decided to throw at him. If he made good time, I'd have just enough of a window to slip out the front and be gone before anyone got wise.

I helped myself to a cigarette from the box near the window and lit it with one of the wooden matches from a bowl beside it. Then I moved behind a potted palm near the corner to keep myself hidden just in case JB or Amelia had started sending out their dogs. Sure, I had the gun. But two bullets wouldn't get me far, not against the full deck they had stacked against me.

Best-case scenario: I'd be tearing down the road before midnight, flames in my rearview and the devil off my tail.

Worst-case? I'd end up like the others who crossed JB and Amelia – tortured and forgotten.

Bins better come through.

That's when I saw Weasel Face poke his head into the room.

Time to move.

I pushed my way through one of the spinning walls, angling for the windows on the far side of the first floor that opened onto the side patio that bordered the church grounds. I kept my eyes down. No eye contact. Be unmemorable.

I ditched the flashy jacket as I walked, tossing it behind a statue someone had dressed up in a feather boa. No sense making their job easier.

I couldn't tell how close I was to the edge of the house or how far I had to go. Every corridor twisted into another. I stayed along the walls, skirting the thoroughfares, ducking low when I had to. The crowd pulsed all around me, faces flashing in and out like masks at a carnival.

My heart was pounding hard enough to crack my ribs. The air was cold, but I was sweating like I'd swallowed a ghost pepper whole. I must've looked like a man about to implode; wide, twitchy eyes and jerking limbs that didn't match the beat of the party.

I spotted three of JB's goons stopping guests, checking IDs or maybe just sniffing out panic. Then two more joined them, fanning out like hunting dogs.

They'd found the jacket.

Options were slipping through my fingers like water.

Then – luck.

A woman spun one of the partition walls, opening a narrow alley through the chaos. I darted into the space before it closed, clipping her shoulder in the process. Her drink sloshed across her wrist, and she shrieked in drunken indignation, but I was already past her, gone, the wall clicking shut behind me.

I didn't check the room for spies or lookouts. My eyes were locked on the French doors that opened to the patio. Over the wall, I could just make out the burned-out husk of the church. There was no mystery left in its destruction. Virtue had no place in a house like this. Not anymore.

I'd go out those doors, scale the fence, and disappear into the night. I'd ride that car as far as the gas would take me, then fill up and drive until I crossed the border. I'd keep going – Mexico, Guatemala, Honduras, wherever the road led. When the money ran out or the car died under me like a spent horse, I'd go on foot. All the way down to the southern tip of Chile.

And then?

Then I'd find a ship. Head for some island far from memory, beyond consequence. But I didn't dare name it. Not yet. The idea was too fragile. If I thought about it too much, it might vanish, or worse, fate might hear my plans.

No, the destination had to be chosen on the fly. One morning, some morning, I'd wake up, pick a place, and commit to it with all I had left. And when I got there, wherever *there* was, I'd sit on a beach and watch the waves come in. I'd think about this ruined place and everything I did to crawl out of it.

A quick scan told me I was in the clear…for now.

I moved briskly but smoothly toward the French windows. No eye contact, but I didn't look away either. The trick was to blend in, to move like I belonged, even in a house where nothing and no one quite belonged.

Then came the snag.

An older couple stood in my path, blocking the door like life-sized wedding toppers. Too perfect. Too still. Skin stretched taut and polished like porcelain. The man's suit looked like it had been sewn by a tailor who hadn't drawn breath since 1935. It was long-jacketed, high-waisted, cuffs sharp enough to draw blood. Her dress matched: padded shoulders, cinched waist, Depression-era chic with a modern menace.

His hair was slicked back in twin layers of gunmetal and soot, and his mustache was clipped like it had an appointment. His eyes drooped at the corners but sparkled with cold intelligence and the lazy disdain of the ultrarich. She mirrored him with all the regal, rigid, remote sophistication of the wealthy.

They turned to me in perfect sync and lifted their empty champagne flutes toward a tray I didn't have.

"Apologies, sir," the man said with the tone of a man forgiving a waiter for existing. "We thought you were one of the staff flittering about."

The woman nodded, lips pursed like they'd been painted on hours ago. "One doesn't expect someone to stand in front of you *not* offering a drink."

"Sorry," I said, trying to slide past. "Just on my way to –"

"Dr. Francis Sweeney," he said, snapping his hand forward like he expected it to be kissed. "And this is my wife, Dora. You are?"

"Just leaving, but –"

"You look familiar. Where do I know you from?" Sweeney squinted, his gaze tightening like a vise.

"I can't imagine."

"Don't tell me. It'll come." He tilted his head. And then: revelation. "*Robert Johnson!* Dora, look! It's Robert Johnson!"

She raised her brows with manufactured delight. "The guitar player?"

"Do you know another Robert Johnson? My dear boy, where have you been? Haven't seen you in a dog's age."

"I'm sorry, but you've got me mistaken for –"

"The Monte Carlo Beach Club! That was it. I remember glitter. Too much champagne. You played until the sun came up."

"Sure. That was... something," I said, pasting on a smile so thin it barely held.

"Stop your silliness, Robert. You know no one leaves before the fireworks!"

"You know what they say. Seen one aerial starburst..."

Sweeney grabbed my arm. His grip was stronger than it should've been. His breath smelled faintly of roses and formaldehyde.

"Robert Johnson," he said, low and firm, "we've been attending these parties as long as *you* have. And we notice when you're missing."

"And missed," Dora added with a tilt of the head. "Maybe later you'll play *I'll See You in My Dreams* for us?"

"Yes! Where's that guitar you always carry?" Sweeney asked, eyes darting past me, searching for a case that didn't exist.

"I left it outside," I said, grabbing the lifeline. "Let me fetch it. Be right back. You name it, I'll play it."

Their faces lit up with something that wasn't quite joy.

"Go on then, my boy!" Sweeney said, releasing my arm. "Don't keep us waiting."

Time was slipping through the cracks. I had ten minutes, maybe less, before someone figured out I was missing, or someone worse figured out who I really was. I pushed past the crowd and stepped through the French doors into the night.

The air hit me like a wall with humidity and a foul stink of smoke, sweat, and stale piss.

But it wasn't the smell that stopped me cold.

Amelia stood there, flanked by two familiar faces: Silver Teeth and the Little Guy. Her expression was unreadable, save for the tight, reluctant line of her lips. All three of them stared at me like I was a rat that had almost made it out of the maze.

I froze.

Amelia stepped forward, extending her hand as if greeting a dance partner instead of reeling in a traitor.

"There you are, Bobby," she said.

Her voice was soft, even pleasant, but sharp enough to draw blood.

"We've been looking all over for you. It's almost time for the fireworks. What happened to your jacket?"

"I was hot and needed to get some air," I replied, my voice steadier than I felt.

Behind her, over the fence, the burned-out church stared down like a witness, so close, so goddamn close.

Amelia frowned. "JB will be disappointed. He picked that out especially for you. Besides, there's plenty of air on the roof," she said, closing the distance between us.

Her arm slid into mine. The other one swept casually down my back. Her fingers brushed the butt of the gun, just a whisper of contact, but enough to let me know that *she knew*.

Then she took my hand.

"Come," she said, her smile thin and cold. "JB is waiting."

Chapter Eleven
Sunday

Amelia opened the door, and we stepped into the night. She sent the henchmen away. Murder was a private, intimate affair.

Even though we'd escaped the chill of the house, I still felt that cold clinging to my skin. It shouldn't have been like that. Heat rises, cold sinks. That's what science says. But nothing followed the laws of physics in Helman.

This wasn't an ordinary rooftop.

There was a wet bar, a jacuzzi bubbling under a slatted wooden canopy, the kind meant to block the harsh sun for those foolish enough to bathe in hot water beneath a scorching sky. I could picture Amelia up here during the day all splayed out in a tiny bikini, or nothing at all, safely elevated above the filth of the city.

JB Helman sat in his wheelchair near the edge, grinning with outstretched arms like I was a long-lost son returning home.

"There he is," he said, practically beaming. "I was worried you weren't gonna make it."

"He just needed some air," Amelia said smoothly.

"What do you think is up here? Plenty of fresh, untainted air. Come on, let's get to the corner. You'll really catch the majesty of the show from there."

He glanced at me and I understood his nonverbal ask. I grabbed the wheelchair's handles and pushed him toward the edge.

"I can't tell you how excited I am," JB went on. "Haven't felt this way since my pecker stood on its own without pharmaceutical support."

"JB's a child when it comes to fireworks," Amelia said, indulgently. "Everything has to be big and bright and loud."

"Nothing wrong with that," he said with a snort. "Simple things are better, right Bobby?"

"They can be," I replied.

"Of course they can," he said, waving the thought away.

He had me stop at the edge, beside the chest-high concrete barrier that ringed the rooftop. I leaned against it, casting a glance over the crowd below.

They writhed in a semi-controlled frenzy, whipped up with anticipation. Fights were already breaking out in the waiting. The sky was moments from exploding. And so was everything else.

Amelia retrieved a handheld device from the table, a gaudy little box with candy-colored buttons that looked like it had been built by a madman with a God complex.

"For the fireworks," she said, catching my look.

She stood next to JB like the snake at Eve's shoulder, the real engine behind the man who sat grinning in that metal throne. I watched the king and queen of this rooftop purgatory, and something stirred in my memory. Something from a dusty philosophy class I slept through back when I thought salvation came in the shape of a diploma.

Bread and circus.

That's what the Romans fed the mob when things started falling apart. Feed their bellies, blind their eyes. Give them a show while the world rots under their feet. That was Helman's game, to keep the streets drunk and dazzled while he choked the soul out of the city.

The door creaked open again, louder this time, and out walked the young girl.

My angel.

She balanced a tray with three drinks like it weighed more than her conscience. She had changed since I first had seen her at the mines, when they dragged her in like a prize pig. Back then, her eyes still had something flickering behind them. Now, they were just empty glass.

She moved like someone walking through fog, careful, disconnected, as if afraid that one false step might shatter what little she had left inside. When she reached us, she didn't speak, didn't look up. Just offered the drinks like a tired wraith in some hellish tavern.

"Ah, good," Helman said, grabbing a glass with a wolf's grin. He didn't even look at the girl, just tossed the drink back like it was holy water. "Go back downstairs, Maria."

She nodded, a gesture stripped of meaning, then melted into the shadows like smoke in a dying room, no footsteps, no sound, just absence where presence used to be"

The silence that followed was dense, like the air before a thunderclap.

"I have to say," Helman broke it, chuckling as he turned his chair to face me. "This is one of the best Festivals we've ever had."

"The best," Amelia echoed, her eyes sliding over to mine, flashing a meaning only the damned would understand. "A good town. A good show. And a good man."

"You're right," Helman said. "Bobby's been an unexpected gift. Didn't expect all this when you came into town, did you, preacher?"

"No," I said. And I meant it. Not this. Not any of this.

But neither of them knew I was holding one more card than either of them had.

Amelia raised her glass. "To Bobby."

"To Bobby," Helman echoed, clinking his drink against hers with the false cheer of a man used to toasting ghosts.

"That's not necessary," I said.

"But it is," Helman replied, voice tightening just a notch. "You came into this town dead on your feet, selling salvation to people who wouldn't know the Gospel if it shot 'em in the kneecaps. And look at you now, our guest of honor. That's worth celebrating."

They drank. So did I. It wasn't champagne. It was sweet at first, then sour like rot dipped in syrup. Something chemical. Something old. It burned a little on the way down, and not in the good way.

Helman smacked his lips. "Shall we? The people have been waiting."

"I was thinking we let Bobby do it."

Helman lit up like a neon sign. "Perfect! Go ahead, Bobby. Light up the sky like it's Judgment Day."

She handed me the device, the red button pulsing, calling to me like a soul begging passage across Acheron. One push and the show would begin. One push and something, maybe everything, would end.

I hesitated. My thumb hovered.

Amelia's eyes flared in anticipation. "Do it."

And I did.

The sky split open like a wound. Red bloomed first, crimson blossoms bursting against the void. Then gold, green, violet. The crowd below gasped as one, caught in the ecstasy of spectacle. Helman's rooftop became a chapel of fire, and for one terrible moment, I imagined this was what Dante saw when he looked up from the pit: beauty in the service of evil.

And still no gunshot. No betrayal. Not yet.

A minute passed. Then two. Something inside both of them began to curdle.

Amelia turned to me slowly. Her face had changed. No more seduction. Just the raw, unfiltered hatred of a plan unraveling at the seams. She mouthed a word.

"Now."

But I didn't move.

"Goddamn gorgeous," Helman said, squinting into the blaze. "Shame you almost missed it. What was it again? You needed air?"

"It was hard to breathe," I said.

"Don't feed me bullshit, Bobby." His voice darkened, gained weight. "You were gonna bolt. Right, Amelia?"

"That's the way it looked to me," she said, flat.

"That's not true," I lied. "I just needed –"

"Air. Sure. We know. Maybe you were. Maybe we're just paranoid. Misreading things. Misjudging people."

He turned toward me, his smile long gone.

The fireworks kept going burning bright against a sky black as sin.

"Good thing you've got all those Bibles," JB cackled, eyes twinkling like a snake oil preacher drunk on his own sermon. "Got one on you to lay your hand on it?"

"I wasn't trying to leave," I said, but it sounded like a lie even to me, weak and soggy like a confession whispered too late.

"Yes, you were," came a voice slick with smirk and self-satisfaction.

I turned.

Bins.

Smiling like Judas when the silver hit his palm.

He caught the brick of cash Helman tossed without missing a beat. It thumped into his hand like judgment.

"Can't trust anyone these days," Helman muttered, shaking his head as if *he* were the victim in all this.

"Whatever he told you, it's bullshit," I said, heat creeping up my spine.

"Well," Helman said, his voice oily and even, "somebody's a liar. The known scoundrel who'll sell his soul for a hundred-dollar bill, or the holy roller who doesn't keep his promises."

He took a long sip, watching me over the rim of his glass.

"We know Bins. Crooked as a dog's hind leg, ain't that right, Amelia?"

"That's right," she said, walking over like sin in heels, her finger trailing across Bins' shoulder like a razor.

"Bins only plays one tune," she purred. "His own. Boring. But predictable."

I spit on the concrete. The rooftop smelled like ozone and betrayal.

"You sold me out," I said.

Three Days In Hell

"What'd you expect?" Bins replied, flipping the stack of bills like he was fanning himself with absolution. "Last time we met, I was trying to steal your spare change. This ain't ashtray money, Bobby. This is a goddamn upgrade."

He looked at Amelia. "Can I go now?"

She pouted, looping her arm in his like a noose made of velvet.

A bright explosion painted the sky behind them, crimson and gold, blooming like a wound in the firmament.

"You don't want to see the finale?" she asked sweetly.

He held up the cash. "I already did."

He tried to shake loose, but she didn't budge.

Her grip, all delicate fingers and painted nails, was iron underneath.

"Come on," he said, uneasy now.

"What's wrong?" Her voice was still honey, but now there was arsenic underneath.

"Cut it out. Let go."

"You don't like me, Bins?"

He turned to JB, suddenly a schoolboy caught in the principal's office.

"JB… please."

Helman said nothing. Just watched, eyes like cold glass.

Bins started pulling, desperate now. But Amelia held him like gravity.

"Let me go!" he yelled, voice rising.

Then she let go. Just like that.

He fell backward, landed hard. Amelia's life was sharp and bright, like glass breaking.

"Relax," she said. "It was a joke."

"It wasn't funny."

"Sure, it was. It just wasn't funny to *you*."

She bent and picked up the cash he dropped, offered it back like an apology wrapped in butcher paper. He reached for it. She took his hand.

Then she *cut* him.

The blade moved so fast it wasn't a gesture; it was punctuation.

Bins blinked, confused. He didn't fall so much as melt to his knees, staring dumbly at the blood that spurted from his throat like a fountain built in Hell.

His hands went to his neck, but it was too late.

His fate had already slipped through his fingers.

Helman laughed. Not because it was funny. Because it was expected.

Bins gurgled before he collapsed, his eyes still wide with the realization that the last bad deal he made had finally cashed out.

I turned away. His blood was already drying into the cracks of the concrete.

"What the hell was that for?" I asked.

"I'm sorry," Amelia said. "Did you want the pleasure?"

"No."

"Why not?" she asked, cocking her head like a curious child. "He betrayed you for money. He smiled when he thought you'd die. Didn't bother him at all."

"I'm not a killer," I muttered.

"Before the sun rises," she said, smiling like the Devil's favorite daughter, "you will be."

More fireworks clawed at the sky in bursts of red, green, and gold, burning flowers blooming in the dark. JB giggled like a schoolboy drunk on cherry bombs.

"It's go-time, Bobby," he sang. "Time to earn that paycheck. Two in her head, just like we said."

He made a finger-gun and pantomimed the shots. "Pow-pow!"

Amelia didn't flinch. Just smiled like a lioness at the zoo.

"He's not here for me, *papi*," she said. "He's here for you."

Then to me, with eyes glittering like ice above a furnace: "Do it. Shoot him, Bobby."

JB didn't move. Didn't blink.

He watched the fireworks like a man watching his own victory parade.

When I didn't act, she raised her voice.

"Shoot him!"

He finally turned, dragging his chair around to face her. Still smug. Still king of a crumbling hill.

"Looks like you pulled the short straw, sweetheart."

That's when I stepped back, slowly, like a man letting go of the rope in a tug-of-war where both ends lead to Hell.

I reached behind me, pulled the gun free.

It felt heavier than it should have like the weight of *choice*.

I pointed it in their general direction, and for one split second, both their eyes locked on mine – *watching*, *waiting*, hoping to see where justice, or its counterfeit cousin, would fall.

When the barrel settled, only one of them changed.

Amelia's smirk didn't shatter. It softened. Into something like disappointment.

She saw it in my eyes: I hadn't come to kill her husband.

And even then, standing on the edge of betrayal, she didn't beg.

No tears. No performance. Just a quiet, accepting nod like a sinner finally finding her name in the right book of the damned.

"Really? JB?" she asked. Just that. Nothing more.

"That's always been your problem, Amelia," he said, grinning like a grave robber. "You thought you were smarter than me. But I played you better than a fiddle in a funeral band."

He chuckled and sipped from a glass that had long gone empty.

"Bobby and I made a deal. A *rich* one."

Her eyes narrowed on me, scanning for a crack. "Money?"

JB waved a hand at the sky like he owned the night.

"Is there anything better?"

She didn't even look at him. Just me.

"There's not enough money in the world to keep you breathing once my brother finds out. He'll scorch the earth for vengeance. You didn't buy a future, JB. You bought a countdown."

JB grunted. "What'd *you* offer him, darling? Besides what you already gave away for free."

She smiled, but there was poison in it.

"Everything that's yours."

He blinked. Like he'd just been hit with a language he didn't speak.

"Everything?"

"Your house. Your title. Your throne. *Me.*"

JB looked at me, then the gun, suddenly unsure whether the heat at his back was fireworks or the first flames of Hell licking his heels.

He shifted in his seat.

"You sure your brother's gonna like that?" he muttered.

"Bobby's my choice," she said, her voice a hammer. "And I'm his blood."

JB's smile cracked. He tried to glue it back on with bluster.

"Come on, now, Bobby. You're a man of principle, your own kind, sure, but still. We made a deal. Don't be the kind of man who breaks one."

Amelia turned to me, eyes hard as diamond-tipped bullets.

"How much?" she demanded. "How much to kill me?"

I could barely swallow. There was no spit to be found in my mouth. "Fifty thousand."

She scoffed. Looked away, as if the number itself offended her.

"That's a drop in the bucket. I offered you *gold*, and you're reaching for gravel."

"Shut your trap, Amelia," JB barked.

But she didn't stop. She leaned in like a knife twisting itself.

"No, *you* shut your trap. Your time's been up for a long time. You're just too scared to read the clock."

JB snapped. "Shoot her, Bobby! What the hell are you waiting for?! Shoot her and walk out clean!"

The gun shook in my hand.

The world spun; there were too many voices, too many ghosts in the room whispering different sins.

I tightened my grip.

JB was strapped to a chair, but Amelia?

She was dangerous even when she smiled. I'd seen what happened when you let her close. I liked breathing.

She stepped toward me.

"Please," I said. "Don't."

"Or what?" she whispered. "You gonna shoot me, Bobby? Do you really that in you to murder in cold blood?"

"I saw what you did to Bins. You didn't even blink."

"That was different."

"How?"

She smiled again. That same dangerous smirk.

"Because Bins was a pawn. You? You're a king. And the only thing between you and the crown…"

She tilted her chin toward JB.

"…is him."

"Shut up, Amelia!" JB barked. "You got what's coming, and you know it. Go on, Bobby. Shoot her already. Your money's over there."

He pointed toward the door. I followed his finger and saw the metal briefcase.

Amelia's bravado cracked, just a hairline fracture. For the first time since I'd met her, something like worry flashed across her face.

"You think this is going to work?" she asked JB. "You think you're going to get away with it?"

"Absolutely," he grinned, no hesitation, no fear. "You thought you had yourself a winner, huh? Thought your charms would play him like the rest of us?"

He snorted. "Please. He's fresh off a woman who gutted him. You're not his salvation; you're his revenge."

He turned to me. "She thinks she knows men. She doesn't know shit. But don't worry, sweetheart, I'll make sure it's an open casket. Let your people say goodbye to what's left."

Amelia swung her glare to me. "Don't believe him. He's going to kill you, too. He *has* to."

"Wrong," JB said, all smug now, riding high.

He jabbed a thumb at Bins' body on the floor. "See that? That sad sack ratted Bobby out. Came crawling to us. So, guess what? That's our killer. We slice him up good, leave him next to your corpse – boom. Case closed. Bobby gets paid. *Hell*, your brother might even *thank* him for it."

"You son-of-a-bitch," she growled.

"Now, now," he grinned. "Don't be like that. You just got outplayed. Thought you could use Bobby to knock me off? Cute. But I had you pegged from the jump."

He tapped his temple. "I got more up here than you ever did."

Her expression turned surgical.

"Well, you got that right."

His face twitched. "What's that supposed to mean?"

"You heard me. You've always had to *overcompensate*. Couldn't measure up elsewhere, so you played the 'smart' card."

"You're a real nasty bitch."

"I'm honest. I'll go to my grave knowing one thing; you never sired proper offspring."

His voice cracked like glass. "Shut your mouth."

"You *can't* sire children, JB. Not when you chase after things that still play with dolls. Little girls don't make babies. But that's what you like, isn't it?"

And then he moved.

People don't expect speed from a wheelchair. It's a prop. A trick. A sympathy ploy.

But JB exploded from that chair like a mine going off, slapping Amelia so hard she spun.

The *crack* echoed like a gunshot. She hit the floor beside Bins, hair wild, lip bleeding.

JB turned to me, panting, triumphant.

"Well? What are you waiting for? Do your goddamn job."

I stared.

"You can walk."

"What?"

"You can walk."

"I heard you." He laughed. "What's your point?"

"All this time…"

"You thought I was helpless? I never said I couldn't walk. You just *assumed*."

He adjusted his cuffs. "Smoke and mirrors. A little theater. Image is everything."

"How'd you know *that* was the play to make against me? You didn't know my history. You didn't know my brother."

He gave me a long look, reading me like a book already halfway finished.

"You're not complicated, Bobby. You saw the chair and thought 'brother.' You saw a broken man and got soft. I could see it on your face. You've got guilt stitched into your skin like you missed one call too many. And now you're out here trying to make amends with a loaded gun."

He grinned. "How messed up are you? You're just like the rest of this town. Carrying a weight that keeps crushing you every damn day. Running into the fire because you think the pain makes you *better* somehow."

"You're a real piece of shit."

"Lower than a man who screws another man's wife?" He shrugged. "Splitting hairs, don't you think?"

Then he gestured toward the case again.

"My deal stands. Money's there. Take it. You're gonna need every second to get out of here."

He leaned in, voice dropping cold.

"When they figure out Bins didn't do it, and they will, because I'll *make sure* they do, *El Mochomo* will come hunting. And when he finds you?"

He paused.

"They'll put a tire around you, Bobby. Douse it in gas. And *light it*."

He smiled, certain of his triumph, the cruel curve of his mouth forged by years of small, private wars. "For the life of me," he said, smug and slow, "I don't know why people never wise up. Weakness has its reason. People hand themselves over before they even know what they've done."

All my life, I'd walked into fire with gasoline shoes. It didn't matter how many signs warned me off; hell, some people even meant well. But I always took the wrong turn, eyes open, hands out, begging to bleed. I wasn't moving forward. I was going in circles, wearing my own trail deeper with every stumble, spiraling like a soul circling the pit, one level closer to the bottom each time.

"Pull the damn trigger!" he barked, as if that could save him now.

Amelia didn't flinch. She stood like marble, so beautiful, tragic, and untouchable. Death had already kissed her, and instead of shrinking, she glowed. Some people wear doom like perfume. Her eyes held no fear, only the calm recognition of inevitability. Her finger drifted along her neckline, tracing the edge like a blade, waiting for the moment that would decide everything.

Killing isn't hard. It's movement, an impulse given shape. A twitch of the finger. A knife drawn. A steering wheel turned just a bit too far. The act itself is cheap. What comes after is where the price gets paid. For some, it's passion. For others, policy. And for a damned few, it's justice – rough, final, and biblical. But no matter why you do it, you're left with it. It follows you, settles into your bones. It builds your afterlife one brick at a time, like mortar laid by your own guilty hands.

Yeah, I pulled the trigger. Twice.

The first caught his throat and cut off that silver tongue mid-sentence. The second planted itself in his skull like punctuation. Final. He looked at me, wide-eyed, trying to drink in the last drops of a world that no longer wanted him. Then he dropped face-first onto the concrete. The crunch of bone was soft, sick, like someone snapping a communion wafer.

No one heard. The shots were drowned beneath the last gasps of an air raid siren, or maybe just fireworks. It didn't matter. The city was too used to noise, too used to death, to care.

Below, the crowd staggered out of the compound like the condemned after a prison riot. Broken, dirty, alive. Barely. The Festival had ended and so had two days of sanctioned madness and sin. They'd return to their dry little towns, crawl back under their rocks, and wait for the next invitation to raise hell.

Amelia didn't move at first. She watched it all unfold like she was watching a stage play she'd already read the ending to. She gave Hellman's body a nudge with her open-toe shoe, not out of curiosity, but confirmation. A woman like her knew better than to believe in clean endings. Once satisfied, she spat on what was left of him and walked over, her heels ticking like a metronome marking time in purgatory.

Three Days In Hell

She placed her palm on my gun and pushed the barrel gently down. Her touch was light, final. The way a priest closes the eyes of the dead.

Below, the sounds had started to fade to a low hum, the drunken laughter and distant crying signifying the slow return of routine. Morning had come, but not salvation. Just another day in Helman, where survival was a full-time job and sin paid better than virtue.

I stood at the rooftop's edge, watching the human tide drift through the streets, leaving behind their filth, their regrets, their proof of the inferno we built for ourselves. You lock desperate people in a box and call it a party, and you'll always find blood in the morning.

I didn't realize she was beside me until I felt her fingers weave through mine. The hand without the gun. She was radiant. Victorious. Not in love, never that, but basking in the power vacuum her husband's death had created. That was always the point. Their marriage had been a chess game played with razors, and now the king was off the board.

I thought of the woman at the Motel Indigo, the one who told me to stay away. She'd been right, of course. They always are. But no one ever listens to the truth when it doesn't flatter. Like Cassandra she was gifted with foresight, cursed never to be believed.

"What's on your mind, amor?" Amelia asked.

"Cassandra," I said.

"Cassandra? Who's she?"

"A prophetess. She saw the future, but no one listened. You know what happened to the ones who didn't believe her?"

She smirked. "No. What?"

I turned toward the sun cresting the horizon, a slow, blood-orange eye opening over the ridgeline. "Just ask the Greeks."

She gave me a half amused, half puzzled look then wrapped her arm through mine, resting her head on my shoulder like we were some postcard couple frozen in time.

"A beautiful day begins," she said.

Her eyes fell to the pistol still clenched in my hand.

"You can let that go now."

And so, I did.

Epilogue
Fifteen Years Later

Amelia was right.

Helman's death, and her anointing me as his righteous avenger, transformed me overnight. I wasn't just the man who pulled the trigger. I was a legend, a myth wrapped in blood and smoke. The town embraced me like a prodigal son returned from exile, forgiven of sins I hadn't even confessed. Funded by Cartel money, they threw a five-day bacchanalia that ended with a parade down *Calle del Fuego*. The crowd crowned me at the gates of Helman House. Amelia stood at my side, a queen in a silk dress, kissing my cheek as though sealing some Faustian bargain.

And that was the peak. That was the mountaintop. Everything after was descent.

Two days after moving in, it was clear that nothing about the town had changed. Nothing about me had changed. Not really. Sure, I had a mansion, a pool, a hot tub, and a woman who devoured life and me along with it. But indulgence curdles quickly when it's served daily. The pool became a water-filled grave of boredom. The hot tub, a tepid basin of broken promises. The guests? Strangers with names

I didn't remember and stories I didn't want to hear. Amelia filled the house like she was restocking a brothel, until one night I snapped and told her to shut it down. Even the sleek Helman car couldn't deliver me from the rot. I'd drive to the edge of town, stare down the long blacktop out to nowhere, and think: This is the moment. But it never was. Something always dragged me back.

Ten years blinked by. Then another five.

Sometimes I walked the streets. People nodded as I passed, their heads bowed more out of habit than reverence. Their lives hadn't improved. They still slaved under the same sun, endured the same grind. The only thing that shifted was time itself, crawling like a wounded animal toward the next Festival, the next sanctioned bloodletting. From the rooftop, I watched them transform, year after year, like beasts breaking free from their cages. They tore each other apart under the guise of tradition.

I called it the "Red Hour."

Bread and circus. Pain and spectacle. That's what kept Helman breathing.

I tried to save it. I did. I poured money into the town like a priest spilling wine on the altar. I rebuilt downtown. I restored the farms. I hired experts to find new veins in the old mines. I even rebuilt the church, hired an outside crew, brought in materials, and tried to breathe faith into a place long abandoned by it.

It all failed.

Workers vanished. Supplies disappeared. Crops died in the dirt. And the church? It stood there half-finished, hollow as a mausoleum, the altar never consecrated, the pews never filled. Nothing stuck. Nothing held.

Helman didn't rise. It rotted slowly. Quietly. Like a man dying in his sleep.

Three Days In Hell

I had entered the ninth circle and called it home.

Amelia, though... Amelia was different.

Time hadn't touched her. While I wore every year like a scar, she glided through the decades untouched, her beauty impervious, her smile practiced and perfect. In public, she was everything the town needed: charming, warm, obedient to the fantasy. At the Iguana, she laughed with the townsfolk and wrapped her arms around me like we were Eden reborn.

Behind closed doors, she gave me everything I thought love was, at least in the beginning. She made a religion out of lust. She could be tender, yes, but it was the hunger that defined her, a hunger I mistook for passion. But love, real love, is a quiet thing. And we never had quiet.

Eventually, even fire runs out of air.

I don't know exactly when the shift happened. Somewhere around year eight. Maybe nine. About the time of my accident.

A flight of stone stairs. Too much tequila. That's the official story. That's what Amelia told the doctors. And the town nodded and whispered and filled in the blanks space.

But the blank spaces matter.

The blank spaces are where the truth hides. They're the negative space around a crime scene. The silence between gunshots. They separate the narrative from the confession. And I've been studying them ever since.

Now I sit in a wheelchair on the same rooftop where I once stood victorious, watching the same tired cycle repeat. The Red Hour comes and goes, and I'm still here – older, slower, broken in ways no surgeon can fix.

And Amelia?

She still smiles like a promise. Still leans close and whispers sweet things that taste of arsenic and perfume. Still wraps her fingers around the push handles of my chair like she's holding the reins to a beast that forgot how to roar.

Fifteen years later, I am the king of a town built on dust and delusion.

And I can't shake the feeling that Hellman never really died.

He just changed clothes.

If you asked Amelia, she'd tell you I'd been in one of my moods. That I got angry. Violent. That I hurled obscenities and shattered glass without thought or consequence.

She wouldn't be lying.

I was drunk. Hell, I was drunk most days. What else was there to do? I didn't work; I had no need to. Every week we received generous "gifts" from her brother. Sometimes cash. Sometimes gold bars. Sometimes diamonds in little velvet pouches like party favors from a cartel masquerade. More shipments arrived in Helman than ever, deliveries that included new girls, fresh from some borderland purgatory. Some stayed. Most didn't. They passed through town like ghosts, their only proof of life reduced to a line of digits in a bank account I couldn't access and barely cared to withdraw from.

I spent my days on the rooftop, the only place that didn't feel like a padded cell. Up there, bottle in hand, I watched the sun melt into the desert, wishing it would take me with it. Amelia would show up eventually, like clockwork, and we'd argue, not about anything in particular. We just needed something sharp to throw at each other. That was our new intimacy: *mutually assured destruction.* There was no forgiveness, just the joyless sport of two people skilled in emotional cruelty.

Three Days In Hell

That night, I stormed off. Blinded by rage, soaked in liquor. Amelia said I missed a step. That I tripped. That gravity did the rest.

Maybe.

But I remember something different. Something colder. More intentional.

It doesn't matter now. Thirty-eight marble steps later, I was a crumpled thing at the base of the staircase with two shattered vertebrae in my back, a severed line of communication between my mind and legs. Just like that, the past, present, and future collapsed into a chair with wheels.

Amelia spared no expense. She flew in the best doctors, bought the best equipment, transformed a room into a private hospital suite. She even modified a car so I could still drive and still appear human. She installed a chair lift for the pool, so I wouldn't miss out on the pleasure of floating like driftwood in chlorinated water.

And she made sure I knew – *really knew* – that all the money in the world could cushion the blow of a broken spine. That I could have everything, *except escape*.

So, I stayed in Helman. My kingdom. My coffin.

Days at the pool. Nights at the Iguana. Trying to drown the last vestiges of memory in a cocktail of bourbon and pills. But no matter how much I consumed, the picture always came back blurry at the edges, sure, but whole. And what I saw in it was *familiar*. Too familiar. A rerun of my origin story.

New faces had started showing up. Young men. Sharp jaws. Dead eyes. Men with nothing to lose and no fear of losing it. Men like I once was, before the throne, before the stairs. You could spot them easily: hungry, twitchy, ready to sell their souls if it meant never going back to whatever hell they came from.

And now, with the Festival approaching, I couldn't help but wonder – was one of them *next*?

Would someone else take the ride?

I wheeled to the edge of the roof, the same spot where I lost the use of my legs. Same cracked tiles. Same railing. Same cursed view of a town that wouldn't let me go. Every time I came up here, I replayed that night like a warped reel of film, and every time I came to the same conclusion:

I should've thrown the gun away.

Or pulled the trigger on myself.

It's strange, the way life clings to you when it's hanging by a thread you can't even see. You think you want to die until you're *almost there*. Then, suddenly, every breath feels sacred. Every second, borrowed. Every regret, radioactive.

And yet... here I am.

Alive.

Watching the sun set over a town that doesn't change. Waiting for a bullet with my name on it that never seems to arrive.

I wondered if an inch to the left would've rewritten the story. If that tiny distance could've meant a different life, or a better one.

But I knew this was just a fantasy, a child's impractical daydream. Fiji was a wonderful ideal because it was a thought exercise. Making a wish into a reality was much more difficult.

I killed Helman, not Amelia. And I'd never know if I chose wrong, or just chose the wrong evil. If I had chosen the lesser of two evils. But fifteen years later, I was certain that when it came to JB and Amelia, there weren't two types of evil: there was just evil.

And here I was, stuck in a place I never wanted to go, and now could never leave.

Now I understood what JB must have felt those days high up on this hill, overlooking the expanse of his burnt landscape kingdom. His life had become one big conflict. On the one hand, he never had to want again for anything. Money kept rolling in, and his castle was big, impressive, and impenetrable. But there came a time when a monarch became so entrenched in his position that he was imprisoned by it. With the title came paranoia and isolation, with poor ol' JB on the defense, watching intently the new faces that seemed to always amble into town, trying to sniff out the intent behind their sudden appearances. And all of JB's power – whether he was the puppet or the puppet master – became a tightly strung cage restricting his freedom and perverting his perspective.

"There you are," Amelia said from behind me. "You've been out here for hours. Why don't you come inside?"

"Was just looking at the town," I replied without looking back at her. "I like the way it looks at this hour. So still and peaceful."

"That will all change in a couple of days," she said. I heard her high heels ticking against the marble-tiled roof. "I have a feeling that it's going to be the best Festival ever."

"You say that every year," I said without much excitement.

"And I'm right every year," she said.

"Where were you last night?" I asked, keeping my eyes fixed at the town in front of me.

She paused. "At the Iguana. Where else would I be?"

I tilted my head to the side to look at her. "And the man in the blue coat?"

I didn't need to see her full expression to know I had caught her off guard. Amelia took a moment to collect herself, and I enjoyed the little victory of having surprised her with information she didn't think I had. She closed the distance between us and stood behind me. Her arms reached around my head and cradled me as she leaned close to my ear. "Why do you always say such things? A stranger in town before the Chili Festival is nothing new."

She masked her tone, but I knew her well enough to know she was lying. I forced a fake, apologetic smile. "You're right. I'm sorry."

"He's here for *El Fuego En El Agujero*. Another gringo looking to make a name for himself."

"Gringo? He's too soft for the chilis."

"So, did you when you got here," she teased. "But you surprised everyone."

"You think he's got a shot?"

She turned my chair around to face her. Our eyes met and I felt a familiar shiver up my spine. "There's something in his eyes that tells me he can do it."

I nodded. She smiled and put her fingers on my shoulder, giving it a little squeeze. For a slender hand, it seemed heavier than usual. The late afternoon sun set behind us, casting long shadows across the flagstone roof. The day over, people started to leak out into the street. Their voices were expressive, talking quickly and in excited pitches.

Three months after my accident, Amelia had widened the door frame that led to the roof and had an elevator installed so that I didn't have to be carried up the steps by one of the hired help. It was a thoughtful gesture, an act of forgiveness at a time when we were two rabid dogs going for each other's throats. And when I was at my lowest, when she could have made me suffer, she came around the other way, comforting me with kindness and helping my rehabilitation.

She made me lower my guard. She made me think that maybe we had turned a corner. That things had a chance of going back to the old days, the better days. And then the new faces started showing up.

"Maybe I should enter again," I said suddenly. "You know, the former champion, competing one more time. The town would love it."

Amelia frowned. "The contest is for those that have to prove themselves. Not for those who already have."

"Have I proven myself, Amelia?"

"Of course. Look where you sit."

It was a curious remark that could be interpreted in two different ways.

"Maybe I'm still hungry," I offered. "Maybe I got a little left in the tank for one more go at it. Finally get down that Pepper X. What do you think?"

Her hand landed on my gut with the dismissiveness of a doctor checking a corpse for signs of life. "I think it's time to go." She grabbed the handlebars of the chair and steered me toward the door. "Don't worry, Bobby. This will be a Festival to remember. I believe that. I really do."

"Where are we headed, Amelia?" I asked as I saw the top of the steps draw closer.

"It's a surprise. Don't you like surprises?"

She maneuvered me through the door. The elevator was right next to the steps. Even though it was afternoon I could still see the marble gleaming in the dim light, the smooth surface cold and unforgiving, like the polished face of a tombstone. The deeper we went, the more the steps seemed to stretch, a marble tongue leading into the house's throat. There was an unnatural stillness to those steps – no cracks or chips – just an eerie, horrible perfection that dropped in temperature the father you descended. Every step was an invitation to a dark, forgotten place, and no matter how hard you tried to tell yourself otherwise, you couldn't shake the feeling that you were going to lose your footing, to slip, never to rise again.

And then I was afraid all over again.

"Where are you taking me, Amelia?

"Where do you think?" Amelia said, and I didn't have to look behind me to know she was smiling

That same smile she wore on our wedding day. The same smile she wore the night I fell.

"Where else? Down."

And with that, she pushed me –

Not hard. Not far.

Just enough.

www.ingramcontent.com/pod-product-compliance
Lightning Source LLC
LaVergne TN
LVHW040041080526
838202LV00045B/3440